THE SKY OVER LIMA

THE
SKY
OVER
LIMA

Juan Gómez Bárcena

TRANSLATED FROM SPANISH BY

Andrea Rosenberg

Houghton Mifflin Harcourt

Boston   New York   2016

First U.S. edition

www.hmhco.com

Library of Congress Cataloging-in-Publication Data
Gómez Bárcena, Juan, date.
[Cielo de Lima. English]
The sky over Lima / Juan Gómez Bárcena ;
translated from Spanish by Andrea Rosenberg.
pages cm
ISBN 978-0-544-63005-5 (hardback) — ISBN 978-0-544-63006-2 (ebook)
1. Jiménez, Juan Ramón, 1881–1958 — Fiction. 2. Poets — Fiction.
I. Rosenberg, Andrea, translator. II. Title.
PQ6707.O5255C5413 2016
863'.7 — dc23
2015037011

Book design by Greta D. Sibley

Printed in the United States of America
DOC 10 9 8 7 6 5 4 3 2 1

To the friends who accompanied me on this journey. Without them, The Sky Over Lima *would resemble slightly less the book I wanted to write.*

To my sisters, Diana and Marta, who know everything about me but still know nothing about these pages.

THE SKY OVER LIMA

I

A Comedy

◇

At first it's just a letter drafted many times: Dearest friend, respected poet, most esteemed sir, a different opening for every sheet of paper that ends up in a crumpled ball under the desk, glory of Spanish literature, most distinguished Ramón Jiménez, peerless bard, comrade. The next day the mulatta servant will sweep up the wads of paper scattered across the floor, thinking they're the poems of the young master of the house, Carlos Rodríguez. But the young master is not writing poems that night. He smokes one cigarette after another with his friend José Gálvez, and together they mull over the exact words to use in writing to the Maestro. They've searched for his latest collection in every bookshop in Lima and found only a dog-eared copy of *Violet Souls,* which they've read many times already and whose lines they know by heart. So now they jot down grand words that a moment later sound ridiculous: Noble friend, immortal scribe, our most intrepid revitalizer of literature, might you, in your infinite kindness, offer a small courtesy to us, your friends across the Atlantic, your ardent readers in Peru — who follow your verses, Don Juan Ramón, with an admiration of which you may be unaware — might it not be too onerous an imposition on our part to humbly ask that you vouchsafe to us a copy of your most recent book, those sad arias of yours, impossible to find in Lima; might it not be an abuse of your generosity to hope to be granted that consideration even though we have not included the three pesetas that the book costs?

When their energy flags, they drink pisco. They open the windows and look out on the empty streets. It's a moonless night in 1904; the boys are just twenty years old, young enough that they will live to see two world wars and celebrate Peru's triumph in the Copa América soccer tournament thirty-five years from now. But naturally they know nothing of all that tonight. They just crumple up one sheet after another, searching for words they know they'll never find. For with the last letter they toss to the floor, they realize that they will never acquire their signed copy of *Sad Arias:* however much they address the poet as an eminent dignitary of literature and the great hope of Spain and the Americas, they will receive not a single line of correspondence in response if they confess that they are only two young masters playing at being poor in a Lima garret. They must embellish reality, because in the end that is what poets do, and they are poets, or at least they've dreamed of being poets on many late nights like this one. And that is exactly what they are about to do now: write the most difficult poem of all, one that has no verses but can touch the heart of a true artist.

It starts out as a joke, but then it turns out it's not a joke. One of the two says, almost idly, It would be easier if we were a beautiful woman, then Don Juan Ramón would put his entire soul into answering us, that violet soul of his — and then suddenly he stops, the two young men look at each other a moment, and almost unintentionally the mischief has already been made. They laugh, congratulate each other on this inspired idea, exchange slaps on the back and two more glasses of pisco, and the next morning they meet up in the garret again with a sheet of perfumed paper that Carlos has remembered to pilfer from a sister's desk. Carlos also takes care of the writing; his schoolmates used to tease him about his feminine handwriting, the letters soft and round like a caress, and the time has finally come to put it to good use. Whenever you're ready, Señor Gálvez, he says, stifling his laughter, and together they begin to sound out those timeless words that require only a sheet of fine paper and a writer with a womanly hand — a poem with no verses, which will appear in no anthology, but that is poised to do what only the best poetry can: name what has never existed before and bring it to life.

From those words Georgina will be born, timidly at first, because that's how they write her: a young lady from Miraflores who sighs over the poetry of Juan Ramón and whose artless sincerity makes them laugh during their pauses. A girl so ingenuous she can only be beautiful. It is she who requests a copy of *Sad Arias,* she who is so ashamed of her own audacity, she who begs the poet to understand and to forgive her. Only the signature is missing, and with it a last name, sonorous and poetic, that the two finally agree on after a debate so long that both the liquor and the pastries run out: Georgina Hübner.

And Georgina begins as simply that: a name and a sealed letter that will travel from hand to hand for more than a month, first in the bodice of the illiterate housemaid, then in the pocket of a lad who charges half a *sol* and a pinch of the maid's broad buttocks for the errand. It will then pass through the hands of two postal workers, a customs official at the docks, and a sailor, and thence to the steamship covering the Lima–Montevideo route in a sack of letters in which bad news predominates. From Montevideo, an unnecessary detour to Asunción, thanks to a negligent postman only thirty days from retirement whose eyesight is too weak to read the delicate handwriting. From Asunción, back to Montevideo by train through the jungle, and then setting sail in the hold of a ship, where it will miraculously be saved from the jaws of a rat that has left many other letters utterly unreadable in the past.

Still Georgina has not yet begun to live; she is still nothing more than a sheet of stationery that, in the darkness of the mailbag, is already losing its last whiff of perfume. First will come three weeks of transatlantic travel in the company of two stowaways who occasionally whisper to each other in a coarse Portuguese, and then debarkation in La Coruña, train, post office, train again, a postal worker who doesn't read poetry and to whom the name of the addressee means nothing, and then Madrid, Madrid at last. It's at some point on the long journey that Georgina begins to breathe and to live — so when she finally arrives at the poet's house, she has become a flesh-and-blood woman, a languid young lady who thrums through a stream of ink and is currently awaiting a response to her letter back in Lima, at her Miraflores estate. A creature as real as the scentless letter that Juan Ramón Jiménez will read that very morning, with hands that are steady at first, but that soon begin to tremble.

Two postal employees, a customs officer who peeks inside the parcel to confirm it does not contain contraband, another sack in which bad news (deaths, miscarriages, unforeseen confinements in sanatoriums and nursing homes, a honeymoon on which the bride's jewelry is gambled away in the Estoril casino) is again more plentiful than good (a traveler who has reached his destination safe and sound, an indigenous man who accepts his mestizo son as his own). By sea to Montevideo in a hold free of stowaways and rats; from the ship to the post office, and from there to the docks once more to set sail for Lima, this time by the correct route, as the nearsighted postal worker has been pensioned and is now enjoying a humble retirement in the neighborhood of Pocitos; from the port in Lima to the local post office, and eight hands later in the leather pouch of the very same errand boy, who again charges half a *sol* and another tweak of the housemaid's haunches. Except this time the package does not fit in her bodice, and she leaves it on young Master José's desk without bothering to glance at the scribbles that she would not be able to read anyway.

> *This morning I received your letter, which I found most charming, and I am sending you my* Sad Arias *at once, regretting only that my verses cannot live up to all that you must have hoped they would be, Georgina . . .*

That night in the taverns the young men celebrate their signed book and this letter written in the Maestro's own hand. They invite their friends, other poets as destitute as they, who arrive at the pub in their horse-drawn carriages. While helping their friends out of their overcoats, José and Carlos urge them to drink, drink as much they like, Georgina Hübner is treating tonight. Then come the explanations, and the toasts, and the letter read aloud; those who believe the story and those who do not, Stop pulling our leg, Carlitos, those stilted lines could not possibly have been written by the author of *Water Lilies* and *Violet Souls*. But then they see the poet's signature and the book that can be found only in the bookstores of Madrid and Barcelona, and they begin clapping one another on the back and laughing uproariously.

Your letter is dated March 8, but I received it only today, May 6. Please do not fault me for the delay. If you keep me apprised of your address — if ever you plan to change residences — I will send you my books as I publish them, always, of course, with the greatest of pleasure . . .

Their friends insist that they must answer the letter; that they must not answer the letter; that Georgina should repay the Maestro's kindness with a photograph, or at least a few postcards of Lima; that great poets do not deserve to be mocked and Carlos and José must confess the truth straightaway; that telling the truth will achieve nothing; that they should put a stop to the joke before things end badly; that things will end badly regardless, so what does it matter. Finally it is José who proclaims, pounding the table with his fist: I say we respond, damn it. And respond they will, but that will be the next day, when the two friends return to the garret in a bleary-eyed haze, armed with the rose-scented paper they've purchased for the occasion.

Tonight, though, they prefer to enjoy themselves. To propose possible responses to the poet, which start out more or less sensible and then grow gradually worse under the counsel of alcohol and euphoria. To emerge into Lima's first light lustily reciting the *Sad Arias*, which, with a bottle of chicha in hand, don't seem so sad anymore. And afterward — and for this they must be forgiven, as by this point they are more drunks than they are poets — to address one another as ladies, loudly calling one another Georgina, pitching their voices higher, hiking up skirts they aren't wearing, and feigning dizzy spells and fainting fits, until finally they squat down to urinate, all together and dying of laughter, in the Descalzos rose garden.

Thank you for your kindness. And believe me to be utterly yours, who kisses your feet.
Juan Ramón Jiménez

◇

Let's suppose for a moment that we had to sketch José and Carlos in a single sentence. That we were allowed to proffer no more than, for example, thirteen words describing them — their existence summed up in the space of a telegram. In such a case, the words we chose would probably be these:

They're rich.

They fancy themselves poets.

They want to be Juan Ramón Jiménez.

Fortunately, no one is asking us to be so brief.

They're rich.

Both of them are, though this is less a coincidence than it is well-nigh self-evident. In 1904, friendship between members of different social classes is a sort of fairy tale, a genre reserved for the particularly naive, like children who drowsily listen to *The Prince and the Pauper* before receiving a good-night kiss.

There exist, of course, circumstances in which this principle is less stringently upheld. Nearly everyone has heard tales of landowners who amuse themselves by granting generous favors to their peasants, perhaps in exchange for the pleasure they get from watching those peasants wait for long stretches in their parlors, caps clutched to their chests and eyes filled with fear that they might stain the rugs with mud. There are also rich, kindhearted widows who sweetly offer advice to their lady's maids, who perhaps even attempt to find them decent, sensible husbands among the footmen of the other women in their ombre-playing circle. And gentlemen who dress up like laborers to tipple in picturesque taverns, exchanging comradely embraces with men whose names they will later forget.

In none of these instances can one find any signs of true friendship, only an artificial camaraderie in which the peasant — or maid, or butler — has the unhappier role. The inferiors respond to the questions, which are often elegantly softened orders, in cautious monosyllables and, humiliated, accept the alms of attention extended by their patrons. The gentlemen, on the other hand, find these little tête-à-têtes, which are convened and dissolved with the ringing of a bell, quite satisfactory and edifying. At some point the servant will leave — *You may go now,*

Alfredo — and the gentleman will remain lounging in his armchair, the proffered glass of cognac, which the shy servant has not dared to sample, still untouched on the table, and his conscience brimming with the satisfaction of having been generous and humane.

There is, then, nothing for it but to acknowledge that both of our young men are rich. Yet there is no obligation for them to be rich in exactly the same way. The Gálvez fortune, for example, goes back centuries and is associated with an illustrious lineage of prominent national figures. And while it is true that much of the wealth accumulated by those distinguished forebears has evaporated, their descendants in 1904 still retain enough of it to enjoy a comfortable life as well as their unimpeachable reputation, which ultimately will be as valuable as the lost riches. Everyone in Lima knows that José's grandfather José Gálvez Egúsquiza died defending the city of El Callao against Spanish troops in 1866 and that his uncle José Gálvez Moreno was a hero of the War of the Pacific. And with such letters of introduction, who could refuse to offer Master José an important post when he grows up, perhaps a diplomatic mission abroad or even a ministry of culture in Lima?

The Rodríguez family fortune, however, is embarrassingly new. Carlos's father began to amass it only three decades ago, during the rubber fever, when he achieved some success in bleeding the jungle of its resins and its Indians. Before that, he'd been a nobody. Just a door-to-door salesman of soaps and waxes who perhaps dreamed of someday becoming one of the many gentlemen who never deigned to allow him into their homes. Then came the sugar boom, and with it a plantation of four thousand laborers, and winter and summer residences, and horse-drawn carriages, and his own serving staff, so similar to those sour-faced servants who had so often stopped him at the doorstep. There was even a botanical garden of exotic flowers and animals, along whose gravel avenues the grandee would often wander, dogged by his numerous preoccupations. Indeed, the Rodríguez family had everything but the illustrious past that not even rubber could buy: its genealogical tree was littered with little indigenous branches that had to be pruned, for that inglorious lineage is disdained in some salons, at certain splendid galas. It is why the gentlemen bow their heads ten or twelve degrees lower as they pass and the ladies offer up the backs of their hands with their noses slightly wrinkled, as if troubled by an unpleasant odor. As if the Rodríguezes still gave off a faint whiff of jungle ponds, the blood of dead headhunters, vulcanized rubber, paraffin — the paraffin that thirty years earlier Carlos's father had sold door to door at a paltry three-quarters of a *sol* per ounce.

This is the closest thing to a friendship between classes that we can find: a wealthy man from a prominent family and an even wealthier man whose ancestors were poor. Perhaps it is unwarranted to dedicate so many words to this matter, as the novel's own protagonists do not seem to take it very seriously. After all, they fancy themselves poets, and that belief keeps them hovering just above the ground, enjoying a detachment that is disrupted by anything to do with reality and its prosaic conventions. So why would they care that Carlos's family has no distinguished dead and that José's has too many? Poetry, art, their friendship — especially their friendship — transcend all of that. At least that's what they'd say if anyone bothered to ask them. We couldn't care less about that, they'd say, don't you see that we're poets? — and that answer should be sufficient.

It should be sufficient, but it is not persuasive. Because it's clear that they do care about the implications of last name and lineage — we have already noted that it's 1904; at this time, it could not be otherwise — though they would never admit it, and may not even realize it. But that may be why the opinions of José, nephew of the illustrious José Gálvez Moreno, always seem a little more sensible than those of his friend, and his poems fuller, and his jokes about Peruvians, Chileans, and Spaniards funnier, and his girlfriends prettier; and you might even say at times that he also seems taller, except that only recently an impartial measuring tape revealed that Carlos has nearly an inch on him. It was José who created Georgina — Carlos, smiling, delighted, thoroughly inebriated, merely agreed to the plan — and he will also be the one to choose her death if one day, God forbid, something has to happen to her. And what alternative did Carlos have, then, but to agree, even if he didn't want to? He could only toss back another glass of pisco and toast his friend's excellent idea; of what use are the opinions of a rubber man's son when all of a nation's illustrious dead are arrayed against him?

◇

The subsequent letters require more drafts than the first. Something more vital than obtaining a book of poems is at stake now: if Juan Ramón doesn't answer, the comedy is over. And for some reason, that comedy suddenly seems to its authors to be quite a serious thing. Maybe that's why they're hardly laughing anymore, and why Carlos has a solemn air about him when he picks up the fountain pen.

Yet there is no reason to imagine that the correspondence might be interrupted soon. Juan Ramón always answers in the return post, sometimes even dispatching two or three letters in a single week that will later travel together, embarking on the same transatlantic voyage back to Lima. He too seems to want the joke to continue many chapters longer, even at the cost of short and somewhat ceremonious missives. The letters are frankly boring at times, yet as fundamentally Juan Ramón–esque as the *Sad Arias* or his *Violet Souls,* and that is enough to move José and Carlos to memorize them and venerate them during many a worshipful afternoon. Sometimes the quartos arrive splattered with ink stains or spelling errors, but they forgive him even that, with indulgence, with pleasure. Juan Ramón, so perfect in his poems, so *intellijent* — with a *j* — he too sometimes scratches things out with his pen, he too gets confused, mixes up *g* and *j* and *s* and *c*.

So what do they talk about in those first letters?

The truth is that nobody much cares. Not even them. They spend many hours writing the letters, packaging them, sending them; hours exchanging remedies for the flu or discussing the cold or the heat in Madrid or Chopin's nocturnes or the discomforts of traveling by car. It is an unfruitful time that is best kept to a minimum. What does matter — and matters a lot — is the way those letters begin and end. The way they transition smoothly and discreetly from *Señor Don Juan R. Jiménez* and *Señorita Georgina Hübner* to *Dearest friend* in only fourteen letters. Not to mention the closings: *Your most attentive servant, Cordially, Fondly, Affectionately, Tenderly.* This shift, which takes place over the course of seven hundred forty-two lines of correspondence, equivalent to about an hour and fifty minutes of conversation in a café, might seem indecorously rapid. But as the Lima–La Coruña route is covered by just two ships a month and a ship rarely carries more than two or three of their letters, in fact the relationship develops quite slowly, very much in keeping with the period. They are rather reminiscent of those lovers who wait six months for permission to speak to each other through a window grating, and at least one full year for their first chaste kiss.

And of course the word *love* has yet to be said.

◇

Whenever José spots the cancellation marks of transatlantic postage amid his correspondence, he rushes off to find Carlos. They have agreed that they will always read the letters together — after all, both of them are Georgina — and Gálvez scrupulously fulfills his promise, though he does occasionally give in to temptation and peek under the flap of the envelope. They read the Maestro's words aloud on the benches of the university or in the Club Unión billiards room, and then they go to the garret to watch the afternoon fade, deliberating over each word of their response. They often continue writing long past nightfall, and as they polish their final draft, the mosquitoes orbit the oil lamp in smaller and smaller circles until finally burning to a crisp in its flame.

Both of them think constantly of Juan Ramón, but only Carlos pays any mind to Georgina. For José she is merely a pretext, a means by which to fill his desk drawer with holy relics from the Maestro. A dainty portrait, for example. Or one of the poet's unpublished poems. That is José's interest with every letter: how to get more books, more autographs, more Juan Ramón. Carlos, on the other hand, strives to give Georgina a personality and a biography. Perhaps he is beginning to suspect that his character will one day become the protagonist of her own story. So he carefully chooses the words she uses in each letter, giving them the same meticulous concentration he gives his handwriting. He's attentive to the adverbs, the ellipses, the exclamation points. He says to José: Let me take care of this, you're an only child and don't understand the language of women; it's a good thing I have three sisters and have learned to listen to them. Women sigh a lot, and whenever they sigh they use ellipses. They exaggerate a lot, and when they exaggerate they use exclamation points. They feel a lot, and that's why their feelings all come with adverbs. José laughs, but he lets Carlos create, cross out, make over his too-manly sentences. Sometimes he teases him, of course. He calls him Carlota, tells him he's looking particularly comely that night. Go to hell, mutters Carlota — mutters Carlos — without lifting his eyes from the paper.

But José doesn't go anywhere, of course. Neither of them moves. First they have to work out the answers to a great number of questions. Might Georgina be an orphan? Does she have a splash of indigenous blood or the alabaster complexion of the criolla ladies? How old is she, exactly, and what does she want from Juan Ramón? They don't know, just as they still don't know what they're doing, or why it is so important that Juan Ramón keep writing back. Why don't they just forget the whole thing and return to their obligations: studying for failed law courses and looking for flesh-and-blood women to take to the spring dance?

But for some reason they keep writing long after it has grown dark. They don't seem to know why, and if they do know, neither of them says.

◇

They fancy themselves poets.

They met in the lecture halls of the University of San Marcos at that critical age when students begin to cultivate ideas of their own along with their first sparse facial hair. For both young men, one of those first interests — the reluctant mustaches would come much later — was poetry. Up until that point, all their life decisions had been made by their families, from their enrollment in law school to their tedious piano lessons. Both wore suits purchased through catalogs in Europe, they recited the same formulaic pleasantries, and at social gatherings they had learned to offer similar opinions on the Chilean war, the indecent nature of certain modern dances, and the disastrous consequences of Spanish colonialism. Carlos was to become a lawyer to see to his father's affairs, and José — well, all José had to do was get the degree, and his family's contacts would do the rest. Their love of poetry, on the other hand, had not been imposed on them by anyone, nor did it serve any practical purpose. It was the first passion that belonged entirely to them. Mere words, perhaps, but words that spoke to them of somewhere else, a world beyond their comfortable prison of folding screens and parasols, of Cuban cigars in the guest parlor and dinners served at eight thirty on the dot.

Though they're not poets, at least not yet, they have learned to behave as if they were, which is almost as good. They frequent the salons of Madame Linard on Tuesdays and those of the Club Unión on Thursdays; they rummage in their armoires and dig out scarves and hats and ancient topcoats so they can dress up as Baudelaire at night; they grow increasingly thin — alarmingly so, according to their mothers. In a pub on Jirón de la Unión, they draw up a solemn manifesto with three other students in which they swear never to return to their law studies as long as they all shall live, under pain of mediocrity. Sometimes they even write: appallingly bad poetry, verses that sound like an atrocious translation of Rilke or, worse still, an even more atrocious translation of Bécquer. No matter. Writing well is a detail that will no doubt come later, with the aid of Baudelaire's wardrobe, Rimbaud's absinthe, or Mallarmé's handlebar mustache. And with each line of poetry they write, the convictions they have inherited from their fathers become a bit more tattered; they begin to think that Chile might have been in the right during the Chilean war, that perhaps what is truly indecent is to keep dancing their grandparents' dances well into the twentieth century, and that Spanish colonialism — well, actually, in the case of Spanish colonialism, they have to admit that they continue to share their fathers' views, much as it pains them.

How long have they considered themselves poets? Not even they could say for sure. Perhaps that's what they've always been, albeit unknowingly — the possibility of this pushes them to reexamine the trivial anecdotes of their childhoods with fresh eyes. Did Carlos not utter his first poem that morning when, on an outing to the countryside, he asked his governess whether the mountains had a mommy and daddy too? And the gaze with which José, having barely spoken his first words, contemplated the Tarma twilight — was that not already the gaze of a poet? In these moments of revelation, they are certain that, yes, they have indeed always been poets, and so they spend hours combing their past for those signs of brilliance that blossom early in the lives of great geniuses, then pat each other on the back when they find them and declare themselves ardent admirers of each other's poems after yet another long, pisco-soaked night. All at once they are the vibrant future of Peruvian poetry, the torch that will light the way for new literary traditions. Both of them, but especially the grandson of the illustrious José Gálvez Egús-quiza, whose light for some reason seems to shine a little more brightly.

◇

The garret is in one of the many buildings the Rodríguez family owns in Lima's San Lázaro neighborhood, aging properties they don't bother restoring and that seem on the verge of collapsing with their freight of tenants inside them. The building's other floors are rented out to thirty or so Chinese immigrants who work in the noodle factory nearby, but the garret is too dilapidated even for them. Not even those sallow men who slept on the ships' gunwales on their Pacific crossing want it, so José and Carlos are free to visit it whenever they wish.

Its windows are broken, and sunlight streams in through gaps between the planks in the walls. The floorboards are pockmarked with neglect, and somewhere a cat has miraculously survived, even though rumor has it that the Chinese eat cats and it's certainly the case that these particular Chinese are in dire need of sustenance. It is, in short, the perfect place for two young men bored with sleeping in canopy beds and admonishing the maids for failing to polish the silver wine pitchers. They are thrilled by the sensation of poverty, and they roam among the burlap sacks and heaps of dusty junk like the lucky survivors of a shipwreck.

It is there that Georgina is born. A birth marked by words and laughter, tenuously illuminated by light flickering from bottles deployed as makeshift candlesticks.

They visit the garret every afternoon. They enjoy walking through Lima's poor neighborhoods on their way to that building that might have been taken directly from the pages of a Zola novel. A humble murmuring issues from within, muffled by threadbare curtains and rice-paper screens. Two women fighting over a serving of soup. A long monologue in a strange language that could be a madman's rant or maybe a prayer. A child sobbing. They take it all in with a mix of eagerness and pleasure, searching for traces of the poetry that Baudelaire was the first to find in poverty, or perhaps they are searching through poverty in hopes of finding Baudelaire himself. Their visits distress the building's watchman, who as he opens the door for them always pleads, "Master Rodríguez, Master Gálvez, for the sake of all that is holy, please be careful." He worries, of course, that the floorboards in the attic will give way and the young men will be injured, but more unnerving still is the vague, mysterious threat posed by the Chinese tenants.

José and Carlos laugh. They know full well that the tenants are harmless: sad-faced men and women who don't even dare to raise their eyes when they encounter them on the landings. "But they're quiet people, really," they respond, still laughing, from the stairs. The watchman clucks his tongue. "Too quiet," he adds before letting them go. "Too quiet . . ."

Some afternoons they clamber up from the garret to the rooftop. They loosen their cravats and take swigs from a shared bottle. Clustered below them are the houses, the humble little squares, the cathedral's spires. In the distance, the somber silhouette of the University of San Marcos, which they're skipping again. They see the denizens of Lima walking rapidly, slightly hunched, most of them oppressed by burdens that José and Carlos neither understand nor judge. The young men make an odd sight in their smudged white linen suits and their walking sticks, hanging over the abyss as if they were newly bankrupt millionaires threatening to leap into the void. But nobody sees them. In the poor neighborhoods, people walk with their eyes on the ground and look up only occasionally to ask the dear Lord to grant them some mercy, which He rarely does.

Sitting there on the rooftop, they play their favorite games. For the first, they must forget that they're in Lima garbed in fifty-*sol* suits. In one stroke they blot out the colonial bell towers, the adobe walls, the golden hills, the people — above all, those miserable people who seem so determined to spoil their fantasies. Now suddenly they are in Paris, two penniless poets without even a crust of bread between them. They have written the greatest poems of the century, but no one knows it. Incredible verses that open like exotic flowers and then gradually wilt amid the ugliness of the world. A week ago, they spent their last coin on a ream of paper. Yesterday they pawned their fountain pen and their desk. That very morning they sold the last of their books to a junkman and used the franc he gave them — ah, they used that franc to make one final wish on the Pont Neuf and then watched it plummet hopelessly into the Seine. *Plop.* They imagine that it's cold. At night, snow will again blanket Paris, and they will be forced to burn their poems one by one to survive the winter.

Their poverty softens them while the reverie lasts, which isn't long, as daydreams are arduous things that can be sustained only with immense effort. Lima is a place that is impervious to fantasies, and soon they feel the heat of their eternal summer once more, or they notice a gold cufflink gleaming at one of their wrists. Or perhaps the Rodríguez car noisily invades the unpaved streets and the chauffeur pokes his head out the driver's-side window and shouts, "Master Rodríguez! Your father wants you home for dinner!" Then their dream plunges downward like the coin they'll never toss into the Seine, and suddenly they see themselves again for what they really are: two wealthy young men looking at poverty from on high.

"What a God-awful city," murmurs José as he prepares to go down.

But their favorite pastime is the character game. It began by chance during a lecture on mercantile law, when José observed that the professor looked just like Ebenezer Scrooge, right down to his spectacles. They both tittered so loudly that Professor Nicanor — Mr. Scrooge — interrupted his lecture and escorted them to the classroom door, whose threshold they seldom darkened anyway. Out in the courtyard, fortified with alcohol, they continued playing. The Roman law professor was Ana Ozores's cuckolded husband from Leopoldo Alas's *La Regenta*. The ancient and practically mummified rector was Ivan Ilyich before Ivan's death — or perhaps, José added snidely, Ivan Ilyich *after* his death. The widow of the impresario Francisco Stevens, an extraordinarily fat woman, was an aging Madame Bovary. "But Emma commits suicide when she's still young," Carlos objected. "Exactly," Gálvez countered. "She's a Madame Bovary who doesn't commit suicide. One who has the objectionable taste to outlive her beauty and become fat and farcical."

Soon enough everyone's a character: friends, relatives, literary rivals, strangers. Even animals: though they've never seen the cat that ekes out a living in the garret — they occasionally hear it yowling somewhere amid the detritus, perhaps reveling in the knowledge of being among kindred spirits — they are unanimous in their conviction that it belongs in a Poe story.

From up on the rooftop, they decide with unhurried capriciousness which of the people swarming at their feet are the work of Balzac, or Cervantes, or Victor Hugo. Up there it is easy to feel like a poet, to contemplate the square and the adjoining streets as if they were a vast postcard with characters from all the world's literature wandering about. For example, the first fantasies of the schoolgirls who line up at the entrance to the convent school are written by Bécquer. The lives of the wealthy citizens striding across the square are narrated by Galdós — what dull lives they lead, poor things, just like Benito the Garbanzo Eater himself. If you are one of the whores on Calle del Panteoncito, your endless misfortunes are narrated by Zola or, should you become a nun, by Saint John of the Cross. The drunks who stumble out of the taverns, of course, are figments from the nightmares of Edgar Allan Poe. Madmen? Dostoyevsky. Adventurers? Melville. Lovers? If things turn out well, Tolstoy, and if they go sour, Goethe. Beggars? That's an easy one, because poverty is everywhere alike — the lives of Lima's mendicants are written by Dickens, but without fog; by Gogol, but without vodka; by Twain, but without hope.

An implacable arbitrariness also divides the characters into protagonists and secondary figures, and their deliberations on whether or not a particular beautiful woman or a certain picturesque beggar is the main character of a story can go on for quite some time. The matter is not to be taken lightly, as protagonists are, in fact, a rare breed; you have to stumble across them, track them patiently amid the mob of figures entering and leaving that page of the book of their lives.

What would they say if they saw themselves strolling across that square? With what writer would they associate their own footsteps? Would they consider themselves secondary characters or protagonists? These seem like natural questions, ones they should have been asking all along. Strangely, though, they never have. Perhaps it hasn't occurred to them. Or perhaps they feel that their place is somehow there, not on foot in the street but on high, up on the rooftops of other men's lives.

It is an odd game — a frivolous one, even — but, in the end, a fitting one for young men who see literature everywhere they look, for whom everything that happens around them happens just as they've read in books. Indeed, it would hardly be surprising to discover that this very scene — two men who, from their garret, dream of commanding the entire world — also came from one of those novels.

◇

Lima, June 26, 1904

Señor Jiménez:

    Immediately after posting my letter requesting a copy of your Sad Arias, I wished I could retrieve it, destroy it utterly. Why? I shall tell you: I imagined that my behavior was rather unseemly for a young lady. Without ever having met or even seen you, I wrote to you, spoke to you. I was so audacious as to impose upon you, to ask a tedious favor of you, you who are so generous and yet owe me nothing . . .

    I reproached myself for all of this again and again until I was in agony. When one is twenty years old, as I am, one thinks quickly and suffers deeply!

    Yet all of my inquietudes were soothed, all my doubts evaporated, when I received your kind letter and your beautiful book.

    Your mournful verses speak to the heart with the resonant cadence of Schubert's melancholy melodies. I will long remember these stanzas, through which wafts the delicate, gentle perfume of the author's soul.

    If I told you that I liked one part of your book better than another, it would be a falsehood. Each part has its own charm, its gray tone, its tears and its shadows . . .

    I must tell you that, since reading them, I have been haunted by many of your verses. I seem to recognize all around me the gardens, the trees, the longings that you describe in your poems. As if it were here, on this side of the ocean, that you endured and enjoyed such exquisite sentiments.

Do you not also, when you look upon the world, feel that it is made from the stuff of literature? Do you not seem to recognize in passersby the characters from certain novels, the creations of certain authors, the twilights of certain poems? Do you not feel sometimes that one might read life just as one turns the pages of a book . . . ?

◇

They want to be Juan Ramón Jiménez.

In a drawer in his desk, José hoards each letter, each stamp moistened by the poet's precious saliva. Five handwritten poems. Two signed portraits. A book inscribed in purple ink — *with the most sincere affection* — to young Señorita Hübner of Lima. Luckily, Carlos has not attempted to claim any of these trophies, as José must have them all for himself. He can no longer sit down to write a poem without first touching the page upon which, even if just for a moment, the fingers of Juan Ramón once rested. The pen that scrawled *Violet Souls* when its author was precisely the same age that José is now. So young! This is the moment, he tells himself, stroking the watermarked paper as he might caress a woman's skin. And then he waits, sitting at his desk. He grasps his pen firmly, waiting for something to happen. But it never does.

Carlos is amused by the worshipful way that José collects every tiny scrap of Juan Ramón's life with philatelic patience. Yet despite his amusement, of course he does not mock. That is a privilege reserved for José alone. Though Carlos is the one who writes the letters, his objective in doing so is not to obtain those sacred objects. He is unmoved by the thought of an advance copy of the Maestro's next book, *Distant Gardens,* which Juan Ramón has promised to send. Carlos pretends to be Georgina for a different reason altogether, though if anyone asked him what it was, he would not know how to answer.

That store of treasures is the envy of their circle of friends. Of course, calling them friends, even calling them a circle, may be an exaggeration. They are not friends, because before they are friends, they are poets, a profession in which good intentions are as scarce as good poems. And they aren't really a circle, as their habit of forging alliances just so they can later destroy one another, of creating magazines and literary journals driven only by the satisfaction of rejecting the poems of their rivals, has less in common with the purity of circles than it does with the tortured, many-cornered geometry of polyhedrons. But let's call it a circle anyway, and, with a little imagination, let's call them friends too. It's true that the men in that circle admire Juan Ramón, and so they also admire José and Carlos, though with a cold, pitiless passion. They feign interest in the young men's clumsy verses as a way to draw nearer to the great poet. For a time it even becomes the fashion among their group to write to other great literary figures in the guise of imaginary characters, almost always beautiful novitiates or consumptive damsels on their deathbeds. Letters to Galdós, to Darío, to plump Pardo Bazán, to Echegaray. One even writes a moving letter to Yeats in dubious English, to which, incidentally, that cad Yeats does not deign to reply — incredible how much sensitivity it took to write "The Secret Rose" and how little of it he exhibits in failing to respond to the piteous final wish of a dying girl.

◇

Before he was a poet, Carlos wanted to be many other things. A dinosaur-bone hunter. A sea lion toughened by intractable Cape Horn. A missionary to the savage Shuar tribe. An elephant tamer. An imperial grenadier. A pearl diver in the Sea of Japan. At six or seven years old, he even wanted to be a Jew, an appealing profession that appeared to consist of having a very long beard and hair. What he cannot recall ever having wanted to be is a lawyer. That was the first of many desires that were his father's alone and that little by little were inevitably imposed upon him.

Back then they lived near Iquitos, in the middle of the Amazonian rainforest. Throughout his childhood he lived in a series of different houses, always erected near his father's rubber camps, which moved around constantly. The camps were full of hundreds of Indians, their backs bare and covered in scabs, a few white foremen prowling among them. Sometimes you could hear the whistling of machetes chopping a path through the vegetation, mingled with the cries of men who seemed to be suffering unbearable pain in unfamiliar tongues. It's the mosquitoes, his father said when Carlos asked about the yelling. Those savages who work for us can't stand being bitten by mosquitoes.

It was a lonely time; his sisters were still very young, and there were no other children around to play with. Actually, the camps were full of children, but they were not children in the strictest sense of the word: they were the children of the indigenous workers, and so he could not play with them or even look at them, no matter how amusing he found their mischief or how very alone he felt. Pretend they're invisible, his father told him. And in his efforts to do so, to see nothing where in reality there was something, he also learned to see playmates where others saw none. And so Román, his imaginary friend, was born. Since he could choose, he chose for Román to be eleven years old, like him, and also white and not Indian — white as only Germans and polar bears can be — so Carlos could play with him morning, noon, and night.

Román was a boy who inspired a great deal of respect, so much so that Carlos always addressed him with great deference and docilely acquiesced to his every whim; Román was not just white but also a bit of a tyrant. If, when lessons were over, Carlos didn't play what Román wanted, he would go off with his own imaginary friends, children whom Carlos could not see despite his best efforts, just as he'd learned not to see those indigenous children who fashioned swords out of bamboo stalks and merrily tussled over rubber balls.

Carlos and Román did have a good deal in common, so much that they ended up becoming quite close friends. They both preferred playing in the corridors and bedrooms rather than going out into the fresh air. They were both bored during math lessons with Don Atiliano, the private tutor, even if Román could run off to play whenever he wanted and Carlos had to sit there solving trigonometry problems. They both hated Carlos's father's work, that endless procession of porters bearing bundles of rubber, and sometimes even stranger things, like the cart they saw pass by one night full of a dozen Indians slumbering in a heap, clumsily hidden under palm and banana leaves.

Too much imagination. That was the camp doctor's diagnosis. "Don't worry, Don Augusto, your son just has too much imagination." But Don Augusto was not reassured. "Far too much, damn it. The other day he was talking to the air like a lunatic for hours." But the doctor insisted there was no reason to worry. For the excessive imagination, he prescribed more meat in the diet and more trigonometry lessons.

"And what about the rest of it, Doctor?"

The rest of it was a lot of things. For example, it was that for some time Carlos had been spending all day reading poetry in his father's library, verses that, in excess, could end up turning him, as everyone knew — and here the father lowered his voice, covered his mouth with a clenched fist — into an invert. It was that sometimes he cried and hyperventilated for no reason, especially when Don Augusto discussed Carlos's future: enrollment in high school in Lima, and a law degree, and rubber. It was that when he'd been told how one day he'd be responsible for all the family's plantations, the boy had said in a quiet, serene voice, with the same politeness that he used to talk to Román: Then I'd rather die. It was his feminine handwriting. But the doctor wasn't concerned about any of those things either. For the crying jags and agitated breathing, he prescribed exercise, a dry climate, and certain oils to enhance his liver function. For the poetry, he prescribed a thump on the head and more fresh air. For the homosexuality, two years of patience until the boy turned thirteen, and then whores. And for the suicide threats, he suggested ignoring them but, just in case, and just for a couple of weeks, hiding all the knives in the house.

He was a good doctor. He could splint a broken leg, treat malaria, and counteract the venom of a snakebite. But he knew nothing of psychology. And even if he'd had some knowledge of it, the information would have been of limited use in the final decade of the nineteenth century, when the human mind was considered to be little more than an appendage of biology. And so he did not identify the crying fits as an anxiety disorder; those hadn't been invented yet, and even illnesses exist less, or exist in another form, when they have not been named. The doctor also didn't understand that tyrannical Román was the projection of a nascent inferiority complex produced by the combination of an authoritarian father and a passive mother, a mother who was insignificant, not much to speak of. A mother who mattered so little that she has not even appeared in this novel until now.

And so Carlos grows up suffering from anxiety attacks that are caused by the humid Amazonian climate. With inferiority complexes that are the product of a congenitally feeble liver.

But the prescriptions of the doctor who knows nothing of psychology fulfill their mission. At least that's how Don Augusto sees it. Little by little, Román stops visiting the house: he is not just white and tyrannical but also pragmatic, and he would rather find new friends than sneak around to play with Carlos. The death wishes cease after Don Augusto warns the maids not to let the boy into the kitchen. The homosexuality is dealt with at thirteen in a swank brothel for rubber men with a Polish prostitute who is also a virgin, though that's another story. And the humidity issue is resolved a year after that, when the family celebrates the completion of the mansion they've had built in Lima and moves there so that Carlos can start high school.

The poetry problem, however, is never solved. They send the boy off on endless walks, but he always manages to slip a volume of Hölderlin into his underwear. And when it seems that the vice has abated, one afternoon Don Augusto enters his son's bedchamber and finds under his mattress bound proof of infinite betrayals: books of poetry by Rilke, Mallarmé, Salaverry, Bécquer — books whose absence from the shelves of his library he has never noticed because he bought them all off a bankrupt aristocrat and cannot identify a single title. That night, Don Augusto administers many doses of the medicine prescribed by the doctor. He rains down blows with his belt, which a sobbing Carlos tries fruitlessly to fend off. This blow is for French poetry, and this one for English poetry, and these two right here for Spanish poetry, the biggest betrayal of all, *Spanish* poetry of all things. It's clear the boy's a pansy, and an unpatriotic one too, but Don Augusto's going to thrash that garbage out of his body if it takes all night. That's what he says. Because Don Augusto already has three daughters and doesn't want a fourth, not a simpering girl who rolls her eyes in ecstasy over poetry but a real man. There will be no more behaving like a little girl, he says, no more behaving like a sensitive little girl who can't handle being told that the workers' cries are caused not by mosquitoes but by the lash and that the carts that trundle off into the jungle are loaded not with sleeping Indians but with dead ones. He doesn't want another little girl in the house. What he wants even less than a little girl, though, is a cocksucker; he tells Carlos that quite clearly as he administers his final blow: Cocks are not for sucking, they're for goring women, understood? And Carlos understands, and he says yes, but with his voice distorted into an absurd squawk, the voice of the pansy he is and will always be, his father thinks in despair.

And during all this, the insignificant, inconsequential mother listens to the beating from her room, praying an endless rosary.

◇

Sometimes, when he's not composing letters in Georgina's name, when he's not spending his afternoons perched on the roof of the garret, Carlos writes his own poetry. Over the years, Don Augusto has come to accept it. What choice does he have? His son, who is such a sissy in so many ways, has lamentably turned out to be quite manly in others — for instance, in his stoic ability to endure the harshest thrashings for the sake of poetry. In any case, at least he's not the only one with this nasty mania for metaphors. The heir of the mighty Gálvez family is seized by it too — and such company can promise only great things. Don Augusto has even begun to convince himself that perhaps there's no danger after all, as a clandestine reconnaissance of his son's papers revealed references to a great number of women, each endowed with a lovely bare bosom. Even if his son has clothed them in so many complicated words.

The poems, to be honest, are not very good, and at times Carlos is even aware of this, but he does not care. He lost his ambition to become a great writer a long time ago. This fact, which has been noted quite casually here, is actually a great secret. He wouldn't confess it to José for anything in the world. He knows it would disappoint him, because for his friend there is nothing more important than poetry, or, to be precise, all the glory that accompanies it. It is José who talks endlessly of magazines, of literary prizes, of garlands that must be won, of secret spells that have been cast to keep them, the country's finest young poets, from publishing their poems. In fact, he spends much more time talking about these things than he does writing poetry. Carlos listens to him in silence. Though he is not interested in publications or prizes, he's even less interested in contradicting José. And so he ends up agreeing with him, just the way he assented to all Román's whims ten years earlier. Whatever you say, Román — I mean José.

What does Carlos want, then? He himself is not quite certain. It seems to him that he writes for the same reason his father accumulates tons of rubber and his mother has been praying the same uninterrupted rosary for thirty years: Because he doesn't know how to do anything else. Because he wants to be somewhere else. So every time he has to sign a document as the heir to the plantations of Don Augusto Rodríguez, every time he looks at an assignment for that degree he never wanted to pursue in the first place or hears his father and friends, over coffee, vie to see who has killed more Indians in a single day, he shuts himself in his room and writes. Or he lies on his bed and, staring at the ceiling, begins to imagine a few lines from Georgina's next letter. For some reason the two endeavors — writing poems and being Georgina — are mysteriously linked in his head.

For some time neither of the friends is published, though José sends their poems to every newspaper and printer he knows of. But one day the editor of a small journal in Lima summons them to his office. He's a fat, weary man with rings of sweat staining his armpits. The attention he gives them is as bloated and indolent as his appearance. Barely lifting his gaze from his papers, he informs them in a lackluster tone of the reason for their meeting. Someone has told him these two youngsters are in contact with the great Juan Ramón Jiménez. Might they be willing to suggest to the Maestro that he submit a couple of unpublished poems to this magazine — a modest publication, no need to pretend otherwise, but hygienic and quite respectable?

They hesitate a moment before responding. Carlos is trying to picture a magazine at its toilette. And José seems to be in a trance, gazing at the sheen of sweat on the man's face, the massive belly pressed against the tabletop. Someone so stout and sweaty should be barred from being a poet, he thinks, and certainly from being the editor of a magazine on which so many poets depend. In the end it is José who replies. They will mention it to Juan Ramón, of course; he's a close friend and will almost certainly say yes. In the meantime, however, perhaps they might come to an agreement, because as it happens the two of them are poets too, what a coincidence, and also coincidentally, they still have a few poems that have not yet been promised to other publications. (To be honest, they have more than a few of those — indeed, they have nothing else — but of course they choose not to clarify that point.) And coincidence strikes again, because, by chance, they happen to have some drafts of their poems with them.

Faced with such a remarkable series of coincidences — no less than three in just one sentence — the editor has no choice but to accept the papers José is offering him. He shuffles them listlessly. Holding a poem in each hand, he fans himself with one while reading the other. He wheezes. And after a couple of minutes he declares that, all right, while the letters to and from Juan Ramón are making their way across the Atlantic, it won't kill him to publish one of the poems, but unfortunately only one. For example, this one in his hand right here, by José Gálvez, because the one in his other hand, by Carlos Rodríguez — he says it without looking at him; in truth, he doesn't remember which of them is José and which is Carlos — is a little less refined.

José is exultant when they leave the office. Soon, though, perhaps feeling vaguely guilty about his friend's rejection, he makes an effort to convert all the energy of that euphoria into indignation. He attempts to console Carlos with a long series of protests. Who does that fat fellow think he is; he wouldn't recognize genuine talent if it smacked him on the head; the plot against them continues; they have won only the first battle in a long war; and so on. No one is going to write any letter to Juan Ramón, except maybe that fat bastard editor's mother, and that whoreson is never going to get to publish one of the Maestro's poems in his magazine. In his goddamn hygienic, respectable magazine. José even outlines the acceptance speech he will give if he one day wins the National Prize for Literature and Carlos still, God forbid, has not managed to publish a single poem; in it, he credits every bit of his success to him, his dear unpublished friend.

Both of them pretend to be sad about the rejection, but Carlos fakes it a bit more convincingly. His expression is, as always, a flawless simulation. Sometimes, when he gets bored, he lingers in front of the mirror awhile, rehearsing different expressions — joy, disappointment, melancholy, hope. He does it so well that from time to time he has been surprised to find himself experiencing real sadness and yet unpersuaded by his own emotion reflected in the mirror.

Then, in an instant, José regains the happiness he never really lost. He slings an arm familiarly around Carlos's shoulder and offers to buy a round.

"To Juan Ramón! We owe everything to him!" he toasts. "His letters have inspired us!"

And when he says this, he kisses the most recent wax-sealed envelope. He kisses it as a medieval pilgrim might kiss a holy relic. And he also kisses it on precisely the spot where only a few weeks earlier there lingered the greedy snout of a rat. The same rat that, on voyage after voyage, accompanies the correspondence in the hold of the transatlantic steamer.

Carlos lifts his glass to his lips, but by the time he has finished throwing back his drink, he is no longer thinking about the toast or about Juan Ramón — somehow he has started thinking about Georgina. This has been happening to him a lot lately. He finds himself thinking of her not as part of a game or as a pretext, but as someone who has a life of her own. Something akin to a distant cousin who lives in the countryside and whom we don't see often, or a maiden whose beauty we have frequently heard described by others and with whom we hope to exchange a few words at the next ball. Sometimes he even wonders whether it is not Georgina herself, rather than Juan Ramón and his letters, who is inspiring so many of his poems about impossible loves and ethereal muses.

But he says nothing, for that, too, is a secret.

"What about that nun?"

"Where?"

"Right there, right there — the one who's walking under the archway."

"Oh. Secondary, obviously — who the hell wants to read about a nun?"

"Also, she doesn't look like she's broken a plate in her life, so she's more of a Saint John of the Cross character than a Zorrilla . . ."

"What about the old woman begging for alms at the church door?"

"She's got a protagonistic look about her, doesn't she? But a short piece, of course. A story. Twenty pages or so. At most."

"Yes, a short story. A sad one. Very French, or maybe Russian. One of those where the main character starts out a pauper and spends the rest of the narrative sinking deeper into destitution. And those soldiers making rounds?"

"Nothing. That's all they're good for — making their rounds in the background. They haven't even got a page in them."

They've played the game late into the night. Slowly the electric streetlights have come on, and behind the windowpanes in the poor neighborhoods, the flames of candles and oil lamps have begun to flicker. It smells like noodles and white rice. In that building teeming with Chinese, it always smells like noodles and white rice, and sometimes a little like opium too.

"What about that pretty girl?"

"What about that little boy who's playing?"

"What about that coachman beating his horse?"

They keep pressing each other for a long time, even after the figures passing below them have become mere formless masses onto which any sort of character can be projected. But neither seems to have any intention of moving.

At last, when all is swallowed in darkness, when there is nothing left to look at, one of them — it doesn't matter which — asks:

"What about Georgina?"

And the other, whichever he is, doesn't answer.

◇

But after a while this, too, becomes boring. Or at least it bores them. The craze for anonymous letters fades. Nobody cares what Juan Ramón writes to Carlos and José. Back when the two were still at *Most esteemed Juan R. Jiménez,* the Club Unión would be packed to the rafters to hear the letter read aloud, but by the time they reach *Dear friend,* there are only three or four patrons who pay any attention. At this point, Gálvez doesn't even know what trophy to request from the poet; they have it all and yet still they have nothing. Their correspondence has become as insipid as José's and Carlos's poems, which were never truly admired — the two friends were tolerated at salons and readings only as a way to hear the story of Juan Ramón and Georgina.

Other novelties appear. In particular: A young journalist named Sandoval who works as a typographer for the monthly newspaper *Los Parias.* That in itself is already a novelty — someone among their social circle who works, even though he doesn't need to. He always shows up at the club with his hands stained with ink from the Linotype press, and he bears that mark of humility as if it were a war medal. He also has a scar on his temple, produced, he claims, by a policeman's nightstick during a strike, and he points to it proudly every time he talks about class conflict. He's an anarchist. Maybe not one of those terrorists who put bombs in the Barcelona opera house, but a peaceful revolutionary, an anarchist with his feet on the ground, as he puts it, who writes articles in support of the calls for strikes from the dockworkers in El Callao and the Bread Bakers' Union in Lima.

The people in attendance at the club, many of them members of the most elite ranks of Lima's aristocracy, always listen respectfully to Sandoval, sometimes going so far as to applaud a little when he gets carried away talking about revolution and the collapse of capitalism. They consider him harmless, a nice fellow. They even have a vague sense that his demands might be somewhat justified, that perhaps the workers do have the right to something more than living and dying in their factories, though, truth be told, they have no idea what those workers might do instead. How would the proletariat spend their sixteen free hours a day if the eight-hour workday were implemented? In any case, the young poets at the club don't know much about politics. They will know just as little a few years later when, one by one, they abandon poetry and step into their fathers' places at the head of those very factories.

To make matters worse, Sandoval is writing a novel. "I said *novel,* yes. Never poetry," he declared one night, almost scornfully, when someone asked him whether he might write poems. The twentieth century would be the death of verse, he added. Who gives a damn about fripperies and bourgeois sentiment when the final battle of the class war is being waged all around them? Only the wealthy experience that sort of emotion, those existential chasms and desponds, because when men have too much free time, when they do not employ their vital energy in demolishing the walls that divide them from their brothers, then all of that force is used to burrow into themselves, to grub away at themselves and finally concoct all those delicate, artificial emotions. Enough looking within, he continued haughtily, we must look beyond ourselves, because in plantations and factories across the globe there are humble men dying, dying in the flesh, not like those pansies who feel like they're dying of emotions that, in reality, no one cares about at all. And you can be sure that this is only the beginning; now we write novels in order to speak about actions, but in time actions will speak for themselves. That is the real literature, I tell you: action, the force of events, not the words that explain those events. The true novel of the twentieth century will be written not in a garret but in the streets, amid the clamor of protests, assassination attempts, wars, revolutions. And of that novel, let it be known, we are already writing the opening chapters. Once more the room bursts into applause. Dozens of wealthy poets cheering first the death of capital, and then the death of poetry.

José and Carlos don't say anything. And if they do, nobody hears them.

◇

Juan Ramón is a genius. Nobody doubts that, least of all José and Carlos. But the Maestro had his father die on him, and how could you not write sad arias if your father died, especially if you happened to have loved him; who *wouldn't* have the poetic material for pastorals and violet souls and distant gardens if he'd been interned in no less than two sanatoriums and had, on top of it all, fallen fatally in love with a novitiate? The two of them, on the other hand . . .

"The problem's not the poems — it's life," says José. "To write extraordinary things, first you must live them. That's the difference between run-of-the-mill poets and true geniuses: experience. And, honestly, what have the two of us really lived?"

Carlos doesn't answer for a moment, then realizes it's not a rhetorical question. He tugs at the knot in his tie.

"Nothing?"

"Exactly. Nothing. We're still in this dreadful city, always drinking from the same bottles and laughing at the same jokes. The most exciting thing we've done in our lives is this: writing a few little letters to collect autographs from the one man who truly knows how to live. And let's not even talk about muses. You can't exactly say we've had any passionate love affairs. We've slept with a few women, sure, but that's all. And a lot of them were whores. Nobody revolutionizes Spanish poetry by writing about whores."

"I guess not."

"Even if they're expensive whores, like the ones your father gets for you."

"Go to hell."

They're sitting on benches in the university courtyard, watching the morning pass and the students stream in and out of the lecture halls. Carlos thinks about all the times they've done this very thing before: waving goodbye to their parents using their law textbooks as a pretext, then whiling away the hours sitting outside the university doors, smoking and waiting for it to get late enough to go home. In a biographical note about Juan Ramón, Carlos read, *He started out studying law, but abandoned it in 1899 to devote himself entirely to painting and poetry.* Him too, then! Could it be a sign? He can't help wondering whether Juan Ramón also spent many mornings like this one, perhaps with a book of poetry in his hands, and the thought helps allay his boredom and disgust.

"That's what we need," José is saying. "An unattainable muse to whom we can dedicate our finest poems. Without that, there's nothing, you know? Only the sad little scribblings of an amateur. What would have happened to Dante if Beatrice hadn't been a girl, or to Catullus if Lesbia hadn't been a whore? You don't know? Well, I'll tell you. World literature would have gone to shit, that's what would have happened."

He's found a little stick somewhere and is using it to scrawl idly in the dirt as he speaks. Parallel lines that seem to underscore his words, fill in his silences.

"Sometimes I think it is of secondary importance whether a man writes well or badly," he continues after a pause during which his lips and the stick remain motionless. "Real poetry is produced through the beauty of great muses. You don't need anything else — the only trouble is finding those muses in the first place. And until we find our muse, the magazines are going to keep sending back our poems, because they'll keep being what they are: the efforts of children, school assignments. The work of cocksure schoolboys fondling themselves as they dream of the women they'll have when they grow up."

"We have to take a page from Juan Ramón," Carlos murmurs, as if guessing what Gálvez wants to hear.

"Indeed; our friend writes well and always finds himself a good muse. Even a novitiate once! And before that, in the Bordeaux sanatorium, there was that story about the other one, the French one — what was her name?"

"Jeanne Roussie," Carlos answers immediately. They are experts on Juan Ramón's biography. They know by heart his age when his father died and the most intimate minutiae of each of his heartbreaks. They are careful not to forget a single detail, perhaps because they tend to think of all these tragedies as a sort of *cursus honorum* that one must follow in order to write a good book of poetry.

"That's it, Jeanne. Anyway, that's a tricky situation too. Falling in love with your doctor's wife! That's some real drama right there. But he outdid himself with the novitiate. Think of it: the battle between carnal and spiritual hungers, between divine and earthly love ... Oh, he's a true artist, that Juan Ramón. With stories like that, you'd have to be dead inside not to write good poems."

"Well, you once kissed a novitiate, didn't you?"

José indifferently tosses the stick away.

"You should have seen her! She was the kind of girl who inspires nightmares, not verses. When I took off her wimple, I understood why she wanted to become a nun."

Carlos doesn't respond. Out of the corner of his eye, he's been following the progress of José's stick in the dirt: a grid of crowded lines forming a dense lattice. Looking at it, he thinks for some reason of his father. He thinks of Georgina. He's barely listening to José, who's still insisting that the only thing keeping his poems from genius is the absence of the perfect woman, that divine inspiration that would elevate his verses to the very peak of the sublime. Because, sure, they've both had their puppy loves, he continues, but those were conventional, boring, happy stories, far removed from the mythological stature of the loves they find in books, in which, in the throes of passion, the two lovers expire. Though in their case it would be best if only the women died, because otherwise how would they go on to write their immortal verse? Someone definitely has to die, or be locked up in a monastery, or, at the very least, the families have to oppose the union, forcing the lovers to flee across the Andes with hired guns in hot pursuit. But none of that ever happens, he adds bitterly. Everything around them proceeds so easily: The family agrees to the engagement — so why bother getting engaged? — and what's worse, the daughters agree to everything else with horrifying speed, and once they surrender themselves, how can they continue to serve as muses? What else can one do in such a suffocating environment, José asks, besides write stale literary-salon poetry, poetry for summer readings at an aunt's house — light, insignificant verses, written to be read aloud on Sunday afternoons surrounded by lace fans, cigars, and stifled yawns.

"So all we need is a muse," Carlos says to himself, still looking at the drawing.

"A muse, or whatever else we can find. I don't know. A war, maybe. Just picture it: The flags, the parades, the speeches. The spilling of your best friend's blood. That has to be a good reason to write a poem! Verses written on the verge of despair, knowing that at any moment a bullet might mow you down."

"If you don't die first, of course."

"I'm serious; war is the best source of inspiration. Maybe

Homer was a mediocre poet and was saved by hearing about the right war. Who knows. I imagine every soldier has material that could move anyone; it's just that most of them don't realize it. Take my uncle José Miguel. You know, the hero of the War of the Pacific. I've always believed he could have been a great poet. Everybody knows that he blew up a Chilean ship all by himself and that the explosion was so powerful it left him bald and nearly blind. But few know that toward the end of his life, that memory tormented him. He said that at all hours of the day and night, he could hear the screams of the Chilean sailors burning alive and begging to be rescued, for the love of God. With that on your conscience, you could either write the world's best poem or shoot yourself in the head. And you know which way my uncle went."

"Well, I would have written the poem."

"Sure, but you and I are poets. My uncle was a soldier. I guess he did what was most appropriate for his profession."

Carlos smiles.

"So as far as you're concerned, those are our two options: finding a muse or starting another goddamn war with Chile."

José replies in a jocular tone.

"It's either that or tuberculosis, my friend! Maybe we should give that a try. They say that in your final moments, this incredible lucidity washes over you. Apparently the convulsions produce fits of creativity, and we're losing extraordinary poems because we don't give patients blank sheets of paper and ink as they're dying."

"I don't know about you, but I think I'd rather have a muse. Or just live a long life as a bad poet."

They both laugh.

"Maybe so."

For a few moments neither of them says anything. The sun is now high in the sky. The birds are still singing up on the roof of the university, but the young men are hearing them only now. Soon their classmates will come out into the courtyard, shaking off the torpor of the canon law class, all mechanical and gray, like the bureaucrats they will one day become. It's time to go home.

"If only we could invent our own biographies," says José with something like a sigh as they get up.

"At least we can invent Juan Ramón's," replies Carlos, and he finishes the rest of the sentence in his thoughts.

◇

If the idea has a single origin, it is here. And if it has a single creator, then that creator is Carlos alone, however much Gálvez tries to make it his too, gathering their friends together to declare, "Gentlemen, Carlota and I have started writing a novel." Because the truth is that everything begins with something Carlos said, and at first all José did was shake his head in silent rejection.

The conversation could take place anywhere. Perhaps on that bench in the university courtyard, or maybe on the rooftop that always seems on the verge of collapsing, or in a tavern where they're drunkenly passing the time till last call with bureaucratic patience. Carlos, uncharacteristically, speaks. The night before, demoralized once again by the rejection of one of his poems by yet another magazine, José has suggested that perhaps the time has come to forget about their correspondence with Juan Ramón. After all, what has their wearisome prank produced but a bunch of headaches, a few signed sheets of paper, and the nickname, however amusing it might be, of Carlota? They're never going to become better poets like this, much less find a muse who will get them there. And so: To hell with Georgina. But Carlos doesn't agree. For the first time, he refrains from answering with one of the expressions he's rehearsed in his mirror and instead responds with a *No* that arises from deep within him. Definitively: No. His voice trembles, because he is, after all, only a rubber man's son, made to accommodate all José's desires, but even so he does not give in. No, he repeats stubbornly. Why not? Carlos can't really explain. No, I said no. And that's that.

He can't sleep that night. Lying in bed, he mulls over what José said about muses. Just before he falls asleep, he thinks he has found the answer. An argument that, knowing his friend, will absolutely convince him. One that could change the direction of their lives. And so when they meet up again at last, he gives the speech he's prepared for the occasion. A stammering monologue that Gálvez listens to in silence. Or at least he does for a few minutes, with a condescension that might be mistaken for respect. But at a certain point he can't take any more and impatiently breaks in.

"No, no, no, what are you saying, Carlitos, what novel? Stop talking nonsense! We don't write novels, remember? We leave that to Sandoval and his crowd."

José doesn't understand. Or maybe he doesn't understand what his friend is doing having an idea of his own, regardless of what it is. So Carlos has to insist, despite how difficult it is for him to contradict José, despite how often he touches his hair or nervously clears his throat as he speaks. He asks José if he remembers when they said that everyone's lives were literature, and José replies simply, "Yes." Those afternoons up on the roof, when the world seemed to them to be full of secondary characters and only a handful of protagonists? And José answers, "Of course." Those discussions in which they decided what writer was writing the life of each person? And José squawks, "I said yes, damn it." Well, th-this, stutters Carlos, is exactly the same thing. The life of Juan Ramón is a novel too, and chapter by chapter, letter by letter, they have already begun to write it, though they hadn't realized it until now. All this time, they thought they were playing a fairly tiresome prank or collecting a few souvenirs, but what they were really doing was something much more serious: writing the novel of the life of a genius.

José opens his mouth. Then closes it. And Carlos goes on,

stammering less and less. Because while it may be that they don't have their own muse and so will never manage to produce a perfect poem, he adds, in the end, what does that matter? Perhaps providence has reserved for them, Carlos Rodríguez and José Gálvez Barrenechea, a far nobler fate: out of nothing, creating the beauty celebrated by another poet. And who knows, continues Carlos, who can no longer stop himself, maybe that's another sort of perfect poem, the only one that is truly transcendent, molding the clay of words and saying to them: Rise, and go forth. The two of them would resemble God the Father and Creator of all things, were it not a sin to say so, or even think it. They are giving life to the muse with whom Juan Ramón must fall in love, and that story, that tempestuous romance, that fragment of life caught midway between reality and fiction, will be their novel. And if one day the Maestro builds a poem upon the embers of that love, even just one, they will know in their hearts that they've done the most difficult thing of all: that they couldn't be more responsible for the beauty of that poem if they'd written it themselves.

Carlos stops. To bolster his thesis that everything is literature, that the entire world is a text constructed of words alone, he would like to cite Foucault, Lacan, Derrida. But he cannot, because Derrida and Lacan and Foucault have not yet been born. Actually, Lacan has: he is three years old and currently playing with a jigsaw puzzle — it's morning in Paris — perhaps constructing future memories of what he will one day call the mirror stage. So Carlos has nothing else to add.

José doesn't either. Instead he stares, as if his friend had only just now begun to exist.

He agrees with a slow nod.

He smiles the same smile with which he celebrated Georgina's birth.

II

A Love Story

◇

Their novel does not yet have a title or a defined plot. All they know are the names of the two protagonists and the settings they inhabit: a real Lima and a Madrid vaguely imagined from the other side of the Atlantic.

It starts out as a comedy. Or at least it seems that way. The opening pages are full of rich men pretending to be poor and men pretending to be women and squatting down to urinate in empty avenues. There are mistakes and laughter and gluttonous rats that nest in mail sacks; there are bottles of pisco and chicha. A great poet is tricked as if he were a child, and two children pretend to be great poets. There is envy, too, but the kind that is ultimately healthy, bracing, not bitter, as well as a trend among Lima's wealthy youth to write to their favorite authors pretending to be infatuated young ladies.

Perhaps in keeping with this jovial spirit, the letters between Georgina and Juan Ramón are also breezy and light, like notes passed between schoolchildren. For José and Carlos, the authors of the comedy, it is a happy period, partly because they enjoy the writing and partly because they feel like protagonists in their own novel. Telling them otherwise, informing them that Georgina is the sole protagonist, would likely be a fruitless endeavor. They are young, full of ambition and dreams; they are still unable to imagine that there might be a story in the world in which they are not the main characters.

Then comes the revelation. They discover they've been mistaken all along. It is not a comedy. It never has been, even if the drunken revels and the hoaxes and the little blind girls writing to Yeats made them believe otherwise. It is a love story, perfectly in keeping with so many other beautiful books before it, and only they can write it. An epistolary novel on a par with Goethe's *Werther* and Richardson's *Pamela* — maybe even better than those, as theirs will be the first book in history to be inhabited by flesh-and-blood characters. Each letter sent or received constitutes a chapter of the novel. Juan Ramón, Georgina, the friends and relatives to which the two of them refer — they are all characters brought to life in these pages. The poem that the Maestro will one day write to his beloved is the perfect dénouement. And Carlos and José are the authors, of course, clever novelists who shut themselves away in the garret to deliberate over the details of the plot. They say, for example: "The heroine becomes somewhat overwrought in the fifth chapter; we should bring down the tension a bit in the seventh." Or perhaps: "Would you take another look at the latest chapter? I've noticed a plausibility problem in the first paragraph."

It's true, it still feels like a game. In a way, though, it's the most serious thing they've ever done.

Of course, between letters, many things happen. After all, a ship takes no less than thirty days to cross the Atlantic. Everything is slow in 1904, from the length of a mourning period to the time needed to pose for a photograph. And so during the long spells of waiting, José and Carlos's life continues: their mornings playing hooky, their afternoons lounging in the garret, and their nights carousing at the club; their evenings attending plays and concerts; their afternoons sunbathing and swimming in the sea at Chorrillos; their Saturdays placing bets at the cockfighting ring in Huanquilla or at the Santa Beatriz racetrack or at the billiards tables; their Sundays enduring Mass and watching the hours tick by on the sitting-room clock; their ends of semesters forging grade reports; their spring afternoons strolling up and down Jirón de la Unión; their first and third Wednesdays of every month making and receiving visits, drinking hot chocolate and eating cookies, bowing and listening to piano recitals, discussing the weather or the advantages of train travel with prim young ladies who may one day be their wives. All of that is what they used to call life, but now it seems like only a slow and sticky dream, exasperating in the way it passes drop by suffocating drop. As if the whole world has gone mad and only their letters can keep it going. Real life now consists of waiting for the transatlantic steamship to dock in El Callao and unload its supply of letters from the Maestro. Sitting in the club talking about their flesh-and-blood novel and watching the other patrons gradually lose interest in Sandoval's dockworkers' strike, which never quite takes off. Writing the next letter.

To improve their efforts, they consult a book entitled *Advice for a Young Novelist,* a seven-hundred-page tome that is rather short on advice and long on commandments and whose target audience seems to be not a young writer but an elderly scholar. The author, one Johannes Schneider, repeatedly employs the words *dissection, exhumation, analysis,* and *autopsy.* One could not ask for greater honesty, as indeed the book undertakes with Prussian rigor the task of dismembering World Literature, until everything extraordinary and beautiful in that genre is writhing under its scalpel. The boys take turns reading it aloud, but they always end up dozing off, unable to make it past the one hundred and fourteenth guideline. One inspired night, they decide to light the wood stove in the garret with its pages, timidly at first, but when they see it blaze up they can no longer hold back. Laughing wildly, they burn the seven hundred guidelines, page by page, in a celebration reminiscent of a pagan ritual, of a liberation from the old and the advent of the unknown: a new literature that will have no pages with which to warm oneself, only events and endeavors that will make their mark on the flesh and memory of men. They contemplate this as the flames waver and tremble, and their laughter gradually dies out with them; somewhere the cat scampers and howls, and downstairs the Chinese tenants eat or dream or sing old songs about the Yellow River, or simply continue the business of living without thinking about anything, attempting to remain unaware that they are already starting to forget the faces of their mothers and wives.

◇

Perhaps it is too much to call them writers just because they've authored a few letters. It depends on how much importance we grant their correspondence, not to mention how seriously we take the craft of writing itself, which is not really a profession but something closer to an act of faith. The only thing we can know for sure is this: They believe they are writers. And just as with a hysterical pregnancy, when the body swells to harbor a child that will never be born, their position as hypothetical literary figures brings with it some of the same virtues and defects exhibited by actual writers.

And so it is that their first insecurities and fears arise, the welter of anxieties that every creator must inevitably encounter sooner or later. In the end, no author who isn't an idiot — though we mustn't discount the possibility that a good writer may be one — can blindly trust in something so fragile as words, which after all are the raw material of his work. And so both of them are afraid, but, as no two artists are entirely alike, their fears are quite different.

José fears, among other things, that Juan Ramón will find them out and stop writing letters; that Juan Ramón will not find out but even so will stop writing letters; that the men at the club would rather talk about Sandoval's strike than about their novel; that the Maestro is already engaged, or has a muse, or both; that though he and Carlos believe they are writing a set of letters on the level of Ovid's *Heroides,* in fact their work is fit only for a tawdry melodrama. Most of all, though, he is afraid that Juan Ramón will never write the poem for Georgina — or, worse still, that he will write it and it will be mediocre. To be frank, he is afraid the poem will be awful, a monstrosity, a literary abomination, and that, what's more, the ingrate will dedicate it to her; what good will it do to have authored a muse who inspires not ardent passions but wretched little verses dictated by piety, or boredom, or even friendship, which is what men always seem to talk about when they're really talking about women for whom they feel nothing?

Carlos, for his part, is not worried about the as-yet-unwritten poem. His fears are, in fact, just one alone: That Georgina will not be good enough. That after all the letters, after imagining her for so many sleepless nights, they will have managed to produce only a vulgar, insignificant woman, a woman incapable of piquing Juan Ramón's interest. That she is condemned forever to be a secondary character, one of the countless nondescript women they see pass by from their perch above the garret, nameless, pointless. Where are they going, and why would anyone care? His doubts are reinforced every time they receive a letter that is a little more ceremonious, a little stiffer than usual. How do they know Juan Ramón isn't writing a hundred letters just like these every day? One morning Carlos reads an article in the paper about the assembly lines that automobile manufacturers are starting to use in the United States, and that night he dreams about Juan Ramón sitting in his study, feverishly occupied in assembling polite clichés, sealing envelopes, and tweaking paragraphs that are repeated in identical form in letter after letter.

. . . This morning I received your letter, which I found most charming, and I am sending you my book at once,

regretting only that my verses cannot live up to all that you must have hoped they would be, Georgina/María/ Magdalena/Francisca/Carlota . . .

This is the core of his fear, if fear can have precise contours: that his Georgina will end up meaning more to him than she does to the Maestro.

◇

It doesn't matter who tells them about the scriveners in the Plaza de Santo Domingo. Whoever it is, in any case, quickly convinces them that it's the only place for them to go for help writing their novel. And that Professor Cristóbal, an expert in lovers' notes and epistolary courtship, is just the person they need.

If José and Carlos had seen the Professor pass by from their garret, with his shabby hat and his scribbler's gear on his back, they would have quickly declared him a secondary character. And they would have been right, at least as far as this story is concerned. But if daily life in Lima in 1904 had its own novel, let's say a volume of some four hundred pages, then Professor Cristóbal would certainly deserve a protagonist's role, if only for the secrets that have passed through his hands over the course of two decades. Not even all the priests in the city, compiling all the innumerable tales they've heard in their confessionals, could attain a clearer picture of their parishioners' consciences.

The lives of illustrious men begin with their birth and, in a sense, even earlier, with the feats of the ancestors who bestow upon them their last names and titles. Humble men, however, come into the world much later, once they have hands that are able to work and backs able to bear a certain amount of weight. Some — most — are never born at all. They remain invisible their whole lives, dwelling in miserable corners where History does not linger. You could say that Cristóbal was born at seventeen, when he was given a lowly position in a Lima notary office. All that preceded that moment — his childhood, his longings, the reasons for his indigent family's extraordinary determination to provide him with proper lessons in reading and writing — is a mystery. Or, rather, it would be a mystery if anyone took an interest in finding it out. But no one does; nobody cares. And so his biography begins there, in a dingy room piled with papers where the notary ordered him to steam codicils open and keep certain bits of money apart from the rest of the accounting. Like any newborn, Cristóbal obeyed in silence, not questioning the world around him. We know as little about what passed through his head during this period as we do about what took place before his birth.

In 1879 Professor Cristóbal was called to the front to serve as an infantryman in Arauca during the disastrous war against Chile. At the time, of course, he hadn't yet acquired his nickname. And the war against the Chileans still seemed less like a catastrophe and more like a sporting event or a hunting party, a long pilgrimage made so that the young men could wear trim uniforms with epaulets and have their cries of *Long live this* and *Down with that* ring out across the countryside. With the first shots fired came a number of bitter revelations. After a couple of days of combat, the uniforms were soiled with mire and blood, and the young men no longer seemed so young, and it was those newly fledged men, not ideas or nations, who began to die in the dusty ditches. Many of them were no doubt still virgins, which for some reason Cristóbal found saddest of all. That and the fact that his illiterate comrades, which was most of them, didn't even have the consolation of reading their loved ones' letters before they died. One day, upon hearing the dying wishes of a brother-in-arms, Cristóbal agreed to take dictation as the young man bade his mother farewell. On another occasion he helped his sergeant craft a marriage proposal to his wartime pen pal, and before he knew it he was earning his service pay writing the private correspondence of half the company. He was even made Captain

Hornos's personal assistant, a promotion that had a good deal to do with the six sweethearts the captain had left behind in Lima, women who required daily appeasement with promises and poetry.

The war didn't last long. Or, rather, what began as a war and lasted a mere four years on the battlefield became a humiliating loss that would haunt Peruvians' memory for decades. When Cristóbal — now known as Professor Cristóbal — returned to Lima, he did not want to go back to his position in the notary office. It was, it seems, a question of ethics — no more falsified wills for him, no more perjuries to assist the head notary's accumulation of wealth — though, in fact, the matter remains somewhat muddled, as at the time the Professor was really too poor to have principles. What he did have, though, was the firm intention never to serve another master again, and so he began working under the arcades in the Plaza de Santo Domingo.

The letter writers have no superiors and no fixed schedules. In pompous moments, they call themselves public secretaries, a solemn way of saying that they don't even have their own offices, or rather that their offices and the street are one and the same. They occupy a corner under the arches in the square, and there, each morning, they set up their ramshackle desks and wait for customers to come in search of their services. They are sometimes called evangelists because, like the evangelists of the New Testament, their work is to transcribe the words dictated to them by others. And that is all they do from morning to night, at the foot of the columns around the plaza: write letters for the unlettered. They provide a voice to the emigrant who wants to send news home — *Mother, you wouldn't believe how big Juanito's gotten.* They provide eyes to the illiterate young woman who needs to read the note someone slipped under her door. They provide elegant words to the widow or bureaucrat writing to the government to request a pension or a particular post in the provinces.

Professor Cristóbal set up his supplies in an unoccupied corner of the square, and soon that empty space belonged to him so wholly that he even nailed a hook for his hat and jacket into one of the pillars. He has a school desk, its surface marred by scratches and dents, and for twenty years he has arranged the same objects on it, always in the same order: inkwell, pen, penholder, drafting triangles, blotting paper. He also has a case that once contained a Singer sewing machine and now serves as a footstool and occasionally as a storage box where he can keep a few coins. And, finally, there's a portrait of his dead wife, to whom he probably never wrote a single letter or poem.

He accepts only commissions for sentimental correspondence. A cardboard sign on the table states it quite clearly: PROFESSOR CRISTÓBAL: LOVE LETTERS WRITTEN ON REQUEST. But the category of love is broad enough to include the old woman who has visited him every Monday for twelve years to have him write a new petition for pardon for her imprisoned son, letters that, Cristóbal would argue, are charged with as much emotion as the most passionate romance. Dozens of customers line up in front of his desk every day, wringing their hands as they wait, or rolling their eyes, or fulfilling some other cliché of their condition, because the lovers of Lima are as unoriginal as those anywhere else in the world. It is not only the illiterate who come to him. He also helps young people who need gallant phrases with which to woo the objects of their affection. In those instances, Cristóbal is not merely an evangelist but also a poet who must imagine what the recipient of the letter is like and then compose verses to which the aspirants contribute only the wordless fever of love.

When he finishes, he places all his drafts and abortive attempts in a wicker basket, to be used later to feed the wood stove in his kitchen. He jokes about it frequently, saying that all winter long he is warmed by the love of strangers. Romance provides only an ephemeral light, one that burns quickly but leaves behind neither heat nor embers.

At first they don't see anything remarkable. Just a gray-haired, bespectacled old man who doesn't even lift his eyes from his papers when their turn comes.

"Good morning, Dr. Professor."

"Just call me Professor, if you please."

"We've come to consult with you about a problem, Professor."

Still without looking at them, Cristóbal spoke again.

"I'll bet you have. And I'll bet your problem wears a skirt and a bodice."

José smiles a bit late.

"Don't forget the petticoats, Professor."

At that, Cristóbal looks up. The pause lasts only an instant, but in that instant his gaze seems to take everything in. The imported suits. The silver knob on Carlos's walking stick. The gold cufflinks.

"Expensive petticoats, from the looks of it." Then he interlocks his fingers and rests his chin on them. "Let me guess. A little young lady from . . . La Punta or Miraflores, but I'd say it's more likely she's from Miraflores. No older than twenty. Quite beautiful. Regular features, shapely, delicate ears, velvety skin, winsome eyes . . ."

José arches his eyebrows.

"How do you know all that?"

"Well, Miraflores . . . To be frank, I can't see men of your sort falling in love with a poor woman from San Lázaro. As for the rest of it, I don't know if your damsel is actually as I've described her, but no doubt the two of you think she is. I've never met a man who said his beloved was hunchbacked, that she had ill-formed ears or homely eyes. And with regard to the velvety skin, neither of you could possibly contradict me, as you haven't fondled even a ruffle of her clothing."

"And how do you know that?"

"What's even rarer than meeting a man who doesn't think his beloved is beautiful is finding one with a woman who, once she's consented to his caresses, does not then consent to everything else. To which saint will you be writing these letters, then, since you already have it all?"

José laughs.

"Irrefutable logic, Professor. I had no idea mathematics and love went so well together."

"And now comes the easy part. Deciding which of you is in love and which is the loyal squire who rides at his side . . . There's no question you're the one who's in love — you, the quiet one."

He points at Carlos.

"Me?"

"Oh, dear. Your logic has failed you there, Professor," José tells him. "Let's say we're both interested in the young lady, what do you say to that?"

Cristóbal seems unimpressed.

"That the two of you have a closer relationship than I'd realized."

"Don't pay him any mind," says Carlos. "She's not anybody's beloved, at least not yet. And she's my cousin."

"Her name is Carlota."

"My friend is joking again. Georgina. Her name is Georgina."

Cristóbal's expression has grown stern.

"Your cousin, is she? And which one of you is courting her?

For the sake of our business, I hope I'm mistaken about you, because it is a rule of mine never to wet my nib for love affairs between blood relatives. Nor do I place my wax seal on romances between two men, much less produce letters for girls who have not yet been presented in society. Even we scriveners have our ethics, you know."

"There's no need to worry about that. We're not the ones courting her."

"She's hung up on another man. A Spanish friend she's been exchanging letters with for some months."

"A friend, or maybe something more," Carlos adds.

"The truth is, it's hard to tell how things stand, Professor."

"It's hard to tell, but my cousin, you know — she's smitten."

"She can't think about anything else, poor thing."

Cristóbal focuses on his papers again.

"I understand. And I suppose you want me to help her with the next letters, is that it? Put a little polish on the correspondence to see if we can reel this Spanish fellow in?"

"No, she takes care of the letters," Carlos answers, his voice suddenly harsh.

"We are asking a much smaller favor, Professor. The girl insists, you know, on writing the letters herself. She's a romantic, his cousin is. The one we're not so sure about is that friend of hers."

"We're concerned her affections might be unrequited, you see. That he's only stringing her along," says Carlos.

"That even if it seems like he's ready to pluck the hen, the only thing he really wants to take off her is her inheritance."

"That's why we need your advice, Professor."

"We were told there's nobody in Lima who knows more than you about love letters and how to interpret them," says José.

"If you could give us your impression as to the gentleman's intentions . . ."

"Or tell us if there are signs he is going to make some noble gesture, like perhaps writing her a poem or two. That's just the sort of thing she longs for, you see."

Professor Cristóbal twirls his eyeglasses between his fingers as he listens.

"Yes, I see. So let's just get right down to it: Do we or do we not want the courtship to end well?"

"We do, we do."

"Of course we do! All we want is for his cousin to be happy."

The scrivener nods, pleased.

"I'm glad to hear that, because I also refuse to dip my nib to swim against love's tide. Indeed, you might say that's my golden rule in this work: love above all else. Even a poor man has ethics. You understand."

"There's no need to worry about that."

"I don't help seduce married women either. That's another rule that's not up for discussion."

"You can rest assured that everything is quite ethical and wholesome."

"And very romantic. We're romantics too, you know."

The Professor claps his hands together loudly.

"Then say no more. But if you want my opinion, we're going to need the chap's letters. So if you could —"

Before he's finished the sentence, Carlos has already placed a packet on the table.

"Here are his letters, and hers are at the bottom. You can't say we haven't been thorough."

Cristóbal accepts the bundle of letters and warily examines both sides of it.

"And how is it that you have hers too? Does your cousin write them and then just stick them in a drawer?"

"She mails them, but she makes a lot of drafts beforehand, Professor," says Carlos.

"As we said, she is unable to think about anything else."

"She's completely hung up on him."

"And it's hard to tell how things stand," José adds.

"It's hard to tell," Carlos confirms.

Cristóbal stares at them in silence for a moment, as if attempting to tease out something else behind their words. Then he unties the bundle and gently unfolds the first letter. Almost immediately he looks up from the writing paper.

"What exquisite handwriting your cousin has! I've never seen anything like it. It looks like a doll's handwriting!"

José laughs again.

"That's exactly what I'm always telling her."

◇

It takes almost an hour for the scrivener to read all the letters, and in the meantime José and Carlos wait in silence. They study his reactions, the indifferent or alert expression with which he turns the pages. They fear that at any moment he might look up and offer some crisp commentary. Perhaps:

These are the best letters I've ever read in my life.

Or maybe:

These are the worst letters I've ever read in my life.

But nothing of the sort happens. After folding up the last letter, Cristóbal only takes off his glasses, methodically lights a cigar, and asks them if they've ever seen one of Lima's covered ladies.

"Covered ladies?"

"Of course not," José interjects. "It's been half a century since that was the fashion in this country."

The Professor nods in agreement.

"That's true. But you've no doubt seen that style of dress on postcards or in photographs. Maybe even in the old armoire of a coquettish grandmother . . . am I right?"

"Yes," says Carlos, still uncertain what the covered ladies have to do with his Georgina. Or, rather, with his cousin.

But Cristóbal keeps talking.

"You could still see the last of them when I was a boy. Many years ago. The French styles with their petticoats and corsets had become quite popular, and very few women still wore the old colonial dress. It was something to see: a long skirt that came down to the ankles, so narrow and restrictive that there was barely room to put one foot in front of the other to walk. And a pleated mantle, reminiscent of an Arab veil, that covered the bust and the entire head, leaving only the smallest bit of the face exposed. A little silken cleft through which you could see just a single eye . . . And do you know why the covered ladies left that eye uncovered?"

"So they could see where they were going?" asks José, chuckling.

"To flirt," says Carlos, refusing to join in on the joke.

"Exactly. But don't you think men would find it more tantalizing if they left more of the face or body uncovered?"

"No," Carlos swiftly replies.

"Why not?"

"Because something that shows half is always more suggestive than something that shows everything, Professor."

"And do you think they'd have been more seductive if they'd covered themselves entirely, wrapped from head to foot like the mummies of ancient Egypt?"

"No," he answers cautiously. "Because showing nothing at all has as little allure as showing too much."

Professor Cristóbal claps his hands together so hard that he almost drops his cigar.

"Correct! Even you, who are still novices in this area, who are, shall we say, babes in the woods when it comes to love, understand this basic law, do you not? Love is a door left ajar. A secret that survives only as long as it is half kept. And that roguish eye was the lure that Lima's women tied on their lines when they went out on their promenades. The bait upon which men hooked themselves like fools. Have you heard of the language of the fan and handkerchief? How a woman could speak the language of love without opening her mouth? Well, the same thing can be achieved with batted eyelashes beneath a shawl. A long blink means 'I belong to you.' Two short blinks, 'I desire you, but I am not free.' A long one and then a short one —"

"You know an awful lot about covered ladies," says José in a voice that contains not a hint of admiration. "But as to our cousin —"

"Your cousin," Cristóbal interrupts him with imperious calm, "has forgotten the fundamental rule of love that your friend recalls so well. Perhaps she never knew it. Read the letters yourselves, if you haven't already. Oh, I can see by your faces that you have. Several times, even. So tell me, what is this cousin like?"

José and Carlos exchange glances.

"She's twenty years old . . ."

"She's beautiful . . ."

Cristóbal waves a hand in the air.

"Yes, yes, fine! Regular features, winsome eyes, velvety skin, slender waist . . . I know all that already. I knew it before you opened your mouths. But what is she like? What does she tell us about herself in the letters? Nothing! She hardly talks about anything except literature and poems and . . . whatever else. I wasn't paying much attention by the end, to be honest. It may be that the distinguished gentleman with whom she is exchanging letters thinks her a sophisticated correspondent, but I doubt he could say much more than that. Some women sin in their letters by revealing too much. They approach love naked, so to speak. Your cousin is making the opposite error. This covered lady's so timid that she's cloaked herself head to foot and forgotten to leave an eye showing. And as you said yourself, such prudishness does not work well in the game of seduction. Do you understand?"

For a few moments neither speaks. They stare at the floor like chastened schoolboys. "So . . . Juan Ramón isn't . . ."

"In love? How could he be? He doesn't have anybody to fall in love with! A man can't desire something he knows nothing about. If things were to change . . . who knows? Of course he talks like a bachelor. If you pushed me, I might even say he talks like someone ripe for infatuation. But as things stand now . . ."

Carlos's voice trembles.

"So . . . what do you recommend, Professor?"

"To you two? Nothing. I might recommend something to your cousin. And my recommendation is that she talk about herself a little more. Show a tiny bit of her face so that this Juan Ramón fellow has something to remember when he thinks of her. Something that sets her apart from other women. In short, she should be a covered lady, not a mummy. Are we all set, then?"

But he doesn't let them answer. With a deft movement, he digs in his pocket and flips open the cover of his watch.

"And with your permission, gentlemen, it is time for my midmorning glass of pisco. If it's not too much trouble, I would ask that you pay me the two-*sol* fee we agreed on so that I may, in turn, pay the barkeep his."

José and Carlos hesitate a moment. Never before has a humble man — a secondary character — so insolently reminded them of a debt. Normally the servants, errand boys, and even bureaucrats dare do no more than gently clear their throats. So gently that they might well be asking for forgiveness or permission. With their hats — their caps — clutched tight to their chests. Their eyes lowered. Only when you ask them outright do they name a price, almost always conveniently softened. "Just a *sol*, sir, if you would be so kind." *Just* a *sol*, or a *centavo,* or a coin, because the name of the currency on its own seems to sear their tongues.

"Your fee — of course," says José icily.

And he pays up, or rather he nudges Carlos with his elbow and Carlos pays up. Then they leave.

But they don't leave. As they are moving off, Carlos suddenly turns around as if he's remembered something important.

"Dr. Professor."

"Just call me Professor. What's our little cousin done now?"

The Professor is busy covering the desk with newspapers; sometimes the midmorning pisco leads into the lunchtime one, and then the pigeons flock to preen themselves and coo on his worktable.

"Well, this doesn't have to do with my cousin, Professor. It's just . . ."

"Oh! So it's you! It seems Cupid has been taking potshots at your whole family!"

"It's not that, it's . . . I'm just curious, Professor. That's all. I was just wondering if you've had to write a lot of letters for people you've never met."

"What an odd question! Are you trying to learn all my secrets so you can steal my work out from under me?" He smiles. "Quite a few, actually. Sometimes the customers are wealthy young men reluctant to reveal themselves, and they send me messages through servants or friends . . . like your ingenuous cousin, for example. Then I have to improvise. Drawing from experience, I call it. I ask for a few basic instructions and then imagine what the lovers are like and let the pen do the rest. Once, even, a disgruntled father wanted me to write a letter pretending to be one of his daughter's beaus. He wanted me to say that I was unworthy of her and all sorts of things . . . I didn't accept, obviously. It's a matter of principle, you see."

"But when you invent these romances —"

"I don't invent a thing! A person can write only about himself, even when he thinks he's writing in someone else's name. And so, it seems to me, my letters are always true. At the very most, the only untrue thing is the name signed to each one, don't you think?"

The Professor looks at his watch. Carlos looks at the Professor. José looks at Carlos out of the corner of his eye with an imploring expression. *When the hell are we going to get out of here, Carlota?* it seems to say. But Carlota doesn't seem ready to leave yet.

"And isn't it quite difficult?"

"What?"

"Pretending to be somebody else."

"Difficult? Not in the least! It's as easy as being yourself."

"Even when you're pretending to be a woman?"

"That's even easier! You have to add a few *I don't know*s, *I believe*s, and *it seems to me*s, because women are rather unsure of themselves. And ellipses, too, as many as possible. And then there's the matter of handwriting, which is more complicated than you'd think. But beyond that . . . do you know what the secret is? Imagine that the woman you're pretending to be is one you once loved. And since men are all alike, you can expect that the fellow you're writing to shares your worldview . . ."

"And does it work?"

The Professor laughs.

"Does it work? Well, not always. I'm not going to lie. It's the same as when you fall in love for real. Sometimes it works and sometimes it doesn't."

So he has to write about love. But what does he know about that?

It could be that Carlos is more apprehensive about this than he initially seemed and we must attribute to him a second fear: the terror that the story of Juan Ramón and Georgina will ultimately reveal nothing more than how little his own life is worth. Because in the end all good fiction is rooted in genuine emotion, as the Professor put it, which means that to write about love a novelist must look to his experiences, make use of everything he's learned in a woman's arms.

And what has he learned? What does he know about flesh-and-blood women?

To be honest, almost nothing. It's true that, despite his youth, he already has a bit of experience, but so far he has only ever fallen in love with fantasies. A pretty woman he saw on the street for just an instant. The willowy body of a nymph in a Gustave Doré engraving. A character in a novel. The closest he's come to falling in love with a real person was the night he met the Polish prostitute. If that can even be called love, and if it's even possible to call a woman a prostitute when she is still a virgin.

It happened on the eve of his thirteenth birthday. The next day he would be a man. At least that's what his father kept telling him as they headed off in the horse-drawn carriage toward Carlos's birthday gift. Being a man brings with it a great number of obligations and responsibilities, he said, but also certain privileges. Carlos didn't know if he wanted this or not, either becoming a man or enjoying the privilege his father was about to offer him. Not long ago he'd found a secret compartment in the library with a little book that was simultaneously wonderful and repugnant, full of prints of men and women intertwined, doing things that, no, not on your life. He spent the summer stealthily turning its pages, and at the end of each review his conclusion was always the same: the drawings were disgusting. Some nights he locked himself in the bathroom and studied his naked body in the mirror. He compared his scrawny figure, his hairless chest, with the images he'd seen in the book. On other occasions, in that same bathroom, the drawings briefly ceased to disgust him, but afterward they always filled him with remorse.

At first Carlos thought they were going to downtown Iquitos, to the whorehouses where the young men of Lima made their debut. But his father had a surprise for him. After all, he was one of the richest men in the country. And money, just like manhood, brings with it certain obligations in addition to the associated privileges; for example, the sometimes painful responsibility of frittering that money away just to show that you have it. This was the peak of the rubber fever, when the cities of Brazil and Peru became cluttered with tycoons like Carlos's father, men who suffered the anguish of not knowing how to use their fortunes. The less wealthy among them contented themselves with quenching their steeds' thirst with French champagne. Others sent their dirty clothing by ship to be laundered in Lisbon — two months of waiting so they could protect their imported garments from the impure contact of American waters. In some clubs it was even the custom to light cigars with hundred-dollar bills and, if one didn't smoke, to make wishes with them in public fountains. Ephemeral wishes presided over by the bust of Benjamin Franklin, which wilted and sank before the helpless gaze of passersby.

But Don Augusto was not much interested in horses or cigars. Nor did he care that his servants washed his tuxedos in the water of the Amazon. What he really liked was women, and he was prepared to do whatever it took to ensure that Carlos shared his predilections. To make sure the boy forgot the unnatural temptations that Don Augusto believed were lurking behind every line of poetry, even those that seemed entirely innocent. And so for his son's birthday he could give him only the best: a night in the high-end bordello favored by the rubber impresarios.

They pulled up in front of a mansion built at the edge of the jungle, and Carlos stared at it from the carriage with a mix of fear and fascination. His father had told him that the place was full of virgins from every corner of the world, their certificates of purity filled out in four or five languages. After all, the rubber barons could allow only honorable women into their beds, prostitutes who had not yet had time to ply their trade, even though well before their first periods they'd already been evaluated, sold, and transported. Potential whores who would be sent off to regular brothels after their first night of work, after losing their virtue for an astonishing sum.

The selection process seemed to Carlos to stretch on endlessly. He watched as Hungarian, Russian, Chinese, African, French, and Hindu women were paraded before him. There were Ottomans still wearing their veils, Englishwomen brought over so the British magnates would feel right at home, Portuguese and Spanish women with whom the mestizo men could settle old colonial scores. They were barely grown and almost beautiful, but that beauty was somehow painful. Carlos looked away. He looked at the air between them and pointed at random when his father pressed him. Every time he asked a price, a servant would pull the appropriate card from the stack on the silver tray he carried. The card included not a name or nickname, just the girl's nationality and price. Three hundred U.S. dollars for the Japanese girls. Two hundred fifty for the Egyptians. Only two hundred for mulattas from the Antilles. But Don Augusto shook his head when he looked at the offerings. This one is just a Brazilian — we can get Brazilians anywhere, and she only costs a hundred dollars. Don't be shy. You can choose the best one — my treat. *The best*, of course, meant the most expensive. And in the end that was exactly what Don Augusto gave him: a terrified girl of thirteen or fourteen, no more beautiful than the others but with a more suitable card.

Poland. Four hundred dollars.

While their order was being prepared, Don Augusto gripped Carlos's shoulder. It's going to be four hundred dollars, he said, so you'd better tell me if she bleeds or not. Pay close attention; you never know with these whores. Some of them start working early, offering comfort to the sailors on the Atlantic crossing — they're not even worth the clothes on their backs.

Carlos shuddered. At the mention of blood, all he could think of was how on the first day his father had taken him hunting, he hadn't been able to pull the trigger on any of the animals they'd found for him. All day long, monkeys and wild boars ambled nonchalantly before him, granted a stay of execution by his cowardice. In the end, Don Augusto had furiously snatched his rifle from him and shot them down one by one, piercing their flesh with astounding precision.

The memory lasted only a moment. Someone had just opened the door to the private room, and when he looked up, the girl was already waiting for him.

◇

Carlos knows the polite way to interact with dignified old women, housekeepers, mothers, sisters, chambermaids, and the pious nuns of the Order of Saint Clare, but he knows nothing about how to interact with whores who are really little girls more than they are whores. Perhaps that's why he doesn't move at first. He hangs back, pressing against the door — We'll let you two get to know each other better, his father said before shutting it — while the Polish girl sits on the edge of the bed and waits. She doesn't seem to know what comes next any better than he does. She knows how to deal with Galician peasants, twelve siblings sleeping in a single bed, parents who will sell you for twenty kopeks, the rough crewmen of the *Carpathia,* but she knows nothing about customers who are really little boys more than they are customers. And maybe that's why she is more frightened than she has ever been before, even more than when that drunken sailor tried to drag her to his cabin one dark Atlantic night on the crossing.

Carlos speaks only Spanish, and the Polish girl speaks only Polish. For the first fifteen minutes, though, neither of them says a word. They just look around the room — the velvet drapes, the bars on the windows, the canopy bed she's clinging to — as if the other person weren't there. Then Carlos attempts to muster a few words of greeting. He says, Good evening, and the Polish girl doesn't respond. My name is Carlos, what's yours? And silence. Tomorrow's my thirteenth birthday. He keeps trying out longer and longer sentences, slowly drawing nearer and sitting down beside her.

He doesn't want to look into her eyes, but eventually he can't control his curiosity any longer and gives in. He expects to find in those eyes some trace of rage or pain, the mark of premature old age left by suffering, but instead he finds something else: the startled blue gaze of a girl faintly distressed by a broken porcelain figurine or a lost doll. It is then that he realizes that he'll never do anything with her. That his birthday gift will be to disobey his father for once in his life. He wants to tell the girl that. He does tell her. He says: Don't be afraid, because we're not going to do it. We'll sleep beside each other tonight, but we won't even touch. Tomorrow I'll still be a virgin and you'll still cost four hundred dollars.

She looks at him, unconvinced. She doesn't trust him, of course, because she can't understand the meaning of his words. Or perhaps because, in not understanding them, she is able to identify something deeper that lurks beneath them, between them, despite them — a terrible message Carlos himself knows nothing about.

She is wearing a buttoned summer top, a long blue skirt, pink shoes. They have arranged her hair into two thick blond braids that snake down to her bust, which won't offer much to look at for another couple of years. Out of the corner of his eye, Carlos can see, under the flounces and gauzy swaths of muslin, her tiny chest rapidly swelling and sinking like a frightened bird's. He wants to tell her again not to be afraid, that she can trust him, but at that moment he stops. He sees her small hand slowly reach out and then clumsily touch his body in a trembling, hesitating movement. The gesture has something of a received instruction about it, of an order mechanically obeyed, as if she were administering an unpleasant-tasting medicine or completing paperwork. In his memory, the touch of those white fingers recalls something else. Perhaps the sensation of going back to the jungle. The exotic birds and monkeys he was unable to shoot, his father's disappointment, the ride home. And associated with that memory are so many others: the little volumes of poetry hidden under his mattress, his mother's sighs, the indecent drawings with their edges ragged from endless handling, his father's words just before he had him climb into the coach. *Being a man brings with it a great number of obligations and responsibilities.* His father with a hand on his shoulder and smiling at him for the first time in a long time. His father waiting for him in the hall, maybe reading a newspaper, maybe flirting with one of the girls; her sitting on his knees and him explaining to her patiently, still smiling, that he's a married man, that he's here only for his son, that he's so proud because his son is finally going to become a man.

And then he looks at her. At the girl who quivers and obeys. She has as little desire to be there as he has and yet there she is, uncomplaining. It isn't her birthday and she won't be earning four hundred dollars, but all the same she is participating in this long chain of overseers, mademoiselles, sailors, and human traffickers. A puppet who first moves her hand and later will open her legs, just because Señor Rodríguez has pulled the right strings.

He feels a cold sweat. An electric jolt runs down his back, partly because of those thoughts and partly because, almost without his willing it, his hand has begun to slide down her hip. The hand no longer seems to belong to his body. The girl bites her lip. Her tense little body remains motionless, and she stifles a yelp. Carlos closes his eyes. We'll sleep beside each other tonight, but we won't even touch, he says. Tomorrow I'll still be a virgin and you'll still cost four hundred dollars, he repeats, but still she doesn't believe his words. Gradually he, too, has stopped believing them, because suddenly, behind his closed eyelids, he is imagining the girl leaving the room with her braids still intact, the madam laughing at the gift of four hundred dollars, his father icily shaking his head — he's realized; he always knew — and then the lashes on his back with the leather strap and his mother's prayers and the doctor prescribing spoonfuls of castor oil and summers in the mountains.

But none of that will occur — the hand moving up her torso while she can only tremble; that hand, his hand, touching one of her breasts for the first time. It will not occur, because his father always gets what he wants and this time will be no different. If being a man means he has to crush the Polish girl's body under the weight of his own, he'll do it, he'll press himself against her, that girl who looks like she still plays with dolls, holds afternoon tea parties, and practices embroidery. And it shouldn't arouse him, but it does, and he shouldn't start kissing her or undressing her, but he already has. The girl begins to breathe more heavily, trying not to urinate out of pure terror, and closes her eyes too because she finally believes him, because wordlessly she has understood his movements better than he has, understood the intentions of this terrible boy who is pushing on top of her, still wearing his trousers.

He knows hardly anything about women's bodies. He has a vague idea of the subject that becomes suddenly quite clear and painful, like the revelation experienced by a traveler who thought he knew the desert merely from studying it on a map.

And so he feels himself burning against her body, which now feels as cold and remote as a sacrificial stone. He smells new odors that are somehow familiar. A salty taste he seems to recall from somewhere, as if it came to him in a long dream. As he tears at the bodice and yanks up her skirt, he thinks of the elderly house-maid, Gertrudis, and how patiently she dressed and undressed his sisters. When he feels the pure whiteness of the girl's skin, which tastes like the sacramental host; when he hears the incomprehensible plaints of the suffering girl, praying, perhaps dying, in Polish, he thinks of his mother. When he lets all of the weight of his body sink into her, he doesn't think about anything.

Then, later, everything he has been doing suddenly pains him. He feels like crying. But the dampness on his cheeks is nothing compared to that other, more awful dampness, hot like a wound, underground like a disease, that he feels surrounding his sex. He hears the girl scream and then sees blood, a small smear of blood where his father told him it would be. Blood glistening on the jungle foliage. Red and black spattering the white sheets. He feels as if the rest of his body were the blade of a knife that only today, this very night, has been unsheathed.

He has no idea if this is what love looks like. Whether he is killing this girl who is screaming, writhing weakly beneath his body. He is killing her, maybe, but it doesn't matter. His father paid four hundred dollars for it not to matter.

It all lasts exactly as long as a nightmare does.

And when it is over he begins to cry, and then she cries with him and, stranger still, hugs him. *She's not dead,* Carlos thinks happily, faintly surprised. She isn't dead, and she doesn't hate him. She wraps her arms around him as if he were at once her parents, her siblings, the country she will never see again, the language she will never again hear spoken, the merchant captain who looked after her and kept his word for a whole month. She embraces him as if they were two children who have played and fought and now want to play again.

And suddenly she starts to speak. She murmurs mysterious phrases that he hears and patiently tries to understand. They sound like questions, perhaps, and in the pauses he answers them with others. He asks her if she is thirteen. He asks her if what they've just done was what everyone on the other side of the door expected of them. If her father told her that becoming a woman brought with it a great number of obligations and responsibilities just before he left her at the door. And she answers, in her way, and then falls silent.

The candles have burned out. In the darkness their bodies are still intertwined. Carlos has slowly started to caress her. His hand runs along her silky hair, her milky skin, and she softens and is soothed in the warmth of that contact. They are still crying, but quietly now, without bitterness, and the girl is repeating only a single phrase, like a litany, as if the night had become trapped in place and could not sail forward.

Chcę iść do domu.

When she speaks, her moist lips brush against his ear.

Chcę iść do domu.

And Carlos thinks of those words as he falls asleep and even afterward, minutes or hours later, when he wakes up and discovers that the Polish girl has disappeared and finds his father waiting in the hall to tell him he's finally become a real man.

Che is do domo.

He tries to etch those words into his memory that day, and then for the rest of his life, as he conceives mad plans in which he and the Polish girl are together, against all odds —

Cheis to tomo

— but little by little those plans lose momentum, are put off, abandoned, and finally they die, because in the end she is no longer in the brothel, nobody knows where he can find her, and even if someone knew it wouldn't make a difference, of course, because it's one thing to rebel by reading a few poems and something else entirely to ditch it all for a girl who isn't really a girl anymore — for a whore who probably doesn't even cost a dollar by then, for a foreigner whose last words he has slowly resigned himself to forgetting, the indecipherable sounds becoming jumbled and blurry in his memory, as does the adolescent hope that their incantation might signify something beautiful, that *Cheis torromo* might mean "I forgive you," that *Cheis mortoro* means "I love you," that *Cheistor moro* means "I'll never forget you either, not ever."

◇

The visit to the Professor was a waste of time. At least that's how José sees it, and he makes sure to say so whenever he gets the chance. He never mentions Carlos's two lost *soles*, just his own wasted — and invaluable — time. And what did they get in return? A few useless pieces of advice and a brief history of fashion, neither of which has improved their novel or brought them any closer to the Maestro.

"He didn't even say whether he thinks he'll write the poem. He didn't say anything! The man's a charlatan."

Carlos dares only to half disagree.

"I don't know . . . I didn't think it was so pointless. And I think some of his advice was good . . . in a way. That bit about imagining a woman you've loved . . . Or the part about the covered ladies, for example."

"An old man's idle reminiscences! What about all that nonsense about the language of eyelashes? Ever so practical! Turns out the women of Lima knew Morse code. A long blink to blow a kiss . . . a long one and a short one to reject a suitor . . . How many blinks does it take to say 'I think I'm going to throw up'?"

Carlos laughs. He doesn't want to, but he laughs.

They're sitting up on the roof of the garret. But they're not in the mood for the character game today. The transatlantic steamer has just arrived and, within it, three letters from the Maestro, so similar to the previous ones that it feels like they've read them already. The same old formulas of friendship and courtesy, references to the invention of the cinematograph, an erudite contribution to their ongoing discussion of whether or not all things have a soul (they do, he says) and what those souls might consist of (perhaps this is what philosophers call *essence*?). The only new development is that accompanying these letters are the drafts of several poems. They are from Juan Ramón's new book, to be titled *Distant Gardens,* which will appear next year. But of course the poems do not make a single reference to Georgina. Instead, they include an endless number of twilights and gardens — uninhabited paradises that seem to draw farther away before their eyes or were perhaps always far away, as if they could be contemplated only from the other side of a wrought-iron fence. And there's not all that much to look at in those paradises either. Trees that glumly drop their leaves to the ground. Inconsequential rains, falling on those same trees. Boredom.

Yet José refuses to give up. He cannot believe that Juan Ramón hasn't written a poem to Georgina by now. There has to be one, or maybe even many — hundreds of verses hidden away somewhere. That's what José needs to believe, anyway, as it's been weeks since he's written anything himself. He just sits at his desk and stares at his portrait of the Maestro. If only he could address him as a young poet in need of advice and not as a prim young lady in a skirt and bodice! He would ask him so many things. Indeed, he asks them every night, staring at the black-and-white image, at the portrait's vacant eyes. He asks when Juan Ramón discovered he was a poet, how he was sure he had the talent for it. Whether there's any reason for José to keep sitting there, hunched over his desk, scribbling out drafts that will never astound a critic or bring a lady to tears. Or maybe they will? At least tell me that much, Maestro: Am I already a genius, unawares? Should I persevere in my passion or accept my failure once and for all? But the Maestro does not answer, and so José does not write.

That may be why he's become convinced that Carlos has been right all along. That there is a particular dignity, a solemn, almost sacred dedication, in the act of creating a muse so that a great poet can craft his finest metaphors. And while he waits for those sublime pages, José busies himself reading and rereading the Maestro's poems, finding the mark of Georgina hidden everywhere.

"Listen to this, Carlota!" he exclaims, waving Juan Ramón's letter in the air. "*And suddenly, a voice / melancholy and distant, / has trembled across the water / in the silence of the air. / It is the voice of a woman / and of a piano, it is a soft / comfort for the roses / somnolent in the afternoon, / a voice that makes me / weep for nobody and for somebody / in this sad and golden / opulence of the parks.* It must be Georgina! It's so clear: there's a voice because of the letters, which come from very far away but nevertheless speak to him . . . And because he doesn't know her yet, he weeps for nobody and for somebody . . . Don't you see? For nobody and for somebody! It's quite clear!"

Carlos doesn't say anything. He keeps looking down at the square from on high, as if there were something to decipher there. Darkness is falling. Soon there won't be enough light for José to keep reading him the poems.

"I think I'm going to go see him again," he says suddenly, as if setting down a burden.

"Who?"

"The Professor . . . if that's all right with you."

José looks up from his papers.

"Professor Cristóbal? What for?"

"I don't know . . . It's just a thought."

José hesitates for a moment. Then he shrugs.

"Whatever you like. As long as I don't have to go with you."

He doesn't say anything else. But a few moments later, Carlos hears him muttering other lines with the reverence of prayer:

> *And there are attempts at caresses, / at glances and fragrances, / and there are lost kisses that / perish upon the waves.*

> *She always spoke in blue / she was exquisitely sweet . . . but / I could never even learn / if the hair on her head was blond.*

> *I have a beloved made of snow / who does not kiss and does not sing. / She is now dead for me / and I can never forget her.*

◇

For the novel to be perfect, they have to know their character down to the most minute detail. What kind of writers would they be if they did not know whether Georgina was short or tall, whether she was writing from a seaside resort or from a garret, whether she was married or unmarried or a widow or a nun? A good scrivener, says the Professor, must know his customers better than they know themselves. And that inevitably goes for novelists too. Carlos thinks he once heard that Tolstoy — or maybe it wasn't Tolstoy but Dostoyevsky or Gogol or some other Russian — stopped writing his novel for a whole month because when he got to a particular scene, he didn't know whether his character would accept or refuse a cup of tea.

Do they know that? Do they know whether Georgina even likes tea?

Carlos imagines her as fair, wan, maybe ill. Vaguely sad. Also quite young — she almost seems like a child. She has blue eyes and fragile hands, very white, as if they were made of snow. She is timid and sensitive as only truly beautiful women can be, and perhaps that is why her lips quiver when she rereads Juan Ramón's letters every night, in the secret intimacy of candlelight. The hand holding the paper also trembles. It will tremble even more when she writes out her reply.

Georgina is the Polish prostitute once more.

The Polish prostitute if, six years later, she were still a virgin.

The Polish prostitute if she were neither Polish nor a prostitute; if, instead of having been born in Galicia and sold for twenty kopeks, she'd been born in a mansion in Miraflores and at her coming-out had received gifts of four hundred dollars.

The Polish prostitute if she often wept just as she had in bed with him, but with tears born not from her fear of being raped but rather from the solidarity she shows toward certain minor tragedies — a poem that moves her, the aching beauty of a sunset, the suffering of a kitten with an injured paw.

The Polish prostitute if she had learned to read and write and with those pen strokes — again the hand trembling — told Juan Ramón all the things that Carlos would have liked to hear.

Statements full of sighs:

I have thought of you so very often, my friend . . . ! A cousin showed me your book, Violet Souls, *so full of sighs and tears, and it moved me deeply. Your sweet, soft verses offered me companionship and comfort.*

But why do I recount my poor melancholy things to you, on whom the whole world smiles?

And some days I awake at dawn filled with such sadness . . .

Her life takes place not in a bawdyhouse but in a setting as splendid and cold as marble. A labyrinth of trellised gardens, of ornate chambers with canopies and frescoes and brocade upholstery, afternoons of making and receiving visits, of playing the piano for stern old women. Long evenings in which she sits in the dining room waiting for guests or waiting for nothing — waiting for another day to end and, at the same time, fearing that this is all she'll ever have. Sometimes she stays in the garden a long while, sitting beneath the trailing vines — Carlos can almost see her by his side — watching the bumblebees and the moths that orbit the flame of the oil lamp; like her, they are confined in a prison that cannot be seen and that, morning or night, will surely scorch their wings. Sometimes she snuffs out the lamp to free them. But other times she succumbs to cruelty and does nothing, only watches, until the maid comes running out with a shawl in her arms and strict orders for the young lady to come into the house immediately.

That setting contains few characters and only a couple of emotions. An authoritarian father who does not let her write letters that are as long as she'd like. A mother who is ailing or dead. Every once in a while, the sense that, all around her, the world has briefly turned unreal — *Do you not experience the same thing, my dear Juan Ramón?* — the suspicion that everything may be a stage set, the rehearsal for a play that has no audience or director or opening night. And above all, the six thousand miles of distance that separate her from the only human being who seems to understand her, the person who makes her feel alive again, fully alive, and whose letters slumber tucked away inside the piano.

José imagines her brunette and young, almost a child. His Georgina has dark skin and indigenous features; were she wearing a vicuña wool poncho, she might even be mistaken for one of the women who come down to the city from the high Andean plateau once a month to sell their humble wares. Indeed, she bears a striking resemblance to a servant girl his family dismissed two or three years ago, though he doesn't tell Carlos that. The girl had been beautiful and happy; José always thought of her as an Inca princess in servant-girl guise, though as far as he knew the Incas had at least been able to read the knots of their khipus, and Marcela couldn't even recognize her own name in writing. But she liked poetry, or so Master José believed, and so he used to interrupt her in the middle of her duties to read her his early poems. Marcela would sit down to listen, the feather duster or broom still in her hand, and as if entranced she would repeat all those cadenced, beautiful words whose meaning she did not know. In fact, she was entirely ignorant, or so José believed, and her lack of sophistication fascinated him.

"Oh, dear Marcelita! If only we could all be like you and look at life with the blessed innocence of the songbirds and flowers! Only you, who know nothing, can be absolutely happy . . ."

The maid agreed, sincerely convinced. No doubt she was happy if Master José said so, as José was very intelligent and always right about everything. But between her twelve-hour workdays polishing the silverware and the recent news of her mother's death back in her impoverished village, she hadn't had a lot of time to think about happiness of late.

"How I envy you, dear friend! Knowledge is a cumbersome burden that I must bear everywhere upon my shoulders, like wretched Sisyphus . . . Of course you don't know who Sisyphus is — you have that luck too! I would love to unlearn all my knowledge and become simple and unfurrowed like you!" Marcela was touched by these words. She was moved to tears imagining the unknown pains the young master suffered, and perhaps to offer him comfort she began to let herself be taken in the kitchen, under the rhododendrons in the garden, in the wine cellar, in her narrow servant's bed whenever José's mother fell asleep. Even once in Señor Gálvez's office, knocking over an inkwell in the process and ruining a number of documents whose value was docked, of course, from Marcela's wages. It was in her illiterate arms that José learned all that books and the well-mannered women who read them could not teach. Because Marcela knew how to kiss with her mouth open, and moan, and writhe when a lady would have stayed still, and her hands, those hands that seemed to have been made to take care of guests' hats, had also learned to stimulate places that a virtuous wife should know nothing about. José would remember her lessons for many years, and the words *passion* and *desire* would ever be bound in his recollection to this memory. As would the word *impossible,* because naturally the story comes to an end, a dénouement elegantly wrapped up by the Gálvez family with no consequences other than a dismissal, a small severance of fifteen *soles,* and a solemn promise from Marcela never to see their son again. And the son played at being glum for at least a couple of nights — he may even have entertained the mad notion that love between a wealthy young man and a maid was possible, a foolish delusion that we can by no means credit in 1904.

Now the maid he will never see again has been transformed into Georgina. Georgina is Marcela had Marcela not been raised an illiterate housemaid and, instead of scrubbing the floor tiles in the hallway on her knees, had spent her time reading the Symbolists and the Parnassians. It is she who attempts to slip certain insinuations into the letters to Juan Ramón with the same coquettishness with which she used to forget to latch the door to her room. But Carlos never allows that Georgina to show herself. When the two poets meet in the garret to compose a new letter and José offers one of his ideas, Carlos roundly rejects it. No, he says. Georgina would never say that. Or perhaps, almost shouting: Georgina is a young lady, not a harlot! Accustomed to always being right, to having his ideas eagerly embraced, at first José is startled by Carlos's determination, which becomes more self-assured with each letter they write. Finally he laughs heartily. He is amused by the stubbornness with which his friend defends each of Georgina's qualities.

You're acting like you're in love with her, he says.

But he doesn't stop Carlos. In the end, he cares as much about having his version of Georgina prevail as he once did about the maidservant — that is to say, very little. He is interested only in the poem, the poem that Juan Ramón still has not written. And if in order to write it the poet needs a blond muse instead of a *morena,* a frigid young lady instead of a mischievous flirt, then Carlos's ideas are quite welcome.

"You should see Carlota," he will say at the club later. "You couldn't hire someone with such feminine handwriting. It makes you wonder. And he knows the girl better than you fellows know your own mothers and sweethearts. Anyone would think he was writing a diary, not composing letters, and that at night he puts on a shawl and goes about like one of Lima's covered ladies."

Carlos ignores their laughter. José might not care about Georgina, but Carlos cares even less about what their circle of friends thinks. Or that they've all started calling him Carlota, or that they bow in greeting and pull out his chair for him when he sits down at the table. If you please, madame. Carlos has time to think only about important things. Like finally figuring out how Georgina takes her tea: Two cubes of sugar. A splash of milk. And maybe, but only if her father isn't looking, a bit of anise liquor in her cup.

◇

My esteemed friend:

    You ask what Lima is like, this beloved city of mine, which some call the Pearl of the Pacific, or the City of Kings, or the Thrice-Crowned Villa in honor of some old anecdote I no longer recall. You ask me to write about all this, and it occurs to me that the best way to do so is to imagine that you are here with me. Or even better: To imagine that we are both high up in the bell tower of the cathedral. From there I could point out every corner of my city and all its many beauties . . .

    Or better yet: Did you not once mention that you are a painter? Imagine, then, that I am giving you instructions for painting a landscape. This beautiful view from the sky over Lima, always misty, changeable, so nurturing of inventions and fantasies . . . Suppose, if you wish, that we are painting the canvas together. And that, as with all canvases, my manner of painting it, of adding colors and textures, also creates a sort of portrait of me.

    Imagine first a network of streets and houses, so perfectly laid out that you could draw it with a T-square. Do you see it? From afar it looks like the grid of a beehive or the mesh of a lattice. But if you focus your gaze a little, its geometry unravels into life, into rooftops and awnings, elaborate rows of balconies, the arches of city hall, the Plaza Dos de Mayo, the path of the Rímac River as it plunges toward the ocean.

    All that you see there at your feet is my beloved Lima.

*Within its borders, as you see, there are a good number
of yellow hills and fields. A lovely golden yellow that you,
my distinguished friend, would have to search for in your
palette, as it is not the yellow of melancholy and death that
pervades your poems, but a lively yellow, like a bonfire.
The color of the sun worshipped by our Incan ancestors so
long ago.*

Here, everything, even the colors, means something else.

*The sea? Do not paint it so close to the city. Place it a
few inches farther away on the canvas — that is, two long
leagues. They may call it the Pearl of the Pacific, but the
name is a deceptive one, because Lima is more a timid
jewel, a gemstone that tiptoes away from the ocean without
ever daring to lose sight of it, as if it both feared and craved
its waters. Paint it blue, but a blue that, I suspect, is not
the same blue as the Spanish seas. And in the distance
place a port, and call it El Callao, and scatter a few
transatlantic ships among its wharves, massive saurians
cloaked in steam and rust but somehow beautiful, because
they will, in the end, be the bearers of this letter.*

*Farther out, somewhere on the horizon, is my home,
one of the many estates in Miraflores. And perhaps it is
better this way, that you cannot see it. I have said that a
person's manner of looking at a city reflects that person's
soul, but it is no less true that a house holds the spirit of
the people who inhabit it. And I feel so distant from its
walls! A stranger in my own bedroom, in the dining room
where I while away the hours, so that even in calling it
my home I am obliged to lie to you. Inside it there are
only rules and reprimands, so inflexible that they might
have been drawn by the same T-square used to lay out*

the streets. *A lattice that might at times be called a cage, its bars made of bowing servants, of lectures from a father who does not find this or that to his liking, the riding frock and the gown for receiving visitors, endless dinners that always seem to feature the same plate of soup. Lessons from a young ladies' charm manual, a work that knows so much about protocols and so little of life! It is excruciating sometimes to be a woman, to be a daughter, to be nobody!*

If you wish to know my soul, you should not look at that house. Nor at the geometric avenues, rigid like the instructions of a strict tutor. I am not myself in my house. Only far from it — far, too, from the heart of that city where gentlemen in top hats and women in their street gowns promenade. In my walks, I seek a different, unknown Lima. Because to keep painting this canvas, you must know, my dear Juan Ramón, that there at the edges the strict grid becomes chaotic, twisted, full of unpredictable sinuosities and bends and leaps. I love to wander through those poor neighborhoods, down those dirt alleys where no one has to pretend to be anything. Where the people shout out with unpretentious, authentic words and you can stop to watch a sunset or a flower growing in the crevices without being bothered. My soul more closely resembles those little dead-end streets, those picturesque lots, and I return home with the hems of my skirts soiled with dust and the satisfaction of having lived something real, something beautiful . . .

Oh dear, what strange secrets I am confessing to you, my friend!

The Professor has liked the last few letters. "This is something else," he says, "now your cousin is really letting herself go, showing her face a bit." He also praises the delicate handwriting once again, and when he does, Carlos lowers his eyes.

"So . . . you think there's a chance?"

"Of what?"

"Of making her fall in love."

"Making her fall in love? Who?"

"Making him fall in love, I mean. You know, Juan Ramón. The Spanish poet."

"Oh! Well . . . who knows? But one thing's for sure: the beguiling eye of this covered lady has been unveiled! No doubt about that!"

Carlos goes to ask for his advice every week, whenever Georgina receives a letter or is getting ready to write one. I've never met such a solicitous cousin before, the Professor says every time he sees Carlos join the queue. He always comes alone, but Cristóbal doesn't mention José's absence. He seems to remember him only one morning when he insists on rewriting a particular passage of the next letter and Carlos refuses.

"You see, she wants to write it without anybody's help," he insists.

"But she's not making you come all the way out here every week for no reason."

"Well . . . actually, Georgina doesn't know I come to see you."

Cristóbal raises his eyebrows.

"Oh! So she doesn't know I exist?"

"No."

"And if she doesn't know, how do you transmit the wisdom gained from our chats?"

"Well ... I pretend it's my idea, you know? I ask her, she shows me the poet's most recent letter or one of her numerous drafts, I gently offer an opinion ... When she listens to me, the look in her eyes ..."

He stops himself.

"Go on, say it, say it. The look in your cousin's eyes. You know, we've talked so much about her and I still don't know even know what color her eyes are. I'm curious. What is this cousin of yours like? And don't tell me she's beautiful and shapely; that's old news."

Carlos accepts the cigarette the Professor offers him. He allows himself to speak of her only as long as it takes him to get from his first puff to when the ember of the cigarette almost burns his fingers. In that interval he has time to describe her in intricate detail. Georgina's whole life, summed up in the life of a cigarette. When Carlos drops the butt to the ground, Cristóbal bursts into laughter.

"So she's got blond hair and blue eyes, does she? I thought your friend said she had a darker complexion."

Carlos doesn't look away. For the first time he feels a rush of genuine pride.

"He can say whatever he likes. Who would know better than her cousin?"

Cristóbal looks serious all of a sudden.

"True, true. What's more, it's clear you love her. Unlike your friend — he doesn't like her all that much."

"You think so?"

"A blind man could see it," says the Professor, and refuses to utter another word.

◇

The Professor has already warned him about the importance of making drafts. Letters are like serial novels, he said: once you've messed up, there's no fixing it. That was the experience of Alexandre Dumas, who, because he did not make outlines as he should, ended up killing off a character in one episode and then resuscitating him three or four installments later. Apparently he wrote so many serial novels at the same time that he used to make miniatures of his thousands of characters and arrange them on a bookshelf according to an established code so that he could recall with a glance whether they were dead or alive. Regrettably, one day his maid decided it was time to clean those little figurines, dirty as they were, and with a single sweep of her feather duster brought a whole generation of the departed back to life.

Such is the case with Georgina as well, or rather with her sister, who exists and does not exist at the same time, depending on which letter you consult.

They don't realize it until Juan Ramón's next delivery arrives. It is a shorter, more formal note than usual. His tone is cautious, and even the color of the ink is different. *No doubt there has been some sort of mistake or misunderstanding,* the letter starts, with no beating around the bush. Yes, that must be it, surely he has misunderstood something — there are so many subtleties that are lost from six thousand miles away — but for some time he has been mulling over a contradiction that has arisen. He would like to know why in her third letter Georgina talked about her sister, Teresita — do you remember, my friend? — and now, only fifteen letters later, there is no trace of Teresita, and what's worse, in Georgina's last letter she wrote that she was an only child. He humbly inquires what he has misunderstood — because he's sure that's all this is, he repeats, just a misunderstanding — and how a woman who is no doubt sincere in every facet can in one letter be an only child and in another love her sister, Teresita, so fiercely.

The letter closes with *Best wishes from your loyal servant* and not the usual *Anxiously awaiting news of my dear friend.* In terms of formulas of politeness, it seems their relationship has been set back six or seven months.

At first Carlos and José blame each other. "All that time spent writing and rewriting the letters, and you didn't even realize we were handing out sisters and then snatching them back? If you took this more seriously, these things wouldn't happen," and so on. Then they blame the Professor. "Two *soles* to read some wretched letters and he doesn't even find the errors?" Then the one to blame is Juan Ramón, though they can't really pinpoint why; their rage is simply directed at him for the first time. In the end nobody is to blame. Everything is forgiven, but it is all infinitely sad, without any hope of consolation.

"Well, what now? What solution does your idol Cristóbal have for us?"

"None, because he doesn't know about it and he's not going to find out. What do you want me to tell him? That my cousin forgot how many sisters she has?"

"Damn it," says José, summing everything up quite succinctly.

But in the end Carlos does venture to ask him, at least in a way. One morning he drags out the question as much as possible and finally reminds Cristóbal of Dumas's serial novel and the lead figurines. He asks how Dumas solved his problem, and the Professor laughs at the question. Easy, a cinch, really: He changed the genre of his novel. He changed it from a swashbuckling novel to a supernatural one with hexes and witches and men who die and are later revived, and so the readers were satisfied. Most satisfied of all, though, was the revivified dead man, who got to stay alive until the end of the novel.

Changing the genre. It's not a bad idea, and Carlos hastens to implement it. His romantic novel briefly takes on tinges of tragedy — of course the real tragedy will come later, though he doesn't know that yet — and he writes a long chapter, a five-page letter in which Georgina finally bares her soul. It has been so many years, and yet she still cannot get used to the idea that her sister is no longer with them, poor thing — as if Georgina had not spent an entire night beside her white casket, feeling that she too was drowning; as if at the funeral she had not bent over the coffin to kiss her dead sister's purple lips. That loss had enveloped her in a persistent air of melancholy and guilt — after all, it was she who had asked Teresita to gather lilies from the riverbank. And tisanes and excursions to the seashore and six months in a sanatorium had all been useless against that constrictive pang that still strangles Georgina's lungs.

The coincidence makes me tremble, the poet replies in the next post, both ashamed and deeply moved. *Are you aware that after my father's death I too was sent off to sanatoriums to purge my soul of sorrows, perhaps the same ones that trouble you?*

Georgina is aware of nothing.

◇

For months now Sandoval has been promising a strike that will paralyze all of Peru. The longshoremen in the ports and the railroad engineers rising up as one to tear down the foundations of capitalism together. That strike will never happen, but Sandoval keeps menacing the country with it every afternoon at the club, as if it were only a matter of days or minutes before the social revolution would finally break out. The patrons have learned to listen to his long-winded speeches with skepticism. The ritual is repeated every day with little variation, from the time he rings at the door until he loosens his tie to speak: Sandoval handing the waiter his overcoat, hat, and gloves, conspicuously displaying the ink stains and calluses on his hands, looking for a stool on which to prop one of his boots as he speaks, with the grave and somewhat ridiculous expression of a fencing student preparing to deliver a thrust with his foil. They are studied gestures intended to allow time for interested listeners to approach, but most are already tired of waiting for the strike, the revolution that never comes and that matters to no one. Sandoval, undaunted, keeps preparing harangues that can hardly be heard above the clacking of billiard balls and the clinking of plates against the marble tabletops.

Because the strike, and with it the end of capitalism, is in fact already written. Indeed, everything has been set down in the pages of Bakunin and Kropotkin, so the future of nations holds no secret to men of understanding. In Sandoval's language, a man of understanding means an anarchist. And that hypothetical anarchist would have only to sit and read the writing on the wall for the future of Peru, and really even the whole world, to be clear to him. Perhaps those assembled would like to hear those predictions?

Nobody answers. Usually no more than seven or eight patrons are sitting in his corner of the room, and they pay him only sporadic attention from behind their unfurled newspapers and glasses of whiskey. Sandoval scans their faces, looking for support, a gesture of approval that might spur on the rest of his speech. Not finding one, he simply keeps talking. It is 1904, he says, and from there he spins off into prophecies based on his theory that all of history's major milestones occur at five-year intervals. So five years later — which is to say, in 1909 — the eight-hour workday will become reality. Ten years — that is, 1914 — and a great war will break out among all the world's nations. A war that will go down in history as the first in which nobody goes off to battle because the proletariat has at last understood that its enemies are not on the other side of the trenches; despite Alsace and Lorraine, the wealthy Frenchman will always, when it comes down to it, be the German capitalist's brother; similarly, notwithstanding Tacna and Arica, the Peruvian sugar tycoon will always be the friend and compatriot of the Chilean landowner. In twenty-five years — that is, 1929 — the mirage of capitalism will collapse in an explosion that will push all the millionaires out the windows. Thirty-five years — that is, 1939 — and another war will break out, one in which the proletariat will go to battle because for the first time the conflict will be between social classes, not nations. Forty years — that is, 1944, give or take a year — and the communists will square off against the anarchists for the first time. (We must be honest, Sandoval confesses in a murmur, and recognize that the communists are ultimately just as dangerous as the capitalists, not to mention much more organized.) Eighty-five years — that is, 1989 — and the last foundations of communism will be toppled. Just a century from the present day — that is, 2004 — and nothing of note will happen; everybody knows that reality rarely indulges in round numbers in producing its significant milestones. A century and ten years — that is, 2014 — and anarchism will have managed to vanquish the last of its enemies and will hold sway in the remotest corners of the earth. The end of History.

Carlos is not interested in politics. He's not really even certain that he knows what terms like *anarchism, means of production,* and *Marxism* mean. But there is something in the passion with which Sandoval addresses his audience that he is instinctively drawn to. And so he sometimes pauses in his game of billiards or his conversation with José to listen to Sandoval, to learn, for example, when belief in God will finally die off (around 1969, after the final Catholic council, which will be celebrated in honor of Friedrich Nietzsche). And it is in fact while listening to Sandoval that it first occurs to him that, just as History has an end, so too should their novel, and that dénouement, which he cannot even imagine, fascinates and terrifies him all at once.

Anyone who saw them walking together — from high up in a garret, for instance — would think that they were friends. And perhaps they are. It all depends on whether one believes that friendship between rich men and men who have to earn their living, between protagonists and secondary characters, between young men in linen suits and old men in grease-stained felt jackets, is possible. The two of them, at least, seem to believe in this kind of friendship, and so on some days Carlos accompanies Cristóbal to the tavern to polish off his midday glass of pisco. Alcohol sparks my creativity, the Professor explains, which is why most of my customers show up after lunchtime. People who are in love notice everything, and they've figured out I write my best letters when I'm drunk.

When they drink, Carlos is forbidden to mention Georgina. Cristóbal doesn't like to combine letters with alcohol — that is, work with life. Instead they talk about a great many other things, or rather Cristóbal talks about a great many other things while Carlos listens. He talks about the last covered ladies he met as a child. He talks about the scrivener's ethic, which is as complex and strict as a priest's but can ultimately be reduced to a single principle: never, ever swim against love's tide. He recounts many memorable anecdotes from his professional life, such as the time a young woman asked him to compose a response to the letter he himself had written that morning.

Carlos listens patiently. Perhaps because those anecdotes are helping him write his own novel. Or perhaps because in fact, little by little, they are becoming friends. Or maybe just because the Professor is the only person with whom he feels that Georgina is alive, that in some way she actually exists.

"You know what? There was a time when I wanted to write novels and then sell them one by one, door to door."

"And why didn't you?" Carlos asks.

"Well, I did become a writer of a sort, don't you think? I've invented quite a number of love stories . . . They say that when *The Sorrows of Young Werther* was published, the young Germans who read it felt sorrow even more acute than the protagonist's. They were so profoundly affected by his despair that apparently a wave of suicides washed over the nation. Think of it, the pragmatic Germans blowing their brains out because of love — well, because of Goethe, at least. But my efforts are no less worthy; because of me, a hundred people around Lima haven't so much married a husband or a wife as they have my work . . . And so a person must take great care with words . . ."

That was another of his favorite topics: words.

"Most people believe my work is a sort of business deal, a simple exchange . . . the customers provide the emotions, and I provide the words. That's the way they'd sum it up, at least in their heads. If only it were that easy!"

"So that's not how it works?"

The Professor feigns horror.

"Of course not! Well, it might work that way for the illiterate. They come to me with a letter they cannot read and a piece of paper to answer it, and I am their eyes and their hands. For them, then, sure. But with the wealthy youth it's a different story. Let's say, for example, that you are the customer and you want me to write a love letter for you. Because while you no doubt write and read well, even very well, you don't know what to say to your sweetheart. For instance. As you see it, the transaction is as we described it a moment ago: on one side, emotions; on the other, words. Very easy, or so it seems. But that's not the way it is at all! Because before I give you those words, you don't actually have anything. No, don't look at me like that. You have nothing. You feel some things, of course, I'm not saying you don't, but they are only the symptoms of an illness: rapid pulse, apathy, perspiration, melancholy, confusion, bouts of euphoria, dizzy spells, shortness of breath, fatigue, a sense of unreality . . . the whole lot. And you also have a natural inclination, of course, the emotions of a dog that wants to mount a bitch, that's all. But love — where is it? It's not there yet because nobody has given it words. Love is a discourse, my friend, it's a serial novel, a narrative, and if it's not written in your head or on paper or wherever, it doesn't exist, it remains only half done; it is ever only a sensation that believes itself an emotion . . ."

"But you —"

"I write it. That's what they come for, really, the swains and sweethearts, and that's why they wait for hours under the punishing sun. They come so that I can write that emotion for them, show them what love should be, what they should feel. That's what my business consists of. The important thing is not to gratify the sender — after all, I don't even know him — so much as the customer, who comes for his romance the way a loyal reader goes for the latest installment of his serial novel. The more heartbroken the love I invent for them, the more wretched I make them on paper, the happier they leave. If you could see them, elated to feel all that nonsense! Because from that point on they will truly begin to feel it, and that's what matters. And the same goes for the letters' addressees, who also want someone to write them a beautiful story and are ready to fall in love with anyone who pulls it off. They look at themselves in the mirror of the other's letter: if they like what they see, it's a done deal. And when they get married, if they get married, it may be that one night the two of them will sit by the hearth to read the letters they sent to each other, and then they will remember — will *believe* — that they actually lived that tempestuous love story I created for them . . ."

Carlos fidgets on his stool.

"But what you're saying can't be true. There has to be something more . . . I mean . . . love is something more than words, isn't it? It has to be. It's something born deep within us, something that cannot be betrayed . . ."

He pounds his chest passionately as he speaks. But Cristóbal is unfazed.

"Deep within! Right, and a century ago, when thirteen-year-old girls were betrothed to doddering geezers without objecting in the slightest, tell me, didn't those beauties have the same guts inside them that you do? I'll tell you what was going on: back then people didn't read romantic novels, and so nobody had given those girls the words to feel anything other than what they were feeling." He stops and claps Carlos on the shoulder. "Open your eyes, my friend; love, as you understand it, was invented by literature, just as Goethe gave suicide to the Germans. We don't write novels; novels write us."

The Professor knocks back his drink in a single gulp. Then he looks at Carlos with curiosity, as if noticing his existence for the first time.

"And what about you?"

"What about me?"

"Christ, what else? Is there a woman in your life? A fiancée, a lover, anything of the sort? You should know that if you ever need to invent a good passionate story for her, I would be happy to do that for you. I've charged you in friendship."

Carlos waves his hand weakly as if the question were somehow not pertinent.

"No, I . . . Actually, I don't have anyone."

Cristóbal rolls himself a cigarette as he listens.

"Why not? I mean, you're quite a catch; you must have plenty of candidates. At the very least you have marriage in your future, I'd say."

"Yes, but now's not the time to be thinking about that. I have to focus on my studies. Also, my parents . . ."

He stops and looks away.

"Your parents what?"

"They'll know how to find the woman who's best for me," he says at last, regaining his composure.

"Oh! I see." Cristóbal smiles, his cigarette now between his lips. "My skills are of no use on that score in any event. But it's good you're taking it that way. Arranged marriages are the happiest ones — as long as you haven't filled up your head with certain words, of course. If you wish to preserve that equanimity, promise me this: Avoid romantic novels at all cost! Those vile words will make a marriage go sour for no reason at all."

Carlos doesn't say anything for a while. He stares at the glass the Professor has just emptied.

"What about Georgina?" he says at last in a metallic voice that sounds so unlike his own. "So she isn't in love either?"

Professor Cristóbal laughs so hard that his cigarette falls on the table and then rolls onto the tile floor. He is still laughing as he bends down to retrieve it.

"Oh, no! Your cousin is in love, of course she is . . . But that's because, unlike you, she has read far too many novels."

◇

Carlos is twenty years old. At that age his father was already making a living from his rubber plantations, and his mother was married and about to bring him, Carlos, into the world. And that's nothing compared to his paternal grandfather, who at twenty was already dead — dead, with a widow and two orphaned children, but without even the twelve *soles* needed to pay for a coffin; that's how he was. There aren't men like that anymore, Don Augusto often says. Men today are cut from a different cloth; at twenty they still act like children who want to keep larking about. The day will come when men still won't have a wife or kids or a job or a house or even the desire to have any of those things by the time they're thirty.

He's exaggerating, of course, though he says it with such conviction, such seriousness, that you almost believe him.

But normally Don Augusto doesn't waste his time philosophizing. Who knows what will happen with the youth of tomorrow, and who cares? It's still 1904 — actually, they just celebrated New Year's Day of 1905. So much time has passed, and in that time, many letters, and Don Augusto has to focus on that for now. On that and on Carlos and his twenty years of age. On making sure the boy finishes his degree, beating the *ius connubium* and *ius praecepta* into him if necessary, and then, after he descends the steps of the university, leading him straight to the church to be married. But as the degree seems to be more of a long-term objective, it might be a good idea to look for the fiancée beforehand. Get the lay of the land, as Don Augusto says, which entails sending and receiving invitations to drink hot chocolate and eat pastries with Lima's most distinguished young ladies. Helping Carlos choose a good match, or perhaps even arranging it for him. Men today, as Don Augusto knows quite well, are like children.

There's no need to rush, of course, as marriage will soon be something only the poor do, only nobodies who have no inheritance awaiting them and can't travel to Europe just to kick up their heels a bit. There's no hurry, but there's no harm in keeping his eyes open. Cultivating friendships in prominent circles and at social gatherings, with the hope of seeing powerful influences blossom in them. Opening a path for his son that will take him from the tearooms and foyers to the boudoir of one of the Tagle-Bracho daughters, or even a Quiroga. *Get the lay of the land, open a path, cultivate, harvest* — these are the sort of terms used by a man for whom life has never been anything more than a jungle to attack with machetes.

The Rodríguezes have it all except a last name and a past, so the ideal prospects for Carlos are young women from families that have lost it all except their last names and their pasts. The Sáez de Ibarras, their fortune squandered in the casinos and brothels of Lima. The Lezcárragas, recently fallen on hard times thanks to an unlucky business decision in the wine trade. The Ortiz de Zárate y Toñanes family, which frankly never did have much to its name beyond dubious links to a handful of national heroes. It is houses like those that the Rodríguezes honor with their visits on the first and third Wednesdays of every month. Only in those shabby parlors, in those enormous, servantless dining rooms, in those libraries sold volume by volume to ragpickers, does the Rodríguezes' nouveau riche odor seem to go unnoticed; there is no better cure for an overly sensitive sense of smell than becoming *nouveau pauvre*.

But Don Augusto is looking for more than a daughter-in-law, as Carlos is well aware. He is worried less about his son's marriage than about the possibility of using that marriage to project a fantasy that the Rodríguezes are finally aristocrats — indeed, that they always were. Ever since Carlos's father was a boy, he has been obsessed with that idea, his desk piled high with books on heraldry and documents showing that in the last century the family was this or that. He never found any Spanish ancestor, let alone a rich one. Only Achuars or Quechuas, and half-breeds, and quadroons, who in the baptismal records are invariably listed as "peasants" or "sons of the people" — plus one great-great-grandfather whom a jesting priest labeled a "son of the earth." But he must persist, paging through the manuscripts until he manages to turn the past into what it is supposed to be. Don Augusto has inherited the whites' prejudices along with their money and manners, and it is always jarring for him to look in the mirror after having loudly declared in a café that the Indians must inevitably be slaves because of the blood running through their veins.

A genealogist convinced him that records of those illustrious dead could be found in the parish registers in Spain, and Don Augusto financed his trip across the globe to explore the motherland's churches and chapels, an investigation that is still ongoing. After five years, two thousand five hundred *soles* — pesetas in Spain — and very few certainties, the scholar still occasionally sends letters with hopeful news. In the Santander cathedral he has found a Rodríguez who, if he is not mistaken, is Don Augusto's grandfather's great-great-grandfather's great-great-grandfather; there are some vague indications that the family may be related to the Duke of Osuna and three or four other Spanish grandees; a fifteenth-century baptism certificate could be the key that links the Rodríguezes to King Ferdinand, of Ferdinand

and Isabella fame ... and so on. Each new discovery justifies an outlay of a hundred or two hundred pesetas, which Don Augusto pays without hesitating.

In reality, his confidence in the genealogist is purely statistical. Don Augusto understands something of arithmetic; indeed, it could be argued that he has amassed his fortune thanks to his head for numbers — or rather, to be precise, to his ability to substitute numbers for people. When converted into figures, the genealogy issue is clearer in his head. It goes like this: He was born in 1853. Assuming twenty-five years for each generation, that means his parents (two of them) must have been born in about 1825, and his grandparents (four) in about 1800. None of them, according to the records, appear to have had noble blood. But why not keep going backward? He had 16 great-great-grandparents around 1750, 64 ancestors in 1700, and 1,024 around 1600. During the time of the conquest of Peru, there were at least 8,192 of his forebears roaming the earth. Was it really possible that they were all malodorous Incas, that none of them had come ashore from the ships of Pizarro and de Almagro? And so on: 262,144 in 1400; 4,194,304 in 1300; no fewer than 67,000,000 humans in about 1200. Had not a single one of them a coat of arms, a quartered shield to bequeath to him? It was practically redundant to confirm it; statistically speaking, they'd already been made nobles, were perhaps even the descendants of kings. Yet patience, and a smidgen of humility, prevent him from going all the way back to the first century. Something tells him that at that point he would have so many millions of ancestors, so very many, that it would have to include the world's entire population, even Jesus Christ Himself, if it weren't heresy to think such a thing in the first place.

For his part, Carlos prefers to know nothing of his father's aspirations. Sometimes he even manages to convince himself that nobody is thinking about the question of his marriage with any seriousness, that his family is making and receiving all these visits for exactly the reason it seems: the pleasure of talking about the weather and ranting about the government, eating pastries, and exchanging home remedies for migraines. Counting the angels that pass, one by one, during the conversation's many awkward silences. But to understand the truth, he has only to watch any one of the young ladies arrive, decked out as if for a wedding — her own? — and hear her mother taking every opportunity to comment on how hard-working Aurorita or Cristinilla is. And Aurora and Cristina and Jimena and Mariana look a little at him and a little at the brocade curtains, the embossed silverware, or the dazzling gold of the galleries and bedchambers, as if all of it — son, house, precious objects — were being offered as a packaged set.

And so for a while he feels a cold sweat every time a receiving day approaches. He wants to tell his father to stop looking. That he doesn't want to find a wife, that he's not going to go down to the parlor today, no matter that Fermín Stevens's seven charming daughters have come to visit. But in the end he always gives in, and later, in the dead of night, he feels a pressure on his chest that keeps him from sleeping. As if his father had sat down on top of him and were staying very still, staring at him. He remembers the Professor. Could it really be true that words can cause harm? Not just the words one reads but, and especially, those one utters. Those from which, now so long ago, Georgina was once born. Because today Georgina seems much more real than the succession of women, some of them still girls, who parade through his house day in and day out, petulant and flustered.

What would he do if Georgina were one of them? Would he recognize her? Would he request her company? Would he tell his father, *The Hübners are the best family for us*?

Some of the girls he receives are pretty, but Carlos doesn't even notice. He's spent his whole life looking at cartoons and postcards of women as if they were flesh and blood, and now he is looking at the parade of flesh-and-blood women as if it were a well-worn deck of postcards and cartoons. Characters taken from a novel that has been closed and forgotten. Georgina, on the other hand . . . Because only when he thinks about her is the burden on his chest alleviated, as if someone had made his father get up and leave the room. As if what he senses on his body were not pressure but the lightest touch of a caress, so delicate that he has to close his eyes just to feel it. It is Georgina, coming to visit him. Or not, but what does it matter? It's better not to open his eyes so he can keep believing it, or to open them and see her at last, because she is not like the others. She is not interested in the drapes or the etchings or the silverware. Georgina wants to look at him — only at him.

And then the novel grinds to a halt.

They know, having gleaned it from one of the few pieces of Professor Schneider's advice they actually managed to read, that something extraordinary must take place in the middle pages of every novel. Just before that episode, the plot must seem to falter for a moment — the beginning of the second act — passing through a low spot or valley, a brief plateau of boredom, and then that *something* happens. Often a character who seemed indispensable to the story dies, or maybe one who seemed like he was going to die survives. The others learn to appreciate life more, or perhaps they don't learn anything. And that's that.

But their novel will never emerge from that valley. It simply ends, before the peak has even been contemplated. It is brusquely interrupted, like a volume from which the last pages have been torn out: Juan Ramón has stopped answering their letters. A week passes, then two, a month — an entire month goes by and still they have no word from the Maestro. The day comes again when the ship should arrive from Europe, and nothing happens. What they do have is plenty of time to come up with explanations. The Maestro has grown bored; the Maestro has found a novel or a muse more to his liking; the Maestro has forgotten about the tiresome girl from Miraflores and their disjointed, humdrum novel. The Maestro isn't a Maestro at all but an imbecile who needs to be taught good manners, the proper way to treat well-bred young ladies. And of course they have time to blame themselves — such mediocre writers — and others, too, obviously: Professor Cristóbal, and Don Augusto, why not, and Professor Nicanor — Mr. Scrooge — who has given them failing grades in his mercantile law course, and the watchman who doesn't trust the Chinese, and the servant who has no doubt mixed up or misplaced the envelopes, and other characters so marginal that they haven't even appeared in their novel.

Then comes something akin to resignation. What else can they do but wait? And fib a bit when asked about it in the club — Of course we have; two more letters, three actually; you should read the latest poem he sent, dedicated to Georgina. Maybe they lie out of pride. Or maybe they are waiting for reality to accommodate itself to their words. But one night one of the lads at the club seems unusually interested in their responses.

"So he just wrote you, then!" he says, feigning admiration. "And three letters, no less! What does the brilliant poet have to say for himself?"

José and Carlos exchange an awkward glance.

"Well, mostly the same as always . . ."

"The same as always, is it?"

"Yes . . . Nothing special. The important thing is that the novel continues. The novel continues."

The chap starts to laugh, and two or three other patrons laugh with him.

"Well, since you didn't get those letters via the Wright brothers' flying bicycle, I highly doubt you actually had the chance to read them."

"What do you mean?"

He becomes stern.

"Do you two live on the moon or something? You must be the only people in Lima who don't know."

"Know what?"

"Not a single ship has entered or left the port at El Callao for weeks. Sandoval's strike has begun."

To find out, they would only have had to read one of Lima's five newspapers or forty broadsheets — specifically, the front page of any of them. But neither Carlos nor José reads the newspaper. Nor do they attend their labor law class, in which the El Callao dockworkers have been the subject of lengthy and contentious discussion over the past several days. It's been weeks since either of them has set foot in the halls of the university. Or Carlos could simply have bothered to listen to his own mother's prayers, whose novenas and rosaries have, of late, made mention of the strikers. She asks the Lord for there to be peace in Peru and for everyone in the port to go back to being as happy as they used to be, and the Lord will end up listening to her sooner or later, because the Lord always answers the prayers of those who wish for nothing to change.

His father is well informed on the topic and is delighted when Carlos asks him about it. At last his son is showing some interest in business. He tells him about the thirty-five ships anchored in the port. The fourteen thousand tons of rubber going nowhere. The influx of dollars lost every day because of this preposterous wait and the deuced forces of order, which used to do just what their name suggests — impose order by force — and now allow a bunch of jobless, godless layabouts to humiliate the entire country.

"But what is it they're asking for?" Carlos ventures.

"What is it they're asking for? Anarchy! You know what anarchy is?"

Carlos says he does. Don Augusto keeps talking.

"Of course, they claim they're fighting for equality and justice and who knows what other noble ideas ... but nobody actually cares about those things! The workers aren't fighting for justice — they're fighting to become bosses themselves. It's the law of life! And the strikers have this novel idea that they're going to get rich working just eight hours a day ... what do you think of that? You think I got where I am working eight goddamn hours a day?"

No, Carlos does not.

That very morning, as he is reading the newspaper in an effort to get up to date, one of the housemaids comes in to gather up the dishes from breakfast. Without looking up from the papers, almost idly, Carlos says:

"Even you must have heard about the El Callao strike."

The maid stops short, still holding the tray.

"Is it because of my brother, sir?"

"Your brother?"

She bites her lip.

"My brother Antonio, the one who works in the port. He's on strike with all the others — it's no secret."

"I understand."

"But I'm not like him, sir. You don't have to worry about me. I'm not going to cause any trouble."

"Of course not, of course not."

They stare at each other for a few moments. Perhaps the tray clatters in the maid's trembling hands.

"So tell me ... do you know why they're on strike in the docks?"

The maid answers swiftly.

"I don't know. I don't understand those things."

And then, calmer:

"But I think it's because of the length of the workday, sir.

They want to work eight hours, can you believe it? Eight hours a day!"

She tries to laugh, but it catches in her throat. She tries to control her heartbeat, afraid the clattering of the dishware might offend the young master.

"Eight hours, is it?"

"And the salaries too."

"How much are they asking for?"

"Well . . . three *soles* a day, sir."

"You mean that's what they earn now?"

This time her laugh is genuine.

"Oh, of course not! That's what they'd like, sir. They get just under two at the moment."

"Two *soles*!" Carlos repeats, his eyes widening.

"Two *soles*, yes. And a piece of bread costs less than half a *sol*. Of course some people are never happy with anything."

Carlos closes the newspaper. He ponders a moment.

"How much do we pay you?"

"Me, sir? Well . . . the usual. Room and board, and half a *sol* a day. What more could a person want?"

Carlos doesn't answer immediately.

"Nothing, of course. You may go now."

But the maid doesn't move.

"I just . . . I just want to assure you that you don't have to worry about me, sir. I know what's fair."

"Of course you do."

"I'm not like my brother. I'm happy with what I have and I don't cause any trouble. I'm not a revolutionary."

"No, you're not a revolutionary."

And then he thanks her.

◇

The negotiations have begun, says the front page of *El Comercio,* the financial paper, and they go down to the port, hopeful at the news. What they do not know is that the conversations between the chamber of commerce and the strikers have failed; they had already failed, in fact, when the newspaper ink was still drying on the page. And so when they arrive they find the docks teeming with workers trying to prevent the scabs from the Britain Steamship Company from working. Tomorrow *El Comercio* will say that there were no more than two hundred people; the statement issued by the strikers' commission will claim fifteen thousand. To José and Carlos, these numbers are unimportant. In any event, there are enough people to fill the port and even to block Calle de Manco Cápac, so it takes them a long time to push their way through the crowd to the edge of the dock.

In the distance they can make out the ships' rigging, the steamships covered with patches of barnacles and rust. On one of them, who knows which, are the chapters that have not left; on another, the chapters that have not arrived. José and Carlos sit on the breakwater beside the esplanade and contemplate the ships, impotent. Last night, they heard that the Compañía Sud Americana de Vapores and the Britain Steamship Company had offered their regular crews two and a half *soles* to load the cargo, but the strikers' union headed them off with a better offer, and now the city's taverns are full of Russian and German and Turkish sailors who drink until they pass out at the workers' expense. And so the decks are empty — there is no one aboard any of them save a handful of officers shouting at one another. Them and the rat that travels with the transatlantic mail, of course, which is startled to discover that, for the first time, the boat it calls the universe has stopped rocking and creaking to the rhythm of the waves. For the rat, at least, the strike has brought the whole world to a halt.

José flings pebbles from the breakwater into the sea. Between each one, he pauses to grumble a moment. It's vile, an embarrassment, that a few good-for-nothings can bring an entire city to its knees and then stick around shouting and jeering. Carlos has the sensation that he is listening to his father's voice, grown suddenly youthful but just as harsh. José also talks about Juan Ramón: "Do you know what happens when an installment of a serial novel is delayed?" he asks. Carlos does not. "Well, I'll tell you: For the first few days the readers are restless, more curious, eager to keep reading, but as time passes they end up forgetting about it and start reading something else. That's what's going to happen if the letters don't get out soon," he continues. "The Maestro will start a new novel and won't be interested in the old one. That's what's going to happen, Carlota."

Carlos nods mechanically. For the first time he not only remembers Georgina but also contemplates, with curiosity and some surprise, the workers themselves. From the breakwater they seem to form a single body, as if they were a monstrous living thing spilling down the docks and wharves, its skin scaly with hats and faces. From time to time they shout a few slogans, and their roars, too, seem to braid together into a single voice. If José and Carlos had seen one of those lowly men from up in the garret, they would have taken him for a secondary character, but it occurs to Carlos now that as a group, they might somehow constitute a protagonist.

José hurls another stone and, with it, another complaint.

"That bastard Sandoval sank us. If his goal was to ruin our novel, he certainly succeeded."

Carlos shakes his head, still watching the swarm of men.

"I don't think Sandoval cares all that much about us, to be honest."

"He does, I'm telling you, he does. I know that imbecile . . . He was dying with envy over the Georgina business. He wouldn't care so much about these fools otherwise."

Carlos hesitates a moment, seems about to speak, but then says nothing. José turns abruptly to look at him.

"What?"

"What do you mean, what?"

"Don't play dumb, Carlotita, I know you. At this point I know everything there is to know about your silences. What are you thinking?"

"Nothing . . . just something I heard this morning."

"Let's hear it."

"Do you realize they earn only two *soles*?"

"Who?"

"The dockworkers."

"Okay."

Carlos waits a few moments. Then he adds:

"Two *soles* a day, I mean. Not per hour."

"And do you think that's a little or a lot?"

"Are you joking? It takes more than a week's wages to buy a book, for the love of God!"

José shrugs.

"I very much doubt any of them know how to read. So no books; that's one less expense. Also, their income can't be that low if they're able to take this vacation right now. The bastards."

Carlos is silent, shuffling through a number of possible responses. Finally he says:

"You're right."

But he can't get it out of his head. The two *soles*, just a couple of coins, grow in his mind until they fill it completely. Before him he sees the strikers, their shouts becoming louder, the animal bucking and stomping, trying with its immense body to overrun the railroad track connecting the port with the customs office. A group of soldiers, absurdly tiny, braced to stop it. Carlos feels something like admiration, not for their poverty but for the energy with which they are fighting to escape it.

He wonders what Georgina would think of them. Indeed, he wonders it aloud.

"I wonder what Georgina would think."

"About what?"

"About all this. The strike at the docks."

"I daresay she'd be furious at being unable to communicate with Juan Ramón."

"Yes, but I mean their ideas. What would she think of the workers, their demands, the two *soles* . . . ?"

José makes a gesture that might mean anything. But actually it means something quite specific: *What do I care?*

"I think she'd sympathize with them," Carlos adds when it's clear that José is not going to answer.

"Maybe," he replies at last. "You know, that wouldn't be a bad idea for a chapter. Georgina among the workers . . . Consoling them with her presence . . ." He raises his arm and points into the crowd. Slowly he lets his arm fall. "But what use would that chapter be when we can't even send it to Juan Ramón?"

Carlos is still looking at the spot where José was pointing. Among the dockworkers he can make out a few women. They are carrying leather pouches with crusts of bread for their husbands and sons, and earthenware jugs to quench the protesters' thirst. A few chant slogans, raising their voices and their fragile fists to the sky. There is also one young woman with a parasol, elegantly dressed all in white. She looks like a piece of artwork amid the workers' drab overalls. He is struck by her presence. It only accentuates the destitution around her, making it more incomprehensible, more painful, more genuine. She looks like a figure from a Sorolla painting who, wandering from one canvas to another, has ended up, whether by mistake or out of curiosity, in a humble scene from Courbet. Carlos thinks to himself: *She could be Georgina.* And for a moment it seems that she is about to turn her head — Georgina's head — but at the last second she walks back into the crowd, and she and her parasol disappear.

José slaps himself on the shins, stands up.

"So now what? Shall we go? It's obvious nothing much is going to happen here today."

Carlos stands up too. But he doesn't head back to the carriage — he moves in the opposite direction, toward where he saw the girl disappear.

"Hey, where are you going? That's the wrong way."

"I just want to take a look."

"Don't be ridiculous. Let's get out of here. Can't you see these idiots are ready to riot?"

But he follows Carlos. He's not used to obeying and it takes him a while to make up his mind, but in the end he sighs and goes after him.

Carlos doesn't really know what he hopes to find. It's practically superstitious, his fantasy that the white parasol is hiding a face that can only belong to Georgina. Of course he can't share such a notion with José. He can only do what he's doing:

fight his way through the crowd, elbowing and prodding the dark flesh of that animal, which seems to be rejecting them. Even though the strikers turn to look warily at the young men's gold cufflinks and impeccable suits. Even though the slogans that a few minutes ago spoke of equality and justice in rather abstract terms are increasingly filled with invective, with mentions of spilled blood and dead bosses. Even though, seen up close, some women are distributing not crusts of bread or cups of wine but paving stones and iron bars and walking sticks and metal hooks and fireplace pokers. José's voice is distorted by fear for the first time:

"Carlos, let's get out of here, damn it," he says, grabbing his friend's arm.

Just then they hear a metallic banging rapidly approaching. A whistle. The crowd seems to respond to the noise, and José and Carlos are pulled along with it.

"Scabs! Scabs!"

It's a convoy carrying goods to the wharf, and the crowd manages to stop it by hurling stones. It all happens so quickly that there's no time to react. A few men clamber up on the locomotive and haul the engineer out of his cab. Carlos sees them drag him to the ground like a rag doll, but he doesn't feel anything; it's as if the images parading before him were happening in the pages of a book or being projected on a white sheet with a cinematograph. He is unaccustomed to violence, to the notion that ghastly things might suddenly take place before his eyes. Violence is something that's always happened somewhere else, deep in the jungle, far from the clearing where he played with Román.

"Shit," he hears José say above the tumult.

Suddenly a few shots are fired into the air. Or maybe not into the air. In the distance, perhaps, the girl. Is that her parasol, or a soldier's white uniform? The noise of helmets falling upon the paving stones. More gunshots.

"The cavalry! The cavalry!"

Above the agitated faces, the bodies of the first horsemen come into view. There aloft, they might be at the bow of a ship that cuts through the swell of workers, who shout and scatter in all directions. He sees their sabers flash in the air. A man stabbed by a bayonet. Two dockworkers who bring down one of the horses by throwing rocks at its muzzle. José's hand gripping his arm, bruising him, trying to drag him somewhere or perhaps trying desperately not to be dragged himself. Then he sees a horseman pass by him on his left, and at that moment he feels a sudden burning, as if a bolt of lightning had struck him in the face. The sensation is a sharp pang, one that isn't preceded by any sound, that seems to have no origin or explanation. A cold bite that sears his temple and tumbles him to the ground.

As he falls he thinks he sees José turn to look at him. José hesitates a moment and then keeps running.

It's possible that things don't happen exactly like that. Maybe José does not see him fall. Perhaps he too is dragged along by the crowd and could have done nothing to help him anyway. It is possible that the person who looks at him and then runs off amid the uproar isn't even José. But whatever the case, that's how events will be etched in Carlos's memory: him falling and José abandoning him to his fate.

For a moment he thinks he's going to pass out. That's what always happens in his favorite novels. The hero falls, wounded, and the world stops with him. Everything turns black, or white, or red, according to the author's whims; reality disappears into a fog, and that fog does not clear until, hours or days later, the protagonist regains consciousness. But none of that happens.

He is able to feel, almost to count each of the blows he receives — twenty-seven — as the terrified mob tramples his body. He hears shouts, gunshots, horses' hooves scraping the cobblestones. Voices cry out, pleading for help. Then something like silence. The taste of blood in his mouth. And finally some words he can't understand, and the eyes of the soldier bending over him to check his pulse.

◇

The wounded are taken to the Guadalupe house of aid. The first
to be treated is one Florencio Aliaga, who has a bullet lodged in
his groin and is as gray as a corpse. Then the medics come back
for the less seriously injured. Finally they even come to Carlos's
aid, though he has only a few contusions and a laceration on his
face. He is embarrassed to be transported on a stretcher, since his
single wound has already stopped bleeding. But he lets himself
be carried, what choice does he have, while he looks around for
José. He does not find him.

"My goodness, a gentleman like yourself—what were you
doing among that rabble?" the aide asks as he helps Carlos remove his eighty-*sol* suit.

"I was waiting for some letters . . ."

And he doesn't whimper once as he gets five stitches in his
cheek. That's one of the most important lessons he must credit
his father for having taught him: not to cry out, not ever, even
when they're shredding the skin on your back with lashes.

He is afraid they will want to interrogate him, but nobody
seems to be paying any attention to him. The doctors and nurses
hurry from one cot to another, fold and unfold mosquito nets,
push little carts loaded with scalpels and buckets of blood-tinged
water. The aide also leaves him alone. Carlos struggles to his feet
and then sits back down. The room is an immense nave with
dozens of beds along either side, and everywhere are muffled
moans and whimpers as the suture needle sews up wounds or the
forceps dig around in them to pull out shrapnel. Two soldiers are
posted by the door at the far end of the room, but they hold their

rifles listlessly, as if they were laborers' tools. They look like peasants. Perhaps, when they return home and remove their leathers and uniforms, they really are peasants. Now, though, away from their horses, their unsheathed swords, their combat formations, they also look like little boys.

That's when he spots Sandoval. He's going from bed to bed with concern on his face, checking on his comrades, murmuring a few words of encouragement. The doctors eye him reprovingly, but no one dares say anything. He looks like a father anxious about his children's health, pacing back and forth with his hands behind his back and a solemn expression.

"Gálvez!" he says upon recognizing him. "Carlos Gálvez! What on earth are you doing here?"

Carlos — Rodríguez — hesitates a moment. No one has ever mixed up their last names before.

"Actually, I'm Rodríguez. It's José who's —"

"What goddamn difference does a last name make? Haven't you learned anything?" he asks, making a grand gesture in the air, one that blots out genealogies, privileges, the past. "Oh dear, you're injured! What have those butchers done to you?"

His voice sounds oddly tender. He draws near and examines the sutured wound. His eyes fill with pride. He takes off his hat and points to his own scar, also on the left side of his face, in almost exactly the same spot.

"Here's my own baptism gift. A souvenir of the strike of '99," he says boastfully. "A soldier gave me this gift when I was about your age and I too was just beginning to engage in the struggle."

"I'm not in the struggle. I just —"

"Of course, of course. You were just there by chance, right?"

Carlos begins babbling about Georgina, about letters that neither came nor went, but Sandoval interrupts him.

"Martín."

"Pardon?"

"You don't have to call me Sandoval. You can call me Martín," says Martín.

Then, before Carlos can start explaining again, Martín places his hand on his shoulder and adds solemnly:

"And you don't have to say anything. When our enemies bite the dust at last, we will remember sacrifices like yours. We will be able to sort out the wheat from the chaff. Those who were in the trenches from the beginning, and those who will have no place in the new order."

"In 2014," Carlos says, almost without thinking.

Martín scowls.

"Long before that! Why, today alone we have brought the eight-hour workday two or three years closer."

He falls silent. Two beds away, a nurse is closing the eyes of the first martyr of the revolution. Martín clutches his hat to his chest.

"It's a pity it's already too late for our comrade Florencio," he adds.

And he crosses himself, because it's still 1905 and, according to his own calculations, God will not die for another sixty-four years.

◇

A little while later, José appears. He strides confidently up to the bed and hugs Carlos. It's so wonderful to have found him! He's spent hours going from hospital to hospital in El Callao. He felt so guilty when he saw him fall; he shouldn't have left him to the mercy of those brutes, don't think he hasn't been telling himself that, but what else could he do? What would Carlos have done in his place? The same thing . . . the same thing, of course! But the worst is over. Can he walk? Then he's coming with him right now and leaving this paupers' hospital; there's a carriage waiting for him outside.

And he hugs him again, because the most important thing is that everything has turned out all right; everything is forgiven. A sergeant, accompanied by several soldiers, comes to intercept them as Carlos is getting out of bed. He says he can't let them leave, it's impossible. There are procedures and protocols that can't just be shrugged off; recent events have been quite serious, and statements must be taken from those involved. José sighs. He holds out a piece of paper that he has already prepared. The sergeant goes pallid when he sees the last name on the letterhead. He doesn't even dare to read the full document. He returns it, awestruck, and tells the soldiers that it's all been a misunderstanding, that the young men have been released and are free to go whenever they wish. With all due respect.

Carlos returns home at dusk. He's almost all better; the aide has said all he needs is a little arnica and a change of bandage once a day. But his mother does not agree: their personal doctor must be called; Carlos must be kept awake in case of internal bleeding; the criminals who tried to kill her son must be reported to the police. She looks shaken and her eyes are red. She has been weeping and praying all day, ever since the driver informed her of the young man's disappearance and they started searching for him in the jail, the morgue, the hospitals. For the first time in a long time, Carlos hears her shout, and with every shout she seems to become a little more real, filling in that years-long silence. His sisters emerge from their bedrooms and run down the stairs to kiss him, still wearing their nightgowns.

Don Augusto is fidgeting with a snuffed-out cigar. He's anxious too, but he doesn't chastise his son. It's true that getting mixed up with agitators and terrorists was a numbskull thing to do, only Carlos would be capable of it, but in the end, weren't we all young once? And at least the incident pushed Carlos into the fray for a bit of brawling — in short, made him act a bit manlier than usual, which, with regard to his son, is more reassuring than it is anything else. He's not worried about the stitches either; he's seen Indians still standing even with the white of their bones showing through their wounds. What's more, the mark of the injury gives his son rather a determined look, a virility Don Augusto would never have thought possible and that he hopes is here to stay. Nevertheless, he accedes to his wife's demands and orders his servants to fetch the doctor at once, even if they have to drag him out of bed.

And the doctor doesn't find anything. Or, rather, he finds a clean bandage covering a few stitches — extraordinarily neat work, especially for a proletarian hospital, he thinks admiringly — and a small laceration that threatens no consequence more dire than staining the dressing a little. All he needs is a little arnica and a change of bandage once a day, and the doctor starts to say just that, but something in Señora Rodríguez's eyes stops him. So he drags out the checkup a little longer and finally says that, come to think of it, better safe than sorry, so perhaps the boy should also rest a few days to recover from the shock and his injuries. He makes the suggestion without conviction; he's very sleepy and wants to go home. Carlos's mother desperately seizes on the idea. "The doctor said a week in bed!" she announces to her son after seeing the doctor to the door. Carlos says he feels perfectly fine, that he doesn't need any rest, but in the end he gives in. Just as he allowed himself to be carried on the stretcher. Just as, eight years earlier, he endured those doses of liver-strengthening castor oil.

He spends the week in bed, and that week is enough time for a good many things to happen. He finds out about all of it through the papers, which his sisters sneak in to him on the breakfast tray ("And make sure you don't read anything upsetting").

The night of the riot, rocks shatter streetlights all over El Callao and Lima. The next day the people — but who or what is "the people," really? — bury the martyr Florencio Aliaga in a grave paid for by the government. Someone writes a two-column editorial demanding that those responsible for the injured strikers be found, but even if anyone is responsible, nobody finds the culprit. Two days later the negotiations begin. At last the workers and the steamship companies reach an agreement establishing that everything will remain more or less the same, give or take a few *soles*. His mother's prayers have been heeded once more, and the river of reality returns to its customary course, to what has always been and must always be.

One day Martín Sandoval shows up at the house looking for Carlos and is ushered into his bedroom. He comes bearing his own version of events — they have accepted a twenty percent increase in wages, victory is ever nearer, etc. — and a stack of books for him to read during his convalescence. Carlos, who is not allowed to get up even during visits, accepts them wordlessly from his bed: Marx, Kropotkin, Bakunin. He doesn't know what to say. At last he says, "Thank you, they're very nice," and as he speaks, he realizes how stupid he sounds. But Martín doesn't seem to care; he smiles broadly and says he must read them all. On his way out he winks and raises his left fist, and Carlos responds by raising his right. Martín laughs.

That same day, José also comes to visit. Don Augusto interrupts them a number of times during their conversation. He is thrilled to have a Gálvez, a descendant of the heroes of the Pacific, calling at his home. So he keeps reappearing under various implausible pretexts, giving exaggerated bows and plying his guest with wine and cigars that José simply must try and that José does not try. Carlos squirms in his bed. He mutters a few scathing words that his father does not hear. As he sees it, his father is behaving like a fawning footman eager to please his master with a few clever comments, and José receives the offerings with frosty graciousness. Don Augusto also brings in a newspaper describing events abroad and attempts a verbatim recitation of an article on the Russo-Japanese War he's just memorized; in his opinion, he says, despite the Yalu River victory, the Japanese will be utterly vanquished; they'll see when the Baltic fleet of Admiral Rozhestvensky — is he pronouncing that damned difficult name correctly? — rounds the Cape of Good Hope and surprises them from the south; Czar Nicholas isn't going to let a bunch of yellow men from the far ends of the earth tell him where he can and cannot dock his ships. Doesn't José agree? he asks when he runs out of ideas — which is to say, right where the article ended. Gálvez doesn't know anything about the war, but he pretends to reflect a moment. At last he smiles a genuine

smile and says he does not agree, that in fact he and his father believe just the opposite: that the Russians are out of options and
that Japan is going to trounce the czar and the aforementioned
Rozinsky. Don Augusto blinks a moment, stammers, rolls and
unrolls the newspaper a couple of times — *Why don't you just go
away,* thinks Carlos, *and stop making us look ridiculous?* — and
finally says that he hadn't seen it like that, but, come to think
of it, the Gálvez analysis does make sense, that Japan is going to
win and not Russia. Indeed, he has no doubt, and it is so obvious
now that he has considered it carefully, he is embarrassed to have
thought otherwise. He leaves.

At long last, he leaves.

And only then can José perch on the edge of the bed and
tell Carlos why he has come. The novel, of course. Now that the
strike is finally over, a wide array of possibilities will open before
them, and they cannot pass them up. So they must answer the
letters, which have just arrived — did he not say that already? Six
of them, no less, six envelopes that languished a month in the
hold of one of the ships. It takes Carlos a few moments to realize that José has already read the letters, that for the first time he
has not waited for him — that he hasn't even brought them with
him. He hasn't brought them, and Carlos has to say that it's fine,
that it doesn't matter, that he forgives him for that too.

"Since you were sick . . ."

"It's fine."

"I'll bring them to you." José pats the sheets and, below them,
Carlos's knees. "I forgot them, but don't worry, I'll bring them.
You'll see!"

But that's not even the best part. Even better is the fantastic
idea he had the other day and couldn't wait to tell him about.
He was thinking about the novel and suddenly remembered

Schneider's seven hundred writing tips, specifically one of the few that hadn't been expunged from his memory by the fire. The one that talked about the middle pages of every novel and how something extraordinary had to take place in them.

"I remember," says Carlos, propping the pillow up behind him so he can sit up.

"Well, it occurred to me that that's exactly what's needed to pique the Maestro's interest: a little action. The novel has been rather dull so far, don't you agree?"

"Dull?"

"I mean, nothing much has happened. Of course that's not necessarily a bad thing. Schneider said that at the beginning of the second act the story always drags a bit — gets a little slow, let's say. The same thing has happened with us: weeks with those letters rotting in the port. But now . . ."

"Now what?"

"Now the action begins! The strike, to be precise. We had it right there in front of our noses, and we didn't see it. Don't you realize? You yourself said it the other day: you were saying that Georgina would sympathize with the workers. Maybe she'd even go down to scope out the port, don't you think? And that's when the action takes off. Police repression! Stampede! Georgina in peril! She could even get injured — why not?"

"And what the hell does that get us?"

"What do you mean, what does that get us? For starters, a rip-roaring chapter. And then, imagine the Maestro's reaction . . . his transatlantic friend at death's door! That would awaken anyone's emotions, you must admit. Poets' muses are always on the verge of croaking. That's probably why they're muses. And maybe that's what Juan Ramón needs to make up his mind . . ."

Carlos asks for a cigarette. His mother has forbidden him to smoke during his convalescence, but to hell with that. He needs a cigarette. And he also needs a moment to reflect — the time that it takes José to stand up, fetch his coat, take a cigarette out of his case, light it.

"It's just a suggestion, of course," José continues before Carlos has exhaled the smoke from his first drag. "I know Georgina is your thing. But I thought it might make a splendid chapter. Georgina would also talk about the workers and how worried she is about their situation. It fits her personality, don't you think? The concern for people in need. You could put in those things you were telling me in the port. All that stuff about twenty *soles* a day . . ."

"Two *soles*."

"Whatever. What do you think? Don't tell me there's not any material there."

Carlos feels his blood beating against the stitches of his wound and tastes the acrid smoke in his mouth.

"Yes . . . I guess it's not a bad idea," he murmurs.

Gálvez scratches his ear.

"It was actually Ventura's idea, you know? He and I . . . well, let's say he's going to give us a hand with the novel. As long as you have no objections, of course."

"Ventura?"

"You don't remember him? You must know him. Ventura Tagle-Bracho . . . the fellow with the pipe."

Ventura — of course. Carlos remembers having seen him at the club a few times, with his pipe and his somewhat rough manners. He especially remembers the way Tagle-Bracho always looked down at him from the disdainful heights of his last name, whose hyphenated sonority could intimidate even the Gálvezes. He doesn't like Ventura. But fortunately he remembers his mirror mimicry exercises in time and almost effortlessly pulls off what looks like perfect assent. Only his hand betrays him: an involuntary movement, brusque and contemptuous, that drops cigarette ash on the bed.

"I knew you'd agree! That chap has marvelous ideas, you'll see."

"I didn't know he enjoyed literature," Carlos says slowly, careful not to erase the expression from his face.

"He's not exactly an expert on the topic, that's for sure. Indeed, I don't think he's all that interested. But you should hear the ideas he has . . . Incredible ideas, Carlota! You're going to love them!"

José laughs, even pats him on the knee again. Carlos thinks of the mirror and, with a bit of effort, laughs too. His laugh is discreet, expectant, as if it were full of hollow spaces, as if it were prepared to cease at any moment so José can finally describe the sort of ideas he's referring to. But he doesn't.

◇

My dear friend:

How dreadful your letter, and how I trembled as I read it! The paper still clutched in my hand, I saw you in my mind's eye as if in a dream, dragged along in that awful tumult you rendered so eloquently. The lack of bread creates savage beasts. And equally savage and heedless was your decision to so expose yourself to danger! Tell me, would imperiling yourself make these letters arrive more quickly or make that terrible strike finish more rapidly? For a moment, before our very eyes, you became a full-blown anarchist. A modern-day Bakunin, with a lump and a bruise as your trophy. A fine bother you've given us! For once — though it will not serve as precedent — I must acknowledge that your father is not entirely wrong. Do not give me that look; I agree with him. You are a little girl who must be looked after and chided. Yes, chided! Does that provoke your indignation? But a falling-out and a friendship lost are inevitable when a person insists on risking her life for such a trifling thing as a handful of my letters. Instead, let's make up and you tell me whether you are still in any pain from that injury you suffered, the thought of which causes me keen anguish! Are you sure you haven't minimized the seriousness of the incident to protect the nerves of your friend, who is so concerned about your health and life?

Now that my heart has stopped racing, I reread your letter, which despite its horror is also quite beautiful. I

pause several times, entranced, on these captivating lines:
"From the breakwater they seemed to form a single body,
as if they were a monstrous living thing spilling down
the docks and wharves, its skin scaly with hats and faces."
Or this one, no less beautiful: "Above the agitated faces,
the bodies of the first horsemen came into view. There
aloft, they might have been at the bow of a ship that cut
through the swell of workers, who shouted and scattered
in all directions." Ah! Do you realize that you, too, are a
poet? Even if you do not write slim volumes of verse, there
are many other ways to make poetry; one is a poet in the
way one looks at things, and you — and I say this with
all sincerity — truly have that quality. These letters are
poetry! And I, who hope to continue to receive them for a
long time to come, must beg of you to promise that you will
never embark upon such madness again. Do so for your
father, who loves you so much, or even — if you will forgive
my boldness — do so for this humble servant who, here on
the other side of the Atlantic, anxiously awaits swift news
of your recovery and new examples of your poetry . . .

◇

After that, the novel continues on its course as if it had never stopped. Except that's not true; the novel continues, but something has changed. For starters, the settings have changed. The chapters are no longer dictated up in the garret; for some time now, they have descended instead to the mundane reality of billiards halls, opium dens, and cabarets. The novel frequents those haunts along with its numerous authors — at this point they've added six or seven new pens to the project. First the aforementioned Ventura, and then his gaggle of friends, who provoke brawls wherever they go and have a curious habit of taking the opposite position for anything Carlos says, no matter the topic. One of them, a fellow named Márquez, is less interested in Georgina than he is in the countless billiards games over which they hammer out her biography. And, of course, there is José, who has grown tired of sitting on the sidelines and for the first time is attempting to act as master of ceremonies, to decide what Georgina can and cannot think.

The others agree. They agree and Carlos writes.

The settings change; the authors change. And, of course, Georgina herself changes too. After all, her life is made only of the stuff of words, and naturally the ones uttered in the stillness of a garret are not the same ones that are strung together amid the clamor of the singing cafés and vaudeville theaters, or in the smoky somnolence of a clandestine opium den. In such settings, it is no wonder — indeed, anything else is unimaginable — that Georgina becomes a bit bolder, one might say more in keeping with the sight of the cabaret dancers baring their thighs as the authors drink and write. Often Ventura and his friends offer new ideas while groping the dancers' hindquarters or playing billiards. They propose phrases and words that the old Georgina would never have uttered. Though these are only minor details, Carlos fears that they contain the seed of something new, and he forcefully objects to the suggestions. Then it is up to Gálvez to decide the matter. He almost always sides with Carlos, but sometimes, smiling, he embraces some of the newcomers' fancies. These little defeats gnaw at Carlos's pride and blemish Georgina's biography. They stand out like scrawls on an unmarred file.

But José himself is unquestionably the most changed of all. For the first time, he has difficulty making decisions; he contemplates them for long periods, nibbling at the cap of his pen. Sometimes it takes him hours to judge whether it is pertinent that Georgina say something or not. He agrees with Carlos that such decisions cannot be made lightly. In the end everything hinges on these words, and if they ever want the poet to dedicate a book to Georgina, they're going to have to do much better still. And so sometimes, after opting for Ventura's suggestion, he might still be uneasy. He waits for the others to leave and then he calls Carlos over. See here, Carlota, explain to me again why you say this word isn't right. And he listens quietly, with an attention and patience he'd never dare display in front of the others.

You know what? he will say when he arrives at the club the following night, before he's even removed his hat. *I've thought better of it. We're going to have to cut that last paragraph.*

And once more, Ventura and his friends agree. They agree and Carlos writes.

◇

One afternoon the Rodríguez family receives a visit from the Almadas. Carlos has never heard of them before, but they must be an important family, judging by how vigorously his mother scolded the servants on the eve of the big day. You don't know them because they've been living in Philadelphia, in the United States, for the past twenty years, Don Augusto tells him, as if he cared. And so, because Carlos doesn't care, he doesn't bother to listen to the end of the story. He can imagine what it is, anyway: Centuries of grandeur wiped out in a single decade by a failed business, or by debts, or by gambling. Afterward, when all seems lost, a return to the country they once disdained, the only place where their last name still means something. And finally, the girl — because Carlos knows that somewhere in that story there must be a daughter or niece of marrying age, and he also knows that she is the only reason for their visit.

And in fact there is a daughter — or, rather, two daughters. Their names are Elizabeth and Madeleine, and they are presented with a great display of curtsies and polite clichés. Elizabeth is tall, slender, and somewhat pretty, though she is dazzling compared to her sister. Madeleine is fat and clumsy, and her homeliness is indisputable in any context. She has a large mole on her cheek that seems to dominate her entire countenance, and Carlos can't stop staring at it throughout the introductions. "Our Madeleine was born in Philadelphia and doesn't speak Spanish all that well yet," Señor Almada warns, perhaps intrigued by the interest that Carlos is showing in her, "while our dear Elizabeth speaks both languages perfectly. I'm sure you will find her charming company," he adds, smiling. Carlos tries to smile too, and more or less manages it. "Wonderful," he says.

And he doesn't open his mouth again for the next hour.

The daughters don't say anything either. Elizabeth sits motionless in her seat, rigid as a rod, her feet placed close together and her hands on her knees. She looks like the cover illustration of a correction manual for young ladies. Carlos decides not to look at her. He longs to wreck the whole farce, so reminiscent of a livestock market, the cattle remaining silent while their handlers negotiate the price. As for Madeleine, she couldn't talk even if she wanted to, as her mastery of the Spanish language seems to be limited to three phrases: *No, thank you* (when the servants offer her a canapé), *Pleased to meet you* (when anyone enters the room), and *Pardon me?* (the rest of the time, even when asked the simplest of questions). Or perhaps four; she will most likely also say *Thank you for everything, I've had a lovely afternoon* when it is time to go.

The parents talk animatedly, perhaps to make up for their offspring's silence. Señor Almada, for example, takes the opportunity to trot out some of his impressions of the United States. He speaks of his second homeland with the indulgent air used to describe a summer residence that is dearly beloved despite its many imperfections and discomforts. The problem with the United States is the unions, he says. The problem is Italian immigration. The problem is the coloreds. He sees problems everywhere, but the problem of the coloreds is clearly his favorite. He even mentions one Dr. Eldridge in Philadelphia who uses an x-ray machine to whiten colored people's skin. "Yes, just what I said," he repeats, "the ray turns them not completely white but at least tolerably pale." They spend a few minutes discussing the convenience of the procedure, particularly the thorny matter of financing: whether the government should or should not cover the cost of the skin whitening.

Each family takes the opportunity to share lies that the other will then enthusiastically pretend to believe. The Almadas complain of the vices of servants they no longer have, discuss the rents of properties they've already sold, and laboriously reestablish businesses that have long since fallen into ruin or oblivion. They also mention, in passing, the prospect of a trip to Europe. A summer in seaside towns and jaunts down the Crimean coast, which is as far removed from their financial possibilities as the European continent is from Peru. As for the Rodríguezes, they speak at length of their illustrious dead — that is, they spin lies as fast as they can. They choose a few sonorous names, dole out a few honors and achievements among them, and then describe them with an affection and generosity that transcend the centuries. Did you know that Carlos's great-grandfather's grandfather's great-great-grandfather — on the maternal side — was a count in a city you've no doubt never heard of? Or that he is descended from a particular Frenchman who was a general during the revolutions? The Almadas have not heard all that. Or yes, actually, now that she thinks about it, Señora Almada seems to recall having heard of the Marquis Rodríguez y Rodríguez, decorated by Emperor Charles V himself after the Battle of Mühlberg.

At some point the conversation returns to reality — that is, to the front page of the newspapers. Don Augusto mentions the end of the dockworkers' strike, and Señor Almada nods and says that the problem in the United States of America is the workers. Those anarchists need to be taught a lesson, shown a firm hand, but most certainly not condemned to death, he adds, because as everyone knows, the gallows creates martyrs — take the strikers in Chicago, for instance — and they even created a Labor Day, as if they didn't already have all those Sundays for resting. For her part, Señora Almada agrees with her husband on the fundamentals and confesses that while some of them are no doubt good people, she wouldn't say otherwise, nevertheless one might prefer to cross the street when encountering a laborer on the sidewalk. As for Señora Rodríguez, she finds it ludicrous to compromise the health of one's soul in a quest for earthly riches, which are ultimately fleeting, when everyone knows that when Judgment Day comes, rich and poor will be equal, God willing, which He will be. Finally, Don Augusto smooths his mustache and notes that the matter bears careful consideration, which is what he always says to resolve any debate in which he's not quite sure what his interlocutor wants to hear.

Carlos suddenly interrupts. He has not spoken yet, which may be why his words sound unexpectedly brusque. He does not know, he says, whether the gallows creates martyrs or not; whether laborers are better people when viewed from the opposite sidewalk; whether it is or is not God's will for His creatures to be able to eat. But there is no doubt that the dockworkers are first and foremost human beings, that at least they bleed as if they were — because he has seen that blood, their blood, pooling on the ground under their heads — and as far as he knows they eat too. Although, given that they earn about two *soles* a day, they certainly don't eat very much. Because does anyone know how much it costs to buy a piece of bread? Well, according to his calculations it's half a *sol,* which means four pieces of bread a day per family; four crusts of bread and not even a sip of that delicious hot chocolate they're drinking, which by the way costs three *soles* an ounce.

Carlos breaks off, panting. He's not quite sure why he's said all that. The words don't even sound like his own; it is as if Sandoval has spoken through his mouth for a moment. His first thought is that the books Sandoval lent him might be to blame, though to be honest he hasn't understood much of them, and so in that sense Marx's *Das Kapital* isn't all that different from Carlos's textbook on canon law. Nor is it due to the memory of the workers and their wives collapsing on the paving stones in the port, however tempting it is to believe otherwise. No, if he's honest with himself, he has to admit that he simply wants to irritate the guests. To shred the fabric of the wedding that will never be celebrated, not if he has anything to do with it, even if the Almadas will have to go beg at the door of the San Juan Bautista Church, even if the Rodríguezes are obliged to do without coats of arms and continue to stink of rubber and paraffin.

For a moment, the Almadas do not react. His mother breaks in to dispel the severity of the commentary; she smiles and says that her son must still be somewhat agitated after a certain unpleasant incident at the port from which he still has a number of visible wounds, look, look, there on the poor boy's face. Don Augusto clears his throat and says that of course that position too bears quite careful consideration. And then there's Señor Almada, who, rather than being offended, bursts out laughing.

"You sound just like my daughter," he says, oddly jovial. "You know, dear Elizabeth has her head crammed full of these fashionable ideas about workers' rights and aid for the needy. It's clear from a mile off that you share those noble views, my dear Carlos. Maybe you've even been influenced by those Russian and German philosophers that young people are so wild about these days. Ah, we're getting old, Augusto, don't you think? We're all dried up and no longer understand the passions of our children — and they in turn do not understand that time and

God always settle everything back into its proper place, always. But they have good hearts, I say, first-rate hearts. My daughter is such a kind soul that she even helps out at the orphanages and with the Public Beneficence Society — don't pull that face, my dear, I'm only telling these gentlemen the purest truth. In fact, on some afternoons we hold gatherings at our home to discuss politics with family friends, and Elizabeth uses those occasions to take up collections for the needy. You should bring a friend and come along to one of those meetings, Carlos — it's not often that one meets a young person so passionate about social justice."

It is perhaps peculiar to see Señor Almada, a sworn enemy of workers' demands, applauding words like the ones Carlos has just uttered. Yet in his way he is just as Marxist as the revolutionaries, and so there is really no contradiction. After all, only a true materialist would sacrifice his convictions — which cannot be measured or weighed and therefore are not real — to promote an advantageous marriage. And so, in praising a young man's tirade that he in fact despises, he rises, in terms of praxis, to the level of Karl Marx himself.

Everyone looks at Carlos expectantly. His parents, the Almadas, the maid who has come in to gather up the wineglasses. Even the plump younger sister who doesn't understand a word of Spanish. But the most intent gaze is Elizabeth's. Carlos turns to her, and their eyes meet for the first time. Elizabeth, who for some reason doesn't seem interested in the drapes, or the etchings, or the silverware. Elizabeth looking at him — only at him.

It would be a pleasure, of course. And everybody smiles, and celebrates, and says my, how late it's gotten, how time does fly. *Thank you for everything, I've had a lovely afternoon,* Madeleine will say as she leaves.

His problem is women — or, rather, the lack of them. At least that's José's opinion on the matter, which he makes sure to reiterate at every opportunity. Carlos should forget all those fantasies about Georgina and her poems for a while and think a little about his own life. About those women all around him who are beautiful, and young, and exist outside of books, and yet do not interest him in the slightest. He doesn't even talk about them, much less touch them. Yes — that's the real problem, the only one; José knew it the first time he went to visit Carlos in his room during his long convalescence, when he sat down on the bed and the springs didn't make any noise. What the hell is this, Carlota — a bed that doesn't groan is one where there's no screwing going on, and a body that doesn't screw must inevitably house an ailing mind. Make your bed creak, and you'll see how quickly it'll pass, this obsession of yours with port-marooned letters. Mine screeches like a freight train or a factory sabotaged by Luddites. The servants don't get any sleep even when I'm alone in bed; imagine what it's like when I've got company.

But that is precisely the difficulty: Carlos never has company. The only woman who bends over his bed is the maidservant when she folds back the sheets, and he never even tries to grope her rear end. *That's not love,* thinks Carlos, but then what is? He has repeated the word so often in his early poems, and later through the mouth — the hands — of Georgina, and yet he truly understands so little about it. Lay off the Georginas, José repeats. That guff about young ladies sighing languidly in their gardens and giving their first innocent kisses is all very well — useful for inventing muses and writing marvelous letters like these — but you and I don't live inside a novel. You should come with us to the brothels and try to have a little fun for once. I promise you the women there don't lower their eyes melancholically when you kiss them; sometimes you don't even have to kiss them to get things started, if you catch my meaning.

Carlos doesn't. How could he, when his dreams never venture beyond the very real boundary of his bedroom's four walls?

But things are different now. Or at least Carlos needs them to be. So he's going to go to that meeting and do what he has to do to get to know Elizabeth a little better. Why not? Does he have some more enticing prospect? Is he engaged to someone else? No; he's a bachelor, he's twenty years old, and he never visits the brothels. He never touches the pale flesh of the dancers at the vaudeville theater, even though they ask him to. So why shouldn't he talk with whomever he wishes? All he has to do is persuade José to go with him, but José isn't the least bit interested in political meetings or invitations. He's got a prior engagement this afternoon, and anyway, what does Carlos have to lose in making a private visit to the Almada residence, of all places — they invited you, so you go, damn it, I'm not some governess who has to accompany you and hold your hand through all your maidenly obligations. But then Carlos starts talking about the Almadas' daughters, and at that José changes his tune. He guffaws at the jokes about Madeleine and discreetly arches his eyebrows at Carlos's description of Elizabeth's beauty, and after a while he places a hand on his shoulder and says, You know what, Carlota, the club and Ventura and the whorehouses of San Ginés can go to the devil for all I care — this afternoon the two of us are going to accept the young ladies' kind invitation.

◇

The Almadas' mansion is too vast to disguise its decline. Everywhere they look, there are empty corners that might once have contained Louis XV armchairs, a Swiss grandfather clock, silver-framed mirrors, Persian rugs, a Pancho Fierro watercolor — but now only their absence remains, geometric shadows marking the walls and floors. It is impossible to walk through its deserted rooms without thinking about the junk dealers and ragmen who must have haggled over prices for endless hours; the master of the house loosening his bow tie and repeatedly exclaiming "Oh!" at being forced to discuss money; the hawkers, each with a pencil behind his ear, taking measurements to demonstrate that in fact the piano won't fit, they'll have to dismantle the balustrade. But the Almadas are so hospitable and ceremonious that there's hardly time to look around. Perhaps they are hoping that their courtesy, the endlessly proffered cups of tea or chocolate, will fill in the gaps left behind by poverty. And their reverence becomes all the more wholehearted when they discover that Carlos's silent companion is none other than José Gálvez — a Gálvez! — the last name like a magnet that draws everyone's attention. Only Elizabeth seems immune to that attraction — *A pleasure to meet you,* the hand coolly extended, and then the curtsy. Her welcome to Carlos, though, is something else entirely: again that glow in her eyes that seems to prolong the look between them that began at his house. Carlos is unable to keep the hand with which he grasps hers from shaking a little.

Ten or twelve guests are assembled in the parlor. Almost all of them are relatives; indeed, most of them might as well be the same person, bowing or extending the back of the hand again and again. The only one who stands out is a nun, somebody's friend, sheathed in her wimple and holding a little basket to collect pledges for building an orphanage. Everyone peppers José with questions — Did he have the good fortune to meet his uncle José Miguel, the hero of the War of the Pacific, when he was still alive? Is it true what they say, that José writes poetry? — and there is also the occasional distracted, obligatory inquiry to Carlos. At the other end of the room, the immense Madeleine offers him a half smile that requires no translation. And it is even easier to interpret Señora Almada's efforts to position Elizabeth next to Carlos, not to mention the remarkable coincidence that it is Elizabeth herself who happens to offer him pastries and hot chocolate, her gaze lowered and her cheeks faintly blushing.

Then the guests and their hosts sit down around the table. The famous political meeting has begun, though Carlos does not realize it for a few minutes. The discourse is simplified to suit the most naive, the gathered company speaking abstractly of children going hungry and women dying in childbirth in the hospices. Elizabeth ventures a remark from time to time. She chooses her words carefully, glancing furtively at her father and Carlos, seeking approval. Hers are cozy notions to which no one in attendance could object: hunger should be combated with food, poverty with alms, and the deaths of childbearing mothers with additional orphanages. Well-intentioned words, to which the others listen with their eyes fastened on the dessert tray and their lips smeared with chocolate. Though one might think those at the table evinced a certain sympathy for the proletariat, that would not be entirely accurate. The guests' compassion is inspired not by the life of the dockworker or the butcher they encounter on the street but by an ideal worker they've never met because he does not, in fact, exist.

"A real snoozer of a meeting you've dragged me to, Carlota," José mutters to him in an aside. "We sound like a Christian charity club. Lucky for us, at least the view is nice," he adds, nodding toward Elizabeth.

"Don't point."

"Well, what do you say? Protagonist or secondary character?"

"Lower your voice."

"I say she's a secondary character. Do you like her? I think she was flirting with you. We're not going to fight over a secondary character, are we?"

"Would you just shut up?"

After a while, Señor Almada breaks in to offer Carlos the floor. This man, he says, witnessed firsthand the events at the El Callao docks. And so they clamor for him to stand up and tell them all about it.

Carlos gets slowly to his feet. He lifts the napkin he has folded over his knees and uses it to wipe the sweat from his hands. He doesn't know what to say. Now that everyone's listening to him, now that his disquisition on the dockworkers' poverty is awaited with curiosity and sympathy, he no longer has any interest in giving it. He studies Elizabeth's reaction out of the corner of his eye; he feels the searing weight of her gaze right on his lacerated cheek. For the first time he realizes that she never looks at his eyes or mouth. It is that stitched-up flesh that she is always observing, seeming to study it with interest and desire and even a bit of pride, just as a girl might examine the medals her beloved earned in battle.

At last he begins to speak. He sketches the scene of the crowd packed into the port, the train brought to a halt with hurled rocks, the mounted soldiers charging. The account should electrify his listeners, but for some reason it does not; the words emerge as flat and lifeless as a canvas. He has lost the ardor of his first speech. Now it is not Sandoval or Marx or Kropotkin himself who seems to speak through him; now only Carlos speaks through Carlos's mouth. If anyone bothered to transcribe his words, they would find them to be as full of hesitations, adverbs, and ellipses as Georgina's letters. But nobody bothers to transcribe them, of course. At most they listen to him distractedly, uninterested in his dull discourse. Even Elizabeth's gaze seems to have cooled a little. Only Madeleine, who has not understood a word, maintains the same imperturbable smile.

And then it happens. Someone asks Carlos what he was doing in El Callao on the very day and at the very hour of the largest strike of the century so far, and for a moment he doesn't know how to respond. He seeks out José's gaze, as if asking for help. And suddenly José is standing with a smile and begging permission to speak. Those present must forgive him, he says in a confident tone, but the truth is that it was all his fault; his dear friend Carlos has been covering for him for far too long, but the time has come to confess the truth. It was entirely because of him that they were at the port that day, as he has so often chided himself since — how could he not feel regret after what happened? But he has always felt such profound concern for the disadvantaged, those who go hungry, those who are deprived of the bread that God would knead for all of His creatures. And on that fateful day, he wanted — so selfishly! — to go find out whether the shipping-company magnates had come to an agreement with the protesters. He is sometimes possessed by these sorts of whims — sponsoring a student who has not been offered a scholarship or giving a fifty-*sol* cloak to a blind man so he doesn't feel the chill. His friend Carlos attempted to talk him out of it, of course, because Carlos is sensible and prudent and always tries to make him see reason. He might warn him, for example, that the poor student spends his tuition money on women and wine, or remind him that fifty *soles* aren't to be squandered on a destitute blind man who is probably faking anyway and has perfectly functional eyes behind his dark glasses. Though José does not share Carlos's ideas, he knows that they come from his friend's prudence and good judgment, virtues that he admires so much. Well, then: Carlos gave him the same sort of advice that day, to no avail, and he should have listened to him, because as it turned out, no agreement had been reached, and instead they encountered guns and swords. And it was his poor friend Carlos who'd borne the brunt of it, sensible, prudent Carlos who'd lain wounded on the ground, and José had wept during the charge and refused to leave his side — another foolish bit of stubbornness, really, they could have killed him, though they didn't — the soldiers rushing past with their swords held high and him weeping over his injured friend, the injured people, the whole world injured by injustice and poverty and oppression.

José keeps talking a few minutes longer. He describes the way his hand clutched Carlos's as the doctor sewed up the wound; the fearlessness with which he blocked the sergeant who attempted to detain his friend — Under no circumstances, sir, if you wish to arrest this man, you will have to arrest me first. But Carlos has stopped listening. He is conscious only of the evolving expressions on the guests' faces: the smiles, the looks of surprise, of admiration, of suspense. The way even the nun's waxen cheeks seem to flush with an insurgent glow. But especially the face of Elizabeth, who is no longer looking at him, who now is conscious only of José's gestures, José's eyes, José's mouth opening and closing, saying what she so longs to hear. Seeing the intensity of her gaze, Carlos attempts to smile. He smiles until the mask of his mouth begins to ache.

When José and Carlos take their leave, the two sisters accompany them out to the street. It seems they've become accustomed to taking a walk every afternoon right before dinner. And it also turns out the four of them are going in the same direction, what a remarkable coincidence, so José immediately offers the young ladies their coach. He and Carlos can return home on foot, so they won't be in the sisters' way. And the young ladies accept the chivalrous offer, of course, but they would not dream of depriving the young men of their conveyance. "There's more than enough room!" Elizabeth notes earnestly, her eyes fixed on José. Might not the four of them travel together? The lady's voice stresses the word *together*, but certainly not the *four*. José lightly bows his head and responds that, in that case, they will share the coach with pleasure. Also, it's such a lovely afternoon . . . Mightn't the ladies want to join them on their outing? Although, he hastens to add, including Carlos with his gaze, perhaps the two of them should not request such an abuse of time and trust; surely the young ladies have already had the opportunity to visit Lima and get to know its every detail, and so there is nothing they could offer to amuse them.

"None of that, now! We've hardly left the house since we arrived!" Elizabeth lies, perhaps forgetting that not five minutes ago she declared them enthusiastic takers of long walks.

"Pardon me?" adds the younger sister in English, with utmost sincerity.

And so it is arranged: a journey to Miraflores and the beach at Chorrillos and the Barranco cliffs, and then back to Lima at dinnertime.

Carlos barely participates in the operation. He climbs into the carriage and sits next to Madeleine, careful that their knees don't touch. He doesn't speak; he stares at the knob of his cane, smiles politely when obligated, and occasionally gives a brief instruction to the coachman through the little window.

José, though, points out at the landscape and offers commentary ranging from the humorous to the picturesque. When the inspiration strikes, he even tries out a few philosophical musings that have little to do with what he is seeing and very much to do with the particular texts he has studied for the occasion. As she listens, Elizabeth laughs or expresses surprise or feigns deep reflection, as appropriate. From time to time she translates the observations for her sister, who seems rather less entertained or astonished or meditative. In any event, the conversation has ceased to revolve around the workers and their hardships. Nor do the two of them remember Carlos, who presses against the cushions in the carriage and fiddles with his watch chain. Only the homely daughter occasionally turns to look at him and smile.

When the coach reaches Chorrillos, dusk is falling and the ficus and willow trees beside the road cast long shadows. In the silence, they can hear the clopping of the horses' hooves, the creaking of the wheels in the dust. Voices filter in through the curtains. In the estates, the parks, the gardens of the enormous summer villas, they can see swarms of white parasols and black top hats. Perhaps a wind kicks up, and José seizes the opportunity to offer Elizabeth a blanket, though the night has not yet grown cool. Elizabeth accepts. That is her way of declaring her love: allowing José to cover her legs even though the day's still warm.

The coach takes a couple of little-traveled roads. You must see the ocean, says José, the view of the cliffs at Chorrillos. I'll bet you don't have seashores like these in Philadelphia, he adds, and he's not wrong, though only because the states of Maryland, Delaware, and New Jersey stand between Philadelphia and the Atlantic. On some stretches it seems as if the road might dive into the sea, but always at the last moment, on the last outcropping of land, it retreats.

"It's so beautiful," says Elizabeth, barely looking out the window.

They have stopped atop one of the cliffs. They admire the jagged profile of the cliffs, the sandy slopes and precipices that plunge into the sea. Perhaps José, gesturing toward the horizon, recites a few verses he has prepared. Elizabeth listens to them in delight, and after that she no longer sees the disk of the sun sinking into the water but rather what the poetry says the twilight really is or should mean.

"What is that?" asks the younger sister in English, pointing.

At the foot of the cliffs they can see a small cove framed by sheer rockfaces. And in the cove there is something moving: dark and yellow blotches, tumbling amid the foam of the waves. They all shield their eyes with their hands as the light of the setting sun shimmers on the water and blinds them.

"They look like wild ducks," says Elizabeth.

"They look like fishing boats," says José.

But then, little by little, they begin to look like something else. Like naked women swimming, splashing, cavorting in the water, for instance. But nobody says that. And when they finally realize what they are seeing, José and Carlos stare even more intently while the girls blush and cry out in unison.

"Heavens!"

The two sisters raise their hands to their mouths and turn their eyes away at the exact same moment, as if their reactions were synchronized by some hidden mechanism. Ultimately, the decency of every young woman must include a bit of studied theatricality learned through countless governesses' lessons and parish priests' sermons. Elizabeth, perhaps letting herself be carried away in her performance by an excess of inspiration, even hastily raises her fan before her eyes, but through the ribs, through the slats and flimsy paper, something of the immodest spectacle can still be glimpsed.

At that moment, José's body seems to be possessed by a sudden decisiveness. He grasps her shoulder with the determination of a romantic hero. He tells her not to be afraid, that the women are probably prostitutes from the Panteoncito brothel, who come to bathe in the sea. (Indeed they are; Gálvez knows their faces and names quite well.) That there is nothing to fear from them, that though they may be fallen women, they are perhaps secretly worthy in their poverty — are not they themselves, men and women of position, in some way responsible for the moral and physical depravity of those who have nothing? That what they are seeing is not dangerous or fearsome, only women frolicking in the water and displaying the voluptuous truth of their naked bodies. That he is there to protect her from that, from the truth.

He says all this, or something like it, murmuring very close by her ear. But whatever it is he says, it seems to have some effect, and after a moment's hesitation Elizabeth slowly lowers her fan. She swallows hard and says, quite softly, that it's all right. That if he asks it of her, she won't be afraid. That if he says so, perhaps there is no sin in contemplating the innocent beauty of a human body. And so she moves to the window and watches the women without condemnation, without fear, without guilt. It goes basically like this: Elizabeth looks at the whores; José looks at Elizabeth; Carlos looks at José; Madeleine looks at Carlos.

As that look stretches on, Elizabeth strives to seem dignified and beautiful at once. And perhaps she manages it, because José has just bent down to kiss her. She submits docilely to his kiss. Artlessly, the way the whores are taking in the last caress of the sun and the spray of the waves. Every bit of her shivers, softens with the heat of that contact; his body moves slowly over hers — the carriage creaks, wallows — and an underground, aquatic movement seems to uncoil in that embrace. As if something of the sea, of the provocative beauty of the bathers, had slipped in under the checkered blanket.

Carlos averts his eyes; it seems that he too has in him a bit of scandalized maidenhood hiding behind a raised fan. And when he looks away, his eyes meet Madeleine's. The eyes of the homely sister, who is no longer looking at the floor, who is looking at him — the homely sister, at him — and smiling at him at that. Maybe she is expecting something. Or perhaps she too is trying to seem both dignified and beautiful at once, though surely she knows it would require a miracle to achieve the latter. In any case, it is a performance without a public, because Carlos shifts uneasily, clears his throat; he's already stopped looking at her. He hesitates a moment. Then he strikes the roof with his cane and shouts to the coachman that it's getting late, it's time to go home.

From that point on, Georgina changes rapidly. More rapidly even than José loses interest — after only two or three dates with Elizabeth, he decides he's had more than enough. Though those clandestine encounters leave no mark on his life, they leave one on Georgina's. José amuses himself by incorporating Elizabeth's attributes into his letters: her insubstantial chatter, her naive coquetry, her almost endearing credulity, her concern for the disadvantaged. Even a light touch of her natural inclination toward melodrama ("Why are you doing this to me, José? If you leave me, I am capable of anything! Anything, I tell you!").

But he concentrates most of his attention on including more and more references to the little mestiza housemaid, who for him has always been Georgina. And the others do more or less the same thing: fill the letters with any woman who comes to mind, especially those they know well. When somebody, let's say a vaudeville dancer, sits on Ventura's knee and murmurs some indelicate phrase in his ear, he softens it a bit and assigns it straightaway to Georgina. Maids, prostitutes, cabaret singers, florists: they all throw in their two cents — the modest ration of words allotted to each. A Georgina who evokes less and less the innocence of the Polish prostitute and more the eagerness with which the Gálvezes' maid groped between the young master's legs. Her letters are different now:

> But I must tell you that I am also impulsive and fervent,
> and at times I feel my chest consumed by the bonfire of an
> unknown passion . . . Something like a mad desire to live
> and be happy. A feeling of which the rest know nothing

*and that I can only barely mask. Except with you, my
friend! You who with each letter are gradually unraveling
all my secrets . . . !*

Or perhaps:

*Sometimes I think a woman is a little like a flower that
blooms, hoping for something that it does not know and yet
desires, desires so fiercely!*

Or even:

*I do not know, my dear Juan Ramón, whether what I
am saying is right or wrong: I know only that the body
sometimes feels strange and beautiful things of which the
spirit knows nothing, and that disregarding such beauty
might itself also constitute some category of sin . . .*

Carlos is reluctant to copy down these fancies. No, that sentence isn't going in the letter, not a chance; Georgina's not like that, over his dead body. But in the end he always gives in. What else can he do? His character has ceased to belong to him, and José is becoming increasingly inflexible in his decisions. Sometimes Carlos thinks of Georgina, the real one, as if she were a friend who has died, and many nights he wants to weep for his friend — his friend? — just as years ago he allowed himself to be flogged for the sake of muses who existed only in books. I've been telling you to think less and screw a little more, José says, emboldened by his friends' laughter; maybe that chubby American girl, you know who I mean. You had the whole back seat there to do her the favor and you didn't, Carlotita, you ungrateful lout. If a woman's value were calculated by the ounce, you'd have been letting a real treasure get away.

Ventura and the others laugh. They weren't there, they didn't see the fat, homely sister with her enormous mole, but even so they're sure she really is fat and homely, and so they laugh.

When he's alone, Carlos rereads the drafts of the letters. And also Juan Ramón's replies, which are growing ever longer and more affectionate and which have gradually begun to fill with intimate confidences, with little secrets. It seems the Maestro isn't bothered by the new Georgina. Worse still, anyone would say he prefers her, a grotesque scarecrow whose words reek of absinthe and whiskey. And of opium, especially opium, because by now most of the chapters are worked out in the rear of a building on Calle del Marqués that serves as a corset shop by day and a clandestine smoking den by night. It was Ventura who first told them that no Montmartre bohemian ever wrote a line without first inhaling the dense smoke of the pipes and hookahs, and after that nobody could get the idea out of José's head.

They visit the establishment two or three times a week. It's a small, poorly ventilated place run by Chinese immigrants. The space is divided by partitions and folding screens that reveal mysterious scenes: silhouettes that laugh, that dance, that clasp one another in prolonged embraces, that slumber and go quiet for many hours at a time. Even the smoke, so dark and heavy, seems to have a silhouette. Each nook is furnished with a smoking pipe and a few reed mats and cushions where they recline to smoke until their eyes start to wander and their smiles go dull. Sometimes they talk about the letters, or women, or they recite their own poems, which sound like extended yawns. Or they don't talk about anything; they just fall asleep, and the Chinese owners go silently from one alcove to another, covering their bodies with blankets or sheepskins, refilling the opium in the pipes, carrying bowls of some dubious potion that the poets languidly drink.

Carlos joins them against his will. Such a place, he feels, can produce only a character in tune with the setting. That is, a dull, indolent Georgina who laughs at the slightest provocation, who has a glassy look to her eyes and occasionally says inappropriate things. Foolish things that, like the smoke, take a long time to dissipate.

But it's not just about Georgina. Carlos is also alarmed by the relaxation the drug produces in his own body. With each puff he feels as if the mask screwed to his face, the one that is always able to simulate the appropriate expression, were gradually loosening and melting. And who knows what he might be hiding under there — he, of course, has long since forgotten. And so he is afraid. Sometimes, in the depths of his prostration, it seems to him that a woman comes and sits beside him, whispers something in his ear. It is, perhaps, Georgina, but a real Georgina. She emerges from the smoke with all the purity of the very first missives, free of smudges, of incoherencies, of emendations. She kneels at the foot of the mat and touches his head for a moment. It seems to him that she smiles. And then they have long conversations that leave no words or memories, only the feverish taste of smoke, inundating his lungs like an icy, protracted vertigo, a spiral that drags and blurs the outlines of things and behind which only Georgina remains constant. Her gaze, her smile. Her kiss; Georgina's kiss. The chill of her lips on his, her porcelain touch.

"Dlink," she says. "Dlink is good," she adds, inexplicably. And he drinks, drinks infinitely from that kiss, until he empties the bowl that someone is holding to his lips.

◇

My dear friend:

*Will you allow me to call you "dear," to call you
"friend"? It has been four weeks since I've had news of
you. Your charming letters must be waiting for me in the
mailbox of my residence in Madrid; and, knowing that, it
is all the more puzzling that I am still here, a full month
spent in my boyhood home in Moguer, surrounded by
relatives and relics of another era. Of excruciatingly sad
lights and aromas with which I cannot even make poetry,
with which I can no longer do anything.*

*You spoke in your last letter of your own sorrows that
also bear your loved ones' visages and are set in your own
home. A home that I imagine resembles the sort you see in
engravings, with whitewashed walls and palm trees, with
straight windowsills and severe façades and a well with a
pulley. All stone and rigor, just like your upbringing with
your father, who no doubt loves you but who, perhaps,
through loving you too much, poor thing, makes you
miserable. You spoke of the bowels of that piano where
you hide your secrets, these humble letters of mine among
them. Of your tiny, fragile chest, which seems to grow
even smaller when your father approaches. How could I
not understand you, I who between these walls feel the
presence of my own father's ghost? His dead eyes that now
see everything, against which keys and drawers are now
useless. His threadbare words reviving old accusations:*

abandoning my law studies, and the mad notion of becoming a painter, and then the even madder notion of becoming a poet — that's what my father would say. That's what he says now in a voice growing louder and more certain, in my ears, all the time. Here, in what was his house, he sounds ever more powerful.

And then there are the voices of the others, of the living, of us, the family members who stayed here and have nothing to talk about but money and rents. As if my father were only that: the debts he left, which we divide up the way one would the weight of a burdensome, jet-black coffin. The words debase, they soil things; one's mouth is tarnished by talking about pesetas, partitions, inheritances. We are gradually turning into nickel and metal, growing stiff and cold as the music of a coin. I fear that the mere mention of it has also tarnished this letter.

You ask me to tell you what I have been doing and writing. And yet I do and write so little! You, by contrast, do so much, you describe so many trips and meetings with girlfriends and walks along that street they call Jirón de la Unión that I must confess to feeling a little embarrassed at the indolence with which I watch the hours pass — watch them die, because everything dies. Nothing out of the ordinary to recount, except that I am sometimes happy and sometimes miserable. Everything that happens in reality takes place inside my head, or, if you prefer, within the confines of my own soul. (By the way, you haven't said what you think of that little poem I sent you about the soul of things.) What do I do? you ask. I am afraid you will be disappointed: I do little more than walk. Now around Moguer and its environs, and previously through

the cold streets of Madrid. I walk as if in a trance, and I
tend to forget my hat and my cane wherever I go. I wander
through the Retiro, an enormous park. You would adore
it, Georgina. A little green slice of Madrid into which all
of Moguer, with its diminutive houses and its river and
its sad yellow fields, could easily fit. There is also a pond
full of ducks and boats, and beside it a wafer seller whom
I stop to observe a long while. An old man with wafers
and other sweets, spinning a wheel of fortune. Sometimes
the customer wins and sometimes he loses — does Lima
have that sort of confection, are you familiar with such a
thing? — but the peddler always smiles. Nothing seems to
matter to him beyond the act of watching the wheel spin,
of doling out his delights. And I would like to be a bit like
him: to have the spirit of a dog or a child. Of a statue that
welcomes sun and rain alike with the same smile, that
does not despair or understand or suffer, that only goes to
its usual corner to keep being what it is, what it can never
cease to be.

And sometimes, why not admit it to you, dear
Georgina — let's agree that you have allowed me that
license: to call you dear, to call you friend — I imagine you
are walking with me. It would be such a lovely comfort for
me, a light with which to clear away such gloomy clouds.
Because as I walk out there, I go within myself to craft the
reply I will give you on my return. You could say that some
of my letters are worked out step by step, that I write them
with my feet, and sometimes without my cane or hat — if I
told you how often I leave them somewhere, you wouldn't
believe me. I even go walking within my own room, pacing
back and forth like a captive animal that is nevertheless

gentle and sad; I measure out the dimensions of my cage as I await a letter, a familiar hand, the stamps and seals of a certain far-off country. A square cell six paces on each side, bed and washbasin in the center; a total of twenty-four, and then starting over again. If I had taken all those paces in your direction — and if I could walk on the ocean, which is no small thing to imagine — where do you think I would have gotten to by now? My calculations, made with the assistance of an atlas with which I amuse myself in bed, have allowed me to estimate that I'd find myself more or less in the Sargasso Sea. That briny deep where the sea suddenly becomes unmoving land, a shipyard in which one neither comes nor goes. So lieth my soul! To tell the truth, that sea does not appear in my atlas, and I cannot say for sure whether it might be a fable or a myth, but it exists at least in our understanding, which is almost as if it existed in real life.

I would like to reach you, to reach Peru, which also exists but could just as easily not exist — or, rather, I would like for it to be you on my arm as we walked through the tranquil twilit avenues of Madrid. Perhaps you would like to walk with me, and perhaps you would also like for us to stop awhile as we treat ourselves to a wafer or two. Because I would most certainly give you one, Georgina, I would give you a hundred; something tells me that luck would smile on us for one, ten, fifty spins of that wheel. We could gorge ourselves, and laugh, and the wafer seller would laugh along with us. And if I had a photograph of you, Georgina, even if it were only one, I would know what face to affix to those walks that you and I take every morning, every night for you there in Lima. Will you share with me a portrait of the angels' smile? Will I come to know the countenance that is the inverse of my own self, that abides in the antipodes of my soul? Will you tell me, at the very least, whether you are partial to those sweet treats I offer you on our walks . . . ?

◇

"I find your cousin utterly changed of late. I think I liked her better before."

"I think I did too," Carlos says at last, without looking at him.

The Professor drops the latest letter onto the pile.

"Well! Fortunately, the Spanish poet doesn't share our view."

"What do you mean?"

He points at the stack of envelopes.

"Just read the last few letters, my friend. I'd say he's starting to fall in love. I'm telling you, it's going to take a letter or two at most. Good luck for your cousin and for you, and bad luck for me! After the wedding you're not going to need me, of course. It's a shame the custom is to write letters to woo women and not to keep them."

Carlos's face darkens.

"You think so?"

"That you don't use letters to keep a woman?"

"No, that there's going to be a wedding."

"My dear fellow, I'd say so. When a man and a woman do what these two are doing . . . the business generally ends in a wedding. Unless your cousin surprises us again and she's the one who starts resisting the betrothal."

"But they don't even know each other!" replies Carlos, practically shouting.

The Professor tosses back his glass of pisco and wipes the moisture from his lips with his shirt cuff.

"Well, so what? That doesn't seem to have gotten in the way before now. Also, from what I can tell, the Spanish poet is stirred up enough to come track her down. You don't agree? Look at that photograph. And that portrait of Juan Ramón. He's got the cadaverous aspect of the romantic sort of poet who blows his brains out at his lover's grave. Don't deny it. And didn't you say he'd been in three sanatoriums because of failed love affairs?"

"It was only two."

"Same difference! Listen to me, I've got twenty-three years of experience with this sort of thing. It's all in here, believe me. Suggests a passionate sort with little regard for consequences. And your cousin must be delighted, so there's no reason to fret, am I right?"

Carlos doesn't answer. He doesn't even look up. He stares at his hands as if he didn't recognize them.

"Come now, why so glum? You don't seem too pleased for your cousin. And didn't we agree that the most important rule was never to swim against love's tide? Let's drink to them, then, and not discuss it any further. As you see, I'm even violating my policy of never combining drink and work, and I'm only doing it for them — that is, for you."

He snaps his fingers.

"Jorge! Bring two more glasses for my friend and me. We've got a lot to celebrate."

"What's the happy news?" asks the waiter from the kitchen.

"Some friends of ours are getting married."

"That calls for some whiskey, at least! No, no, I insist — it's on the house."

He takes the bottle and fills two glasses to the brim.

"To the happy couple!" exclaims the Professor.

Carlos hesitates a few moments longer. He stares at Cristóbal's raised glass. Finally he raises his own.

"To the happy couple," he replies.

He is dreaming. The dream will soon turn into a nightmare, but he doesn't know that yet. At the moment he's trying to figure out what he and Román are doing in the middle of the jungle. He wants to ask him where he's been all this time, but really there's no need, because they're ten years old again, and they have mustaches and their Roman law texts under their arms. And Román's face still bears the same sullen expression, the same haughty aloofness.

They push through the foliage for hours, creating openings in the bush that seem to lead nowhere, until at last they come across his father. He's sitting in the armchair in his study. He has something in his hand. Or rather he doesn't have anything, not even hands; at first they see only his face, an enormous face twisted into a scowl. They have broken a window with a rubber ball, it's Román's fault, or maybe Carlos's — it doesn't matter, the window is broken and the repair has cost two *soles*. He tells them, "You've cost me two *soles*, you troublemakers." And another fourteen *soles* when, intentionally or unintentionally — it was never entirely clear — they bathed and dried the household mastiffs on the Persian rug in the parlor. And then there was the music box they broke while playing with it and later buried in the courtyard — it cost thirty dollars because of the gems and mother-of-pearl inlay, though it cost the servant accused of stealing it even more dearly. And now Don Augusto is rebuking them for all of that. He is holding something in his hand again. But they don't look at it yet; they look at his mouth opening and closing, detailing their disobediences. "Two *soles* for the window," he says. "Fourteen for the soiled rug," he says. "Thirty dollars for the music box," he says. "Four hundred dollars for the virtue of that foreign whore." And then, raising the pulsing bundle he has in his hand, blood dripping between his fingers, he adds, "And now tell me, you leeches, tell me how much this poet's heart is going to cost me."

He spends the afternoon running an errand, and when he finally arrives at the club he finds that they've already finished writing the letter.

"You were taking forever," José offers as an excuse.

Márquez and Ventura are with him, ensconced in a seemingly endless game of billiards. Carlos wants somebody, anybody, to ask why he was delayed. But nobody looks up from the table. Only Márquez seems happy to see him: We've got an even number now, he says, we can start playing in pairs.

"Where is the draft?"

José curses a missed carom shot and pulls a piece of paper out of his pocket without looking at it.

"It's not a draft."

"What?"

"It's not a draft. It's the final version."

"Final?" Carlos grabs the paper.

"All you have to do is copy it out."

It takes Carlos a moment to understand what José is saying. He drops into one of the armchairs, still holding the paper, while the others continue to call out shots — Orange five in the left pocket — and argue over whether or not to go after a particular one. The first thing he notices is the handwriting. Somebody, probably José, has attempted to reproduce Carlos's handwriting as a diligent schoolchild might, with some success. There remains only a trace of virility at the corners of the capital letters, and a slight tremor in the strokes. He reads the forged letters with increasing worry. Once. Twice.

"What is this?" he asks at last.

"The draft," says Ventura, clarifying the obvious.

"I said it's not a draft," José insists. "It's the final version. It just needs to be copied out."

And Márquez:

"So are you going to play a game or what?"

Carlos can't stop staring at the paper. A waiter approaches to ask what the gentleman would like to drink, and the gentleman barely notices. Everything around him seems to have stopped except the hubbub in the billiards room, where the noise of cues and clacking balls is endless. The woman who wrote that letter is not, cannot be Georgina. Her voice is marred by moments of stridency, awkwardness, vulgarity; the covered lady has suddenly stripped naked and started talking of love and passion as easily as she used to discuss Chopin's nocturnes. It is as if Gálvez's indigenous maidservant has gradually taken over and left nothing of Georgina's former discretion and modesty. She no longer resembles the Polish girl. Instead, she resembles the Almadas' daughter; once again she is sitting in the carriage with José, under the blankets. The two of them giggle, and he can only watch them in silence, listen to them kiss in the darkness. A knot in his throat.

"I can't copy this."

"Why not?"

"Because it's too . . ."

It takes him a moment to find a word.

"Too what?"

"Too . . . bold."

Ventura guffaws.

"Bold! A fine word! You mean Señorita Georgina's gone saucy on us."

Carlos doesn't turn to look at him. He keeps watching José's eyes, which are fixed on the cue ball.

"Georgina isn't like that. You know it."

José shrugs his shoulders.

"Characters change."

Carlos swallows hard.

"I was just talking with the Professor about that."

"Let me guess. He doesn't think it's a good idea for Georgina to change."

"He says he thinks Georgina has been off lately. That at this rate the romance will end in a wedding, and then we won't be able to —"

"The Professor can suck my cock," Ventura breaks in.

They burst into laughter. José does too, though his is a calm laugh, barely showing his teeth; it is the smile of someone with power, sketched out from a distance. Only Carlos remains earnest.

"And what if he's right? What if Juan Ramón wants to get married?"

José's eyes glint. He straightens up from the billiards table before he's even taken his shot.

"We already thought of that. Tell him, Ventura."

Ventura has had too much to drink. He gesticulates wildly as he talks, and with every swoop of his hand a bit more whiskey sloshes out of his glass.

"All right, listen here. The novel has two possible endings. One of them is pious and the other's a little spicy."

"Tell him the spicy one," José says impatiently.

"Well, in the spicy version her father forces her to marry a count or a duke — but she's not in love, of course! He's an ugly old man, and she has eyes only for Juan Ramón! So they have to carry on their correspondence behind the husband's back. Keep in mind that Georgina's a little naughty now. A furtive love!

There's even a servant who helps them and all that. All right. So years go by and—"

"No, the pious ending is definitely better," José interrupts. "Tell him that one first."

"Well, it's just what you'd expect: Georgina becomes a nun. But even behind the convent walls, she finds a way to keep sending Juan Ramón little messages, forever torn between devotion to God and the temptations of the flesh."

"Have you fellows lost your minds?" Carlos says. "Georgina has no spiritual calling, you know that. We made her that way. Together. And—"

Ventura breaks in again.

"And what of it? So we'll make her have one. We can do that, you know!"

José gently intervenes.

"Don't worry about that, Carlota. I know that we haven't made her terribly devout, but it's all worked out. Georgina is going to find God in chapter twenty-nine, with the death of her mother. Really dramatic stuff: tuberculosis!"

"But we already killed off her mother!"

They fall silent a few moments. José is still holding his glass halfway to his lips.

"Damn it, Ventura, he's right. We hadn't thought of that."

"How about an aunt?"

"An aunt could work."

"So her aunt dies, then . . ."

"The death of her dear aunt Rosinda! Really dramatic stuff, chapter twenty-nine!"

Carlos feels as if reality were flickering in and out, as if the sky were lurching beneath his feet.

"So are we playing pairs or not?" asks Márquez, handing him a cue stick.

"But José, don't you see we're destroying the novel? Everything we've built . . ."

José turns back to the game.

"You worry too much, Carlota. We're not destroying anything. There are just some things you don't understand. All those things you wrote were wonderful, quite lovely, very tasteful, but now we've got to stoke the passions a little, all right? Less prudishness. Something pulled from the pages of *Wuthering Heights*."

Silence. And then a new hardness in Carlos's voice and expression.

"I told you not to call me Carlota."

"It's just a joke, my good man. What do you think we should do, then? Tell him the truth?"

"No . . . I don't know. I just mean that we could make sure they continue their relationship . . . as friends."

"Friends, is it? Yes, I'm sure Juan Ramón would be very grateful to you. He'd say, Thank you for opening my eyes and completely screwing up the novel on top of it. That's what he'd say." José lays the cue stick on the table. For the first time, he's giving him his full attention. "Listen. Imagine if at the end of *María* the main character didn't feel like making the trip because when all was said and done the girl was going to die anyway. Imagine if Anna Karenina didn't throw herself under a train or if *Madame Bovary* ended before Emma fell in love with Rodolphe. Would that make any sense? What sort of novels would they be then, do you think?"

"But this isn't a novel," Carlos replies, his voice thin. "I mean . . . I mean, at least that's not all it is. It's a novel, sure, but it's also a man's life."

"Don't give me that nonsense! This was your idea! Didn't you always want the credit for it? Well, here you have it, before all this assembled company: it was your idea. And it was a good idea — a good one, I tell you, the best you've ever had. And now you want to ditch it."

"I didn't say I want to ditch it. I just can't go along with that," he says, indicating the page.

Ventura loses his patience.

"Well, either you're in or you're out!"

José makes a conciliatory gesture to Carlos.

"Don't pay him any mind. Ventura can be brusque, though he's not entirely wrong. To a certain extent that's the way it is, I mean. You've played a crucial role in" — he smiles — "well, let's say in a stage of Georgina's life. We're all quite grateful. But now that life has to move on. Georgina is growing up before our very eyes, you might say. And if you don't want to move on . . ."

"Of course I do! You're the ones who . . ."

He trails off. He thinks about the mirror in his room, about the exercises he performs before it each morning, practicing different facial expressions. He attempts to muster a dignified expression, any one at all: skepticism, censure, indifference. But he fails. He feels like crying. Maybe he is crying — he would need to look in the mirror to be sure. He feels that they are all watching him, but he is mistaken. They are focused on the game again, engaged in a long discussion of a complicated shot.

The draft — the letter — slips from his hand and falls to the floor. Carlos doesn't even notice. But a few seconds later José picks it up. He hands it to him again, along with a glass of whiskey filled to overflowing. He smiles.

"Come on, Carlota. Have a drink. Let's play a game and forget about all this. You're good with the language of women, I admit, much better than the rest of us with all that business with ellipses and exclamation points. When you copy out the letters, you can correct those sorts of details. Whatever you like. But from now on, leave the rest to us, all right? We need to make Georgina a little more passionate. A little more coy. And I think we can all agree you're about as good at licentiousness as you are at bedding girls, Carlota."

Even Carlos is surprised by what comes next. First he feels all his energy gather in his right hand. His right fist. A fist that's heading toward José's face, Carlos realizes a moment after the movement has begun. But it doesn't make contact; the explosion of rage is a halfhearted one. Though his fist is quick, it is too slow to outrun his swift conscience, his almost instantaneous reaction of fear and cowardice. And so what begins as a punch ends up as something else, a sort of girlish slap as his hand changes course midair to swat the glass José is holding out to him to the floor and snatch the paper from José's fingers.

What comes next is another risible gesture: he puts all the intensity of his wrath into ripping the letter into tiny pieces.

His movements are so absurd, midway between tenderness and aggression, between an accident and a deliberate act, that José is too startled to respond for a moment.

"What the hell are you doing? Now we have to write it all over again!"

"That letter can go to hell! And all of you can too!"

Every morning, Carlos tries out dozens of expressions in the mirror: surprise, piousness, adoration, indifference, approval. Especially approval. It is quite possible that he has never practiced his expression of fury, which may be why it is hard for the others to take it seriously. Or perhaps the problem is not his performance, which is perfect, as always, but what the young men think they know about him. Just as a child seems comical precisely when he manages to ape his elders' habits perfectly, shouts and curses seem innocent, almost endearing, in Carlos's mouth. And so after a few stunned seconds his friends react in the only way possible: by bursting into laughter.

"Oh, please do me no violence, my lady!"

"White hands do not offend, mademoiselle!"

"Go on, Carlota! Rewrite the letter and stop diddling!"

Carlos is wild with rage.

"Write it yourselves! Let's see how you do! Let's see you keep your lousy novel going without me."

They continue to laugh uproariously, amused by the fury in Carlos's eyes. Only Ventura has grown suddenly serious. He points at Carlos with his finger.

"If you don't rewrite that letter, we'll break your nose!"

"Leave him alone," says José, pushing Ventura's hand aside. He crouches down to pick up the scraps of paper. "We don't need him anyway. With a little effort, I can mimic his prissy handwriting fairly well. See there, Carlota? My hand still shakes a bit, but damn it all, we need your harlot hand to finish the novel. So sit down already and stop being a bore."

"You can stick the novel up your ass!"

"My ass?" José laughs even harder. "Your Indian blood has started to show! It took a while, with all that blue blood on top of it. What are you going to do now? Beat us with sticks till we bring you rubber?"

At the neighboring tables, the men reading newspapers or smoking cigars or playing billiards turn to look at them. One of the waiters gives them a severe glance from the bar. Still laughing, the destitute poets ad-lib a few more things that Carlota might do: burst into tears, pull their hair, suffer a fainting fit, write to her beloved demanding that he defend her. Or even lay off the letters and play a game, damn it — that's Márquez's suggestion, what he's been saying all along, to no avail.

But Carlos only instructs the errand boy to bring his greatcoat and hat.

"That's right, go take a walk. Come back when your head's on straight."

"I'm not coming back!"

He attempts to simulate confidence, but his hands are shaking, and at one point his hat falls and rolls across the floor.

"We'll see about that, mademoiselle."

The waiter takes advantage of the lull in the action to approach and sternly inform them that making such a ruckus is quite unseemly, that the club's members have the right to enjoy their evening in peace, and that personal matters — he eyes the torn paper and the shattered whiskey glass as he says this — should be settled in the street. His speech is unnecessary, in any event, as Carlos has just left. The bottles behind the bar rattle as the door slams shut.

José tosses back his drink and flings a coin to the floor.

"That's fine, absolutely fine! We're leaving too!"

And then, looking at the door:

"He'll come back," he says.

But Carlos keeps his word. At least for the rest of the chapter.

◇

That night he visits every brothel in the city, his mind a blank. Around him he sees whores waiting, whores smoking, whores engaged in shouted conversations with their procurers, whores talking or laughing or crying — one of them beaten to a pulp and sprawled on a trash heap in an alleyway — whores blowing kisses, whores sighing, whores who on closer look turn out to be male, whores haggling, whores who with a whistle can be summoned to bed or to the paving stones of the alleyway; whores with rooms and without them, with madams and without them, still with teeth and already without them. Sometimes they call out to him when they see him walk by. They call him Sir or Your Excellency — even in the darkness they spot the gleam of his gold watch chain — and offer to give him the best night of his life. Carlos wards them off, waving his hat and crossing to the other side of the street.

He doesn't know what he's looking for. He's drinking from a bottle of whiskey he bought somewhere along the way, and his frequent swigs from it make the uncertainty a bit more bearable. It's a long trip, from Tajamarca to Huarapo and from there to Panteoncito, Barranquita, Acequia Alta, Monserrate. At some point he is seized by a painful thought: nowhere, not even here, will he ever be able to find Georgina. Then he keeps drinking and forgets that too. Midnight finds him in one of the bordellos on Panteoncito, drunk off his gourd and sitting on a sofa while the madam goes off to fetch the girls.

Though the girls do sleep with the customers for money, it would perhaps be unfitting to call them whores. At least, that's what Carlos thinks when he sees them come down the stairs in their long gowns and kidskin gloves. Whores are the other ones, those sordid women he's seen offering themselves up on street corners, the ones who crowd the prisons on the eve of presidential elections and let themselves be taken behind the nettle patches on Colchoneros for a few coins. These women, however, in the garb of elegant young ladies, look like Miraflores maidens interrupted in the middle of a gala dinner. And the madam — though it would perhaps be unfitting to call her a madam — introduces them one by one with feigned enthusiasm.

"This is Cora, the young heiress of the Incas, granddaughter of the grandson of the granddaughter of Atahualpa himself . . .

"The one winking at you is Catalina. She's as Russian as the czar and so affectionate she'd melt the glaciers of Siberia . . .

"That's our dear Mimí. The lustful blood of the French runs through her veins . . ."

Each of the girls has been given something like a Homeric epithet — Cayetana of the sweet kisses; Teresita, shy by day and pure fire at night — and before he chooses, Carlos chuckles to himself just thinking about that, about Homer and *The Iliad*. It's not really funny — it's a joke for drunken intellectuals — but he laughs anyway.

The one he's chosen has a name too, but Carlos has already forgotten it. An eternity has passed since he met her in the hall — almost ten minutes — and the last swig of whiskey has scattered the madam's words until they seem very far away. He vaguely remembers the girls, many of them quite young, waiting for him to choose and watching him with something that might have been desire or hope or boredom. Who the hell has he chosen? Antonia, the novitiate with earthly appetites? Or maybe Marieta with the unfettered imagination? Who knows, and who cares.

In the bedroom he discovers that she's not even pretty. How could she be, when she's not the protagonist of any novel? She has the discreet beauty of secondary characters, designed to entertain for a single chapter and then disappear without a trace. Perhaps aware of her modest role in Georgina's novel, she doesn't even open her mouth. She only sits on the edge of the bed, attempting to smile, waiting.

In the room, nothing happens. Though one might also say that many things happen. He takes off his coat. He tosses back his drink. He murmurs a few words — expectantly, she responds with other words, or maybe with just a smile. He feigns a sudden interest in the window latch. He consults his watch. He lights a cigarette. Then stubs it out. Nothing, to be sure, to justify the five *soles* he will later pay the madam. At some point, with all that nothing happening, the girl decides to take the initiative. The resulting scene is imbued with a peculiar sadness: clumsy caresses, the creaking bed, hands touching places that, no, not on your life. The bodies in a state of half undress, their movement suddenly ceasing. An apology.

"I'm sorry," he says.

"You have nothing to be sorry for, sir," she says.

There is a grandfather clock somewhere, and the sound of its weights and gears makes the silences even more profound.

"I've had too much to drink."

"You should rest, then."

"But I'm going to pay you anyway. Of course I'm going to pay you. I'll pay you for the whole night."

"Please don't worry about that right now."

Carlos shifts uneasily on the bed. He should add something, but he doesn't know what. Or he should at least fill the silence by lighting a cigarette, but his jacket pocket is too far away. She smiles.

"Would you like to tell me what's worrying you?"

Carlos opens his mouth and then closes it again. Antonia, or María, or Jimena counts to ten. When she finishes, she reaches out her hand to stroke his back. Slowly. It's her way of telling him that she's ready for the thing she's second best at in the world: listening. She's not all that interested in what Carlos might tell her, of course, but in a way she considers it part of her job. After all, it's 1905 and psychologists don't exist yet. Priests in their confessionals and whores in their brothels are the only people who help unburden men's consciences. She uses all the experience of her profession to ask a single question:

"You're out of sorts because you're thinking about another woman, aren't you?"

Carlos turns for a moment to look at the mouth that has uttered those words. Her voice is very sweet, much sweeter than a psychoanalyst's would be. But then, when he doesn't respond immediately, the girl apologizes. Forgive me, she says. Forgive my rudeness. You needn't answer. But the young man is drunk and wants to answer, and after a few moments he does so, cautiously, slowly, choosing his words carefully.

He says:

"No."

And then:

"I don't know."

And finally:

"I suppose so."

He doesn't know why he's answered that way. He feels an enormous sorrow and yet a tiny consolation: the touch of her hand on his body. And perhaps because it's so quiet and he feels that something more should be said, he adds: She loves someone else. A man named Juan Ramón, he says. A man named José, he corrects himself. Or maybe neither one, who knows; it's complicated, he says at last.

But the girl doesn't find it all that complicated. To her, all rich people's problems look like mere variations on the same hollow, insipid problem.

A pat on the shoulder. "I understand," she says, though she doesn't really.

And then, since the gentleman has paid for the whole night, they blow out the oil lamp and pretend to fall asleep, but even in the dark they both keep their eyes wide open.

It is the first time a customer has rejected her, and she thinks of nothing else until daybreak. Of that and of Cayetana, the whore from Cusco. The older customers say she used to be stunningly beautiful, but today Cayetana is just a fat, sad woman to whom age has not been kind and who washes the dishes and cleans the bedrooms because nobody wants to sleep with her anymore. Only a few old men, plus Señor Hunter, who is quite young but blind and doesn't much care what body he's mounting. And now she wonders about the first time a customer didn't want to sleep with Cayetana and how long it took the others to follow his lead. When did she start to get old, to make beds that other women would unmake the next day? And then the girl thinks about herself, about her twenty-five years of age, about her breasts that will gradually cease to be firm—but that can't be the issue, impossible, because the gentleman hasn't even seen them—about the unsightly, hairy mole on her neck that Madame Lenotre's doctor didn't allow her to remove; and now, finally, she imagines young, blind Señor Hunter in a few years, perhaps fewer than she thinks, Señor Hunter only a little less young but just as blind, running his trembling hands over her body and whispering in her ear, "Me too, baby, I'm all alone now too." She shudders.

And as for what Carlos is thinking, it's best not to say anything at all.

◇

My dearest friend,

*You must forgive me these lines, even my handwriting
... Oh, I am quite irate! As you can see, even the hand
with which I grip my pen and trace these letters is
quivering. Yes, I know — the etiquette manuals say that
a young lady should be prudent and demure and not
express any intense or excessive emotions. But I daresay
there are moments when the soul cannot be gagged or
thwarted. Don't you agree? And tonight my fury is such
that prim old Saturnino Calleja and his rules of decorum
would certainly disapprove, but I hope that you, my dear
friend, will be able to forgive me. Who else but you, the
loyal confidant of my every thought, even these that go so
contrary to all propriety!*

*It is my friend Carlota who has put me in this state.
Have I mentioned her to you before? Though we are
joined, it's true, by a long-established friendship, we are
also divided by a great many differences! This afternoon
I made the mistake of sharing the secret of these letters
with her. You should have seen how she looked at me, how
scandalized she was! She finds these missives we send each
other quite unseemly: they are so very long, so frequent,
so personal. With a stranger! — you can imagine the to-
do. That I could so freely send you these letters, which go
beyond mere politeness, six letters in a single envelope,
and six envelopes on a single ship, and in them revealing*

so many private things . . . If she had her way, you and I
would discuss nothing more stimulating than the weather.
The rains that fall in Madrid and the summer heat that
scorches the fields of my beloved Lima, or the state of your
mother's health. Or, better still, we would never have
exchanged a letter at all, because what reason on earth
would I have for asking you for a book, and what reason
beyond that would you have for giving it to me? She
stopped just short of calling me brazen! Tell me, please,
that you are shaking with rage as I am. Or do you agree
with her? Do you believe, as she does, that I am just a
capricious, ill-mannered girl, a vulgar girl whose audacity
is offensive or, at best, amusing? Oh, do not be so cruel! It
would give me such pain to hear those words from your
lips — or, rather, from your hand and pen.

No: I know that you share my view of it. That you
too are of the belief that in a conversation between two
spirits there must be neither sheriffs nor jailers, and the
only protocols, those imposed by their own consciences.
Even if the catechisms of propriety declare in the relevant
chapter that a young lady "has the duty first to give her
letters over to her parents in complete confidence" and that
her replies "must express her intentions clearly, without
circumlocutions to muddy them." But oh! What if one's
intentions are precisely that — to make everything an
enormous circumlocution, and for those unnecessary words
to, in some way, be the language of one's soul? Tell me,
please, that you understand me. That you wish, as I do,
to keep writing these letters — to speak tonight, to speak
tomorrow, to speak always.

But let us forget my friend and her dogmas and address each other, please, as we once were accustomed to do. Let me tell you a few more things — so many that I wish this letter would never end . . .

At last it is time to tell the tale of the philanthropic rat, a tale that no one has told and no one ever will if we don't take this opportunity to remedy the situation. It is a rat like so many others, *Rattus norvegicus.* It has shoved off on the Buenos Aires–La Coruña route in the same transatlantic steamer countless times before, though it knows nothing of the existence of La Coruña or Buenos Aires; indeed, it is reasonable to suppose that it believes in no world beyond the hold of its ship. The universe is three hundred feet long and sixty across, and in it the rat lives out its wee life, an endless night full of barrels and boxes and burlap sacks. Like so many workers, it has found a way to eke out a living from the transatlantic mail: it nests in the warmth of the sacks of correspondence, gnaws at the delectable sealing wax, feeds on the letters that crisscross the ocean once every four weeks. It has a special fondness for envelopes adorned with official letterheads, the typed pages that always begin with the same words: *The government of Argentina regrets to inform you.* And so its tiny stomach gradually fills with sorrowful news that will never be read, and in a way that is where that news deserves to be, because why should a mother have to learn that her emigrant son has been carried off by tuberculosis; why not allow her to grow old still believing that the blood of her blood has found in the Americas the fortune that so many dream of? There are some things a person is better off knowing only halfway, or knowing another way, or not knowing at all, and if José and Carlos were writing a fantasy novel, if they believed that the supernatural could insinuate itself into an otherwise realistic tale, we would say that the rat shares that view. That in some murky way it has learned to identify the tragic or needless letters, the ones that should never have been written, much less sent. But admitting such a thing would be the stuff of another genre, one in which the two young authors are not prepared to founder; as we have already noted, their novel is or aspires to be a realistic one — sometimes comedy, sometimes love story, and sometimes even tragedy, but ultimately realistic. They are interested only in the romance between Georgina Hübner and Juan Ramón Jiménez, and not in the life of a rat that reads, and judges, and feels pity for mankind. Such a thing is impossible, and, what's worse, it would ruin their story.

Let's agree, then, that the only reason the rat devours the letters is hunger. Let's also agree that its predilection for sad letters arises from some fact unknown to us — maybe bad news is simply more abundant than good; maybe the rat prefers ink-soaked paper, and, as everyone knows, conveying happiness does not require so many words. It feeds on news that would cause its intended recipient pain, and today it has come to Georgina's twenty-fifth letter to Juan Ramón. It has already pardoned one Spanish emigrant's first message home to his family — *Buenos Aires is huge, Mother, you would be amazed, larger than Santander, Torrelavega, and Laredo put together* — and gnawed at the news of a homely daughter who miraculously had seemed on the verge of betrothal but who, in the end, was not. Now it stops at Georgina's letter. It sniffs it with its greedy snout. It prepares for the first bite, its little lips drawn back over its teeth, perhaps intoxicated by the scent of the writing paper. One might say — but really it is only a manner of speaking — that it understands the envelope's poisonous contents, that it knows that so far Georgina has been for Juan Ramón no more than a small everyday satisfaction, no more significant than a sunny afternoon or an unexpected visit from a friend, and now that clutch of letters is about to change everything. If Juan Ramón reads one more letter, there will be no fixing it; he will have fallen utterly in love with Georgina, transformed her into the muse with melancholy eyes and smoky candles who presides over his poems, and then what began as a comedy — two poets playing both at being poor and at being a woman — will end as a tragedy: a man attempting to make love to a ghost. Everything depends on whether the rat eats the letter or doesn't, but obviously in the end it doesn't, because if the letter were to disappear, the novel would end along with it, and it is to continue on for many pages more.

And so from this point on the book becomes a tragedy, there's no other option — and the rat is entirely to blame. The letter will arrive and the besotted poet will want to travel to Peru to ask for Georgina's hand, and then what will the poor poets do, those boys with scanty mustaches who only a year ago were squatting on the ground, pissing pisco? And tragedy befalls the rat, too, which will never get the chance to gnaw at the envelope. The sailor on watch comes down to look for a piece of cargo and out of the corner of his eye spots movement in the mail sack; then comes the broom brandished in the air, the desperate chase, the shouting, stomping, curses, blows, the refuge that is not reached in time, the crack of the broom against the tiny body. Once, twice, three times. And, afterward, the ascension to the heavens: the rat is carried topside by its tail and, its eyes faltering as it dies, sees that other world whose existence it never suspected — the unknown deck of the ship and above it the blue sky in the middle of nowhere, halfway between La Coruña and Buenos Aires.

This has been life, it has time to think as it is tossed overboard, *and this,* it perhaps thinks as it sinks under the waves, *this must be death.*

III

A Tragedy

◇

After that first night, Carlos returns to the brothel every weekend. The girl is more surprised about this than anyone, as she had not expected to remain part of the novel.

Since the last chapter, she too seems to have undergone a number of changes. She is still a secondary character, it's true, but now there is something subtly protagonistic about her. She even seems a bit more beautiful than before, and so it is a little less inexplicable that he wants to see her again. Perhaps her seemingly insignificant life deserves a few lines of attention — a whole page even.

But Carlos will never read any of the words relaying her humble tale. He will never see her attic room, the bed she shares with Mimí and Cayetana. He will not watch them sleep in one another's arms or fight over the large bottle of perfume. Sometimes they laugh together, remembering a particular old man or a particular crooked cock, and he will never know anything of that laughter either. Hidden under the mattress there may be a photograph of a woman, clumsily patched and repaired, as if someone had torn it to shreds in rage and then remorsefully attempted to piece it back together. A single armoire for all of them, and in it this girl's one street gown, which reeks of mothballs because it's been so long since a customer has taken her out. Not even Carlos has. In front of the barred window, a chair to sit in, to gaze out at a world she barely remembers. And downstairs in Madame Lenotre's room, there's the account book that explains the need for the bars, noting that, in addition to the cost of food, laundry, and beauty products, not to mention the cost of two abortions and one molar extraction, the girl owes the house a total of three hundred forty-five *soles*.

One page. That's more than enough for now. After all, her rickety bed and the book of debts and the pieced-together photograph and the bars on the window will never be important enough to appear in Georgina's novel.

◇

He doesn't even touch her. At least that's what she says, and the girls are intrigued by the revelation. Customers with all manner of perverse predilections have passed through the brothel, but that particular deviancy — paying five *soles* a night in exchange for nothing — is unquestionably the most extravagant of all.

Whenever they see him sitting in the hall, shifting his hat restlessly from one hand to the other, the girls laugh. They call him Mr. Gob-Smacked. Your beau, Mr. Gob-Smacked, is here, they tell her, and she smiles or gets angry, depending on her mood. Mostly she gets angry. Anyone would say she's beginning to have feelings for him. Or maybe what she's really interested in are his generous tips. In any event, she sternly tells them to be quiet while she fixes her hair or adjusts her earrings, and then the girls laugh harder, and the madam scolds them — Shush, you ninnies, he's going to hear you — in vain:

"Is he courting you to ask for your hand in marriage?"

"Has he introduced you to his parents?"

"Remember us when you're a grand lady!"

As a customer he's very easy to satisfy. There's no need to check his thighs for syphilis sores or wash his cock in the sink. No need to fake panting or call him "master" or "stud" or shout out the ridiculous words that her customers find so arousing. All she has to do is lie beside him and talk if the gentleman wants to talk or simply be quiet if, as is sometimes the case, he prefers to spend the night smoking and staring at the ceiling. Sometimes he asks her about her life, and then she shrugs her shoulders and talks about her shared bed and the closed wardrobes, the endlessly increasing debts, the window bars. At other times it is

Carlos who, taking the cigarette from his mouth, delivers some meaningless anecdote.

"I took an exam today."

"I went to the docks yesterday. The dockworkers earn exactly the same amount that they did before, but now there's not a single one protesting."

"This morning I ran into Ventura and he asked me if I'd heard from José and I told him I hadn't — it seems no one's heard from him in weeks."

Afterward he stubs out the cigarette, and as he does so, he lets the sentence trail off, as if he were erasing it. In some way these confessions seem to be linked to the act of smoking those cigarettes and then putting them out, grinding them fiercely against the metal ashtray.

One night he tells her he's a poet. He looks at her solemnly when he says it, as if assessing the effect the news will produce. She doesn't respond immediately. She doesn't know much about poets except that they're very poor men, practically beggars, who always end up dying of tuberculosis. And Carlos, who is always so hale and well dressed, doesn't seem to be either of those things. A little thin, perhaps, though that probably doesn't matter. So she smiles and even nods with feigned enthusiasm when he asks her if by chance she would like to hear one of his poems. Straightaway he pulls out a sheet of paper and reads for a long time in a voice that doesn't sound like his. At first she interrupts him to ask the meaning of certain words. Then she doesn't say anything. She lets *gossamer* and *diadem* and *alabaster* echo sterilely without opening her mouth. When he finishes, Carlos asks her if she liked it and she hastens to say she did, forcing a smile. And she adds: But you are getting quite thin, sir, you should eat a little more and get your strength up — they've just reported another tuberculosis epidemic around here.

Sometimes he doesn't talk or look at the ceiling, and those are her favorite nights. The nights when he lies beside her and pretends to be thinking about trifling things but in reality is looking at her, only at her. It is a new look, one that seems to belong to that other world she can glimpse through the bars, and for a moment it makes her feel less like a whore. She senses that, in a way, he is not looking at her, not touching her — that what he seeks in her body is the shadow or memory of another woman. But still it's flattering, and she wants the feeling to last. All night if possible.

They also talk about love. In that room that smells of carmine and perfume. Lying on the bed where so many men have slumbered far away from their wives. They talk about love — or, rather, Carlos talks about it while she watches him intently. She is his audience. Five *soles* a night, and the curtain is up. He rambles tipsily about tempestuous love affairs, about insurmountable obstacles, about letters, rivalries, anonymous poems, about losses, especially those losses that cannot be remedied. He lights and stubs out cigarettes while uttering strange words. Words that, like his voice when he reads verse, do not sound like his. They sound to her as if they were taken from one of his poems or, more likely, from a serial novel. Though the girl is illiterate and has never read a novel herself, Mimí often reads them aloud to her and they clutch each other in excitement when the prince finally manages to track down the princess. So she knows what she's talking about. Like the characters in those novels, Carlos expects love to give him everything money cannot buy, and she senses that his suffering is born of that conviction. Literature, and maybe even love, has always seemed to her a treacherous luxury. She thinks of Mimí, whose passion for serial novels has also cost her dearly: ten *centavos* a week to buy the latest installment of *The Prince and the Odalisque of the Southern Seas,* which Madame Lenotre unfailingly adds to her account book in the "Owes" column.

Occasionally he also mentions Georgina. Indeed, he seems to talk about her constantly, even when he doesn't say her name. The girl doesn't know much about her. She imagines her to be wan, and very somber, and most of all very boring, languidly fanning herself in her garden and drinking the same endless lemonade. Feeble too — practically moribund. She's not sure why, but she also feels a slight ache in her chest on those nights when Carlos says her name too much. It's a pang of jealousy, but she doesn't realize it. In fact, she doesn't really know what that word means, *jealousy*, since nothing has ever belonged to her and so she's never feared losing anything.

Most likely, she thinks, it's just hunger.

On some nights she is able to ask the young man questions. She feels comfortable in her role as a secondary character, offering protagonists the opportunity to think and reflect on themselves. Her questions are sometimes thoroughly gauche but asked with endearing guilelessness. After each one, she always adds: You needn't answer. But he doesn't mind. One day he even works up the confidence to tell her about the Polish prostitute. Maybe he is answering a question about his earliest sexual experience, or his adolescence, or his first love. Or maybe he's not even answering a question — he just starts talking. She listens to the story with interest, and for a moment she feels that pang again. Especially when she hears the price. Four hundred dollars! On her fingers she tries to count out how many *soles* that is, how many nights with her you'd need to pay for a single night with the Polish girl. But her hands are clumsy and she finally gives up. She concludes that it would be many, many nights. More nights than there are in a year. Maybe more than there are in a lifetime.

She'd like to know if he slept with the Polish prostitute. If he looked at that woman, that girl, the same way he looks at her now. But she doesn't dare ask him. Carlos doesn't explain any further, the story comes to a close, and in the end she decides that they did sleep together. She thinks it, and she smiles. She tells herself that the reason the young gentleman doesn't touch her is precisely that she means something to him, while the Polish girl was just your everyday harlot, a little four-hundred-dollar doll to mindlessly mount. That he stripped off her clothes on the bed or on the floor and maybe even hurt her, because in the end she meant nothing to him. That he must have learned from her, under her, beside her, moving in and out of her, everything a man needs to know about a woman. That over the course of that night, he made her weep more than she'd wept during the month-long Atlantic crossing.

And the truth is that she takes pleasure in these cruel, piteous images. The Polish girl's tears comfort her because she is jealous (hunger pangs again): her Peruvian virginity was never worth a single dollar, let alone four hundred of them, and there is a certain universal justice in that sadness, in the suffering of a pale European girl who must have felt her body becoming less and less valuable every night, one hundred dollars, twenty dollars, twenty *soles*, one *sol*, finally a nickel — just one goddamn nickel to drag her down on the floor and do the usual to her again.

◇

Time passes. José is nowhere to be found. He is no longer attending his classes at the university, nor is he lounging outside them smoking on the bench in the atrium. Everybody says he's writing a novel. Carlos can't tell whether it's the same novel or if he's started a different one, but in any case José seems to be quite busy. He doesn't even go out anymore, and Ventura and his friends say he's changed quite a bit. For a moment Carlos thinks that yes, José must be writing the love story of Juan Ramón and Georgina; indeed, he'd even say that he's writing his own life, and also everyone else's. The life of all of Lima. The whole world contained in its pages.

Carlos goes back to the university. Now that José's not there, he goes as often as possible. He had almost forgotten the classrooms' scent of wood and chalk, the height of the lectern from which all those mediocre professors give their classes. He barely even remembered his classmates' names, much less the import of the law of habeas corpus or the particular subtleties of the Napoleonic civil code. Just a few hours of studying each day — he has so much free time now — and he learns it all, a little late but in time to take his exams. He may not write novels, or letters either, but at least he knows how to do that: pass exams. That's what he thinks as he scribbles his answers and glances at José's empty desk out of the corner of his eye.

His parents are happy and even tell him so. José has turned out to be a bad influence. That business with that Juan Jiménez fellow was just a silly bit of fun. They are proud that, little by little, disappointment by disappointment, Carlos is becoming a real man. Yes, he stays out all night sometimes and that's not

216

good, of course, but who can blame him; he's young, it's spring-time — better that than going around cooing sweet nothings to a decent girl, the kind of girl who's so decent that when she ends up pregnant, she refuses to have an abortion. He is a good son, there's no doubt about it. Someone who will take on the mantle of the family's birthright when they die.

Sandoval seems quite satisfied too. He comes to visit often now, loaded with new books and projects that Carlos accepts in silence. One night he insists on taking Carlos to a political meeting in an apartment on Calle Amargura. According to the organizers, the meeting is secret — there's even a password — but it's a secret no one cares about, not even the police. Most of the people in attendance are Italian socialists and Spanish anarchists who claim to have been behind every assassination attempt in Europe. They confess their crimes in the same tone of voice José used to employ when claiming to have bedded the most beautiful women in Peru. Carlos only half understands them. But at one point Sandoval talks about how "all our ideologies, and even our consciousnesses, are nothing more than a reflection of material reality," and that phrase keeps echoing in Carlos's mind. He thinks about Georgina, though he does not know why. About their fifteen months of correspondence. About the nights when he falls asleep convinced that she is writing and breathing somewhere out there in Lima. And he wonders whether she is a false consciousness like the ones Sandoval and his friends are so animatedly discussing or if there are real ideas in the world too, as real as class warfare and annual steel production.

On some afternoons he makes his way to the garret. After idly chatting with the watchman, he climbs the stairs very slowly, gripping the banister on each step. He likes to study among the worn furniture and burlap sacks. He repeats aloud the elements of rhetorical discourse — *inventio, dispositio, elocutio* — and the punishment prescribed by law for the crime of impersonating another individual: three years in jail. All this in the very same place where he and José once recited Baudelaire, Yeats, Mallarmé. And during his breaks from reading, he thinks about many things. He thinks about the Professor, whom he's been ducking for weeks, taking long detours to avoid passing through the square and running into him beneath the arches and then having to tell him — tell him what? He thinks about Ventura and his friends, who no longer haunt the club and its billiards tables. They have vanished as thoroughly as José himself, and with him those letters he is no doubt still writing and that Carlos will never read, blank chapters of the novel that once was his.

Often he thinks: *I too am a character in that novel.* Everything will be documented in the pages that José is writing, even Carlos's own repeated visits to the whore he never sleeps with. He wonders if there is any explanation for certain things — a chapter, a page, even just a line to say why he feels this need to sleep next to a whore at night. He'd like to understand it himself. He's had time to try out any number of explanations, not in front of the mirror now but in the dusty solitude of the garret. That the whore reminds him of Georgina. That she reminds him of the Polish prostitute. That he needs someone who believes in Georgina. That he feels lonely. He has even considered that perhaps his father might have been right all along and all that poetry has feminized him. Don Augusto warned him so many times as a boy, whenever he caught him with a book of poetry — Mark my words, your taste for metaphors is going to make you an invert. And now here he is, incapable of arousal even in the presence of a beautiful woman, proving his father right nearly a decade after the fact.

He dreams, too, of José's novel. That he's trapped within its pages, forced to do what the narrator commands him to do. It's his worst nightmare: ending up as a pansy in José's novel. Discovering that's what he is only because that's what the narrator wants.

The gentleman's gifts, always as extravagant as they are beautiful. At the moment, for example, he is loaded down with cardboard boxes and tubes that he wants her to open. Look inside and tell me if you like them, see if they're your size. She hates ripping the wrapping paper and cutting the ribbons, but at last she does and goes through the packages in wonder, pulling out petticoats and hats, bodices and skirts, satin veils and shoes and nightgowns. Gauzes so fine that she feels like she's holding air, like someone's sewn stitches through nothing. He says it's his mother's and sisters' castoff clothing, and she pretends to believe him, even though the garments smell new and it's clear no one's had the chance to wear out the hems of the dresses. His mother's and sisters' clothing, sure, if he says so, but at the bottom of the last box she finds a receipt with a figure so enormous, so astronomical, that she cannot even comprehend it.

From now on, happiness will mean this. She's decided it must be so. When she hears the word *happiness* — not that it's heard with any frequency in the brothel — she will remember placing the dresses on their hangers. Seeing her fingers peeking through the sheer muslin. Finding, and not understanding, that astonishing number.

"Do you like them?" asks the gentleman, without a hint of joy in his voice, with something more like aching hope.

"They're — they're for me?"

"For you, if you like them."

It's not the sort of clothing a whore wears. That's the first thing she thinks. It's the sort of clothing worn by the young ladies she sees through the bars, passing by in their carriages. A fleeting sight that lasts just long enough for her to begin to envy them and then watch them disappear, unsure what to do with their memory.

"How could I not like them?"

"Why don't you try them on?"

Yes, why not? She starts undressing immediately, pulling off her skirt, her garter, her petticoats, flinging her shoes and bodice aside. The garments sail through the air in a blind frenzy born of pure happiness. She does it so quickly that she's already half naked when Carlos manages to tear his eyes away and suggests that it might be better if she undressed behind the screen.

He stammers as he says it, still not looking at her, and for the first time she recalls the screen that stands behind the door, a faded parchment-like material printed with flowers, which no customer has required until now. But no one else has given her clothing and shoes, or read her poetry at dawn, so why shouldn't Carlos be the one to request it? The screen — why not. She covers herself as best she can with whatever clothing she hasn't yet removed and slips behind the screen, blushing and silent.

As she finishes getting undressed, she ponders Carlos's discomfort and comes up with a number of possible explanations before finally deciding that she doesn't understand it at all. She is not ashamed of her body and never has been; showing it to her customers has always seemed completely natural to her, as commonplace as a naked babe. But as much as Carlos has looked at her as a customer would, he also watches her as a preacher might, or a policeman sealing off the whorehouse door, or a haughty old woman crossing herself when she sees her on the street. She pauses a moment to study herself, now completely naked behind the shelter of the screen, and in the candlelight her body appears inoffensive. But suddenly an unfamiliar sensation comes over her. A whiff of modesty, as if it were no longer she who was look-ing at her — as if Carlos had lent her his eyes and through them she felt an unfamiliar curiosity about the roundness of those breasts and the curve of that hip. The sensation provokes fear, but also desire and guilt and arousal and hope. She closes her eyes. Then, with a sudden brusque movement, she starts to get dressed.

The first box contains a floor-length white gown with a bon-net, gloves, and garters to match. When she emerges from be-hind the screen, she has been transformed into a figure from a Sorolla painting who has wandered out of her canvas and into a Toulouse-Lautrec brothel. Naturally, she has no idea who So-rolla and Lautrec are, but she does know this: when Carlos sees her, it's as if he were looking at the static image of a painting. He recognizes fear in her eyes, but also desire and guilt and arousal and hope. She smiles nervously, her hands clasped behind her back — Does she look like a young lady now? Can the whore-house still be discerned in her face? — but Carlos doesn't smile in return. He just hands her a parasol, also white, and asks her to open it. She hesitates a moment.

"Isn't it bad luck?"

"That's umbrellas."

Indeed, a parasol is not an umbrella, though they're similar. A parasol is used not to shield from rain but to provide shade from the sun — and why on earth does the young man want her to open it here, in the light of the oil lamp? — but she takes it and minces primly from the bed to the wardrobe and from the wardrobe to the window. Taking small steps like a woman with a tiny dog. What would her mother say if she could see her now, looking like a real lady? And what would Carlos say, if instead of staring at her with his mouth agape he ventured to say something? But no matter. She feels joy wash over her because he is still looking at her, because he's never looked at her so intently as he is right now.

There are many other outfits, and eventually, many nights later, she has tried them all on for him. Maybe he's looking for the dress that suits her best, the one they'll use for their first promenade through the streets of Lima — why else would he give her such sumptuous garments? — but time passes and he proposes no such outing. The clothing remains there, stuffed into one of Madame Lenotre's wardrobes, ready to be used at any moment. Sometimes the young man has a hankering to see her wearing one of the dresses, and then she must try it on and walk around the room, or sit on the edge of the bed, or pretend to be doing something, while he sits smoking in a corner and contemplates her through the haze. And though she does find it strange, she also accepts it easily, because it is all from that same beautiful, alien world where naked bodies are cause for embarrassment, whores are treated like ladies, and men don't sleep with those ladies but instead read them poetry.

She finds some of the ensembles quite amusing. An old-fashioned skirt and mantle, for instance, that look like something straight out of a dowager's armoire, but still the young man asks her to put them on. It all seems rather absurd, him sitting there, her with the mantle over her head, just one eye left uncovered. An eye that, seen so separately from her face, could belong to a virgin or a whore or even a man. Behind the mantle she laughs to herself, because it's laughable, but the young gentleman is solemn.

And then there's the night she tries on the outfit that looks like a little girl's — a summer dress with buttons, a long blue skirt, pink shoes, even little bows for the braids she doesn't have — and when he sees her come out from behind the screen he is gob-smacked; the girls were right to call him that, Mr. Gob-Smacked, your beau Mr. Gob-Smacked. And Mr. Gob-Smacked — who's not really her beau — slowly approaches, as if recognizing her, and reaches out to stroke her face with his hand. The young gentleman, touching her. And then he whispers a strange phrase that seems to come from far away.

"*Che is to moro . . .*"

And at first she pays it no mind, thinking it must be another of those incomprehensible words the young gentleman likes to include in his poems. *Gossamer, diadem, alabaster,* and now, why not, *che is to moro.* But then she thinks that maybe it means something else — that maybe it's like when the prince rescues the odalisque of the southern seas and before he kisses her he tells her he loves her more than life itself, and even though the odalisque does not speak his language she nevertheless understands him, because a person just knows that sort of thing. That's what she imagines as she stands there in her little-girl dress: Carlos telling her in Persian, *I love you, I will take you away with me, I won't forget you either, not ever.*

"*Chcę iść do domu,*" she murmurs, trying to imitate the beautiful sounds she's just heard as best she can.

Carlos doesn't react at first. He blinks and then looks into her eyes, surprised and also satisfied. Suddenly he seems very happy. He patiently repeats the phrase again, a faint smile still on his face.

"*Che is to moro.*"

"*Che is do domo.*"

And then him, slower:

"*Che-is-to-moro.*"

"*Che is to moro.*"

He laughs.

"Better."

From now on, happiness will mean this. She's just decided it. Being so close to the young man, and seeing him laugh, and repeating *che is to moro* till daybreak.

Somebody calls out his name. He is crossing Jirón de la Unión, and amid the hustle and bustle of passersby it takes a moment to locate him. Finally he sees someone emerge from a nearby tavern, staggering slightly and rosy-cheeked from alcohol. Professor Cristóbal.

"Well, well. Look who we have here. If it isn't the concerned cousin."

Then he says:

"You haven't come by in a long time. I thought you were dead, my friend."

"No, no, I wasn't dead," Carlos answers, as if Cristóbal might need clarification on that point. "I've just been very busy lately."

That is certainly the case. He's been avoiding the main square for three months just so he won't run into him, and as a result he has spent a great deal of time walking in complex, exhausting circles around the place. And so it is true he's had no lack of work.

He's carrying a book under his arm, and Cristóbal grabs it from him.

"Let's see what you're reading . . . Oh! *Introduction to Canon Law.* Excellent. For a moment I thought it might be a romantic novel. I was worried about you, but this sort of book poses no danger . . ."

"No, it's not a romantic novel," Carlos answers, confirming the obvious once more.

But that's just what the Professor wants to talk about: romantic novels. He wants to know what happened with Carlos's cousin. Whether she married her Spanish poet in the end. And above all, he adds with a smile, what it is he did wrong to lose his best customer. Carlos tries to smile too. You didn't do anything wrong, he replies, you mustn't worry about that; it's just that my relationship with my cousin has become somewhat strained over the past few months.

He pauses, clears his throat. He is looking for an excuse to continue on his way, but the Professor breaks in before he can find one. His brow is furrowed.

"So you've had a falling-out."

"Something like that."

"And, naturally, you have no idea how things are going with the poet. Whether the relationship has continued or not."

"No."

Cristóbal has started to unwrap a cigar. He watches his own fingers intently, as if the task were a difficult one or as if he were pondering something.

"Well. Let's not worry about her. I'm sure she's found someone to help her, don't you think? Maybe that friend of yours, the one who doesn't much like her . . ."

Carlos doesn't know what to say.

"Yes, I suppose so . . . And now if you'll excuse me, Dr. Professor, I'm late to class at the university."

Cristóbal cheerfully claps him on the shoulder.

"What a shame! I thought we might chat awhile. But I don't want to keep you, of course. You must come pay me a visit at some point. You've abandoned me, my friend. Come and we'll drink pisco and talk about love, yes indeed."

"Most certainly, Dr. Professor. Though to be honest, these days . . ."

"And about the covered ladies, of course. I have so much to tell you about that! Some of it would amaze you, I daresay. For instance, did I ever tell you why they tried to ban the skirt and mantle during the viceroyalty?"

Carlos makes a timid attempt to get away, but the Professor has a firm grip on his shoulder.

"To prevent married women from flirting?" Carlos's tone is the same one he uses to answer when he's called on in the classroom.

"Yes! I remember now I told you that already. But there was another reason I forgot to mention . . ."

"Oh," asks Carlos. Just like that, without a question mark, without the least bit of curiosity. He only looks toward the far end of the street, wishing he could just disappear.

"Well, the authorities also wanted to prohibit them, amazingly enough, because it seems a few fairies had started wearing them too. What do you say to that?"

"Fairies?"

"Sure, fairies — pansies, you know. Imagine that: nancies dressing up as coquettish young ladies so they could snag a kiss or three from strapping suitors. Droll, isn't it?"

Carlos's expression freezes over, but the Professor keeps talking. He is smiling strangely, the sort of smile generally seen only on madmen and clairvoyants.

"Men dressing up like women!" He squeezes Carlos's shoulder even harder. "What do you make of that? It's like something out of a book, isn't it? Tell Georgina about it for me when you see her, which I've no doubt will be before too long. And, of course, give her my compliments on that exquisite handwriting of hers."

He lets go of Carlos's arm, still smiling. Before moving off, he gives him two indulgent pats on the shoulder. It is a quick, familiar gesture that Carlos recognizes instantly. The sound of a man's hand on the shoulder of a child.

It's a narrow bed; with a great deal of effort and a fair bit of discomfort, the three of them barely fit into it. Luckily, they rarely
go to bed at the same time. Cayetana retires quite early, just after
midnight, once it becomes clear that blind Señor Hunter and
the old men won't be coming, or maybe they have come but are
interested in something else that night.

Mimí goes to bed at about four in the morning, and by then
she's already taken care of three or four customers. She's fast. She
knows all the tricks to make men climax as quickly as possible
and just the right words to say afterward, as they lie in bed, to
make them remember their wives or children and want to return
home. Tricks of the trade for a whore in 1905 — in all likelihood,
they are not too different from the tricks of the trade a century
later.

But she doesn't go to bed until daybreak. At least not on the
nights that Carlos comes calling. She climbs the stairs to the attic
with her shoes in her hand and wipes off her lipstick in front
of the broken moon of the mirror. By then, the sun's first weak
rays are bending in through the rafters, and she starts to get undressed without lighting the oil lamp. Cayetana half opens her
eyes and glances silently at the girl's youthful body, the naked
heat of her pale skin in the blue dawn. Then she tries to fall back
asleep. Sometimes she can't.

The bed has seemed narrower of late, and the contact with
the other girls' skin more uncomfortable. Mimí and Cayetana
take up the whole mattress, and she has to fight a little to carve
out a space. Every night is the same thing. She didn't mind in the
past, but now, for some reason, she does. Even the attic seems

smaller. And then there are the bars, which she's never thought about before. She feels as if she can't breathe, like a bird gasping in the hollow of a closed fist. It annoys her that Mimí snores and Cayetana gets up early to make coffee for the girls. It most especially annoys her that Cayetana dreams so often and so badly, and tosses, and kicks, and sometimes cries out. Afterward she says she was dreaming about the blind man again.

Because she has a hard time falling asleep, she often finds herself pushed to one side of the bed as Mimí and Cayetana fight to stretch out their arms, and she tries to think about happier things. She thinks, for example, about the Holy Week celebrations, when the policemen come to seal up the door of the brothel — "You whores are an affront to Christ every day, but especially so the week He was crucified" — and then she and the rest of the girls get to spend seven days doing whatever they like. She thinks about the days when no customers come at all and they play bingo into the wee hours, and Mimí has to help her fill up her cards. About the sweltering afternoons when Madame Lenotre agrees to take them to a cove in Barranco, two long miles of beach where the wealthy bathe in the sea — they may even come across a man they know, accompanied by his wife and children — and they all leap into the ocean naked, laughing and splashing. She thinks about things like that, images full of sun and afternoon naps and dried beans filling the bingo cards, and if she's lucky she falls asleep.

But on other nights she can't help it: the happy memories quickly fade away, to be replaced by thoughts of Madame Lenotre's account book. Behind her closed eyelids she can almost feel the pages of the book turning, marred with sums and debts she does not understand. She wonders how long it will take her to pay them all before she can be free, and she tells herself maybe one or two years longer. It's a lucky thing she doesn't know how to read, much less do sums. If she knew basic addition and subtraction, she would discover that her debt has grown to three hundred sixty-two *soles*, and that paying off such a figure would take exactly seven years and one hundred forty-eight days, assuming she satisfied three customers a night. And that's not counting the food or clothing or the annual visit from the doctor to look for — and inevitably find — symptoms of syphilis.

Nine years and two months if she doesn't work Holy Week and other religious holidays.

Thirteen years and seven months if she continues to eat and drink.

Seventeen and a half years if she gets it into her head to use spermicide.

Twenty-one if she decides to fall ill a couple of times.

Thirty-nine if she bathes every morning.

Forty-five if she's pregnant even just once.

One hundred fourteen if Mimí finally manages to teach her to read and she too makes a habit of buying the latest installment of *The Prince and the Odalisque of the Southern Seas* every week.

But luckily she doesn't know how to count. So she can keep smiling and serenely close her eyes, unaware that every day she lives and breathes means yet another coin owed to the house. Some nights she is so happy, despite the narrow bed and the window bars, that she even ends up thinking about that which cannot be contemplated. She remembers the silver knob on Carlos's walking stick and wonders whether it would be worth enough to pay her debts, should the young gentleman wish to spend the money on her. She dreams about what she would do if she were free, and finally, before drifting off — though she's a little embarrassed to admit it — she closes her eyes again, and instead of the account book she sees the young man in a turban. How amusing, Master Carlos in a turban instead of a hat, carrying a saber instead of a walking stick, crossing the fathomless southern seas and then battling his way into the palace harem. Doing everything to reach her and take her away with him. Far from the evil sultan; far from Madame Lenotre.

It happens one summer night.

For this scene, the one of repentance and forgiveness, Carlos had frankly expected different circumstances. It would take place in his parents' mansion. Outside, it would be pouring rain, and beneath the sheets of water José would bang the door knocker and wait. The butler would take one look at his muddy shoes and usher him in through the service entrance. Then a servant would inform Carlos. But he would not come down immediately. In his fantasy there was some reason for the delay, one unrelated to pride or cruelty. The pretext changed from day to day as he reimagined the scene. The other ingredients would remain unchanged: the night, the rain, the muddy shoes, the maid's scornful expression. He could see himself descending the stairs so clearly that he was even able to identify the suit he was wearing and the title of the book he was holding in his right hand. And as he reached the bottom — after making him wait a very long time — he saw José standing in the parlor, soaked to the bone. José looking at him imploringly, then starting to speak.

What would he say?

That part never quite came together. Even in his dreams it was impossible to imagine José asking for forgiveness.

◇

Reality turns out to be somewhat less generous. It is nighttime, yes, but he is not in his parents' mansion. Instead, he is reading in the garret, so there is no maid, no service entrance. It isn't raining either, of course. In fact, it is quite a pleasant night for a stroll. Furthermore, José doesn't have to wait outside at all. The watchman opens the door for him straightaway, and he climbs the stairs on his own, as he has so many times before, and knocks on the garret door.

Only José himself is just as Carlos has imagined him. He stammers and seems unsure of how to go about this encounter. Maybe he thinks the grandson of José Gálvez Egúsquiza should not have to apologize for anything. Perhaps he even has the poor taste to remember the Rodríguezes' past and compare it with his own illustrious pedigree, and so finds this humiliating scene all the more grotesque. In his hand he is carrying the bundle of letters, his reason for being there, despite all the blood the Gálvez family has spilled for the good of the nation.

His voice trembling, he makes a few false starts.

He says:

"You were right. What we did was vile and deplorable."

And then:

"Something terrible has happened, and I need your help; Georgina and I need you . . ."

And then:

"I've missed you . . ."

There is no rain, no maid, no parents' mansion. Strictly speaking, there's not even a real apology. But Carlos doesn't need all that. He doesn't even need José to finish his speech, those halting sentences mutilated by shame. He goes to José and puts his arms around him; he calls him *brother* and tells him he's missed him too. Missed both of them.

It's not cold, but they light the stove anyway, perhaps unable to imagine listening to a good story anywhere but beside a warm fire. And the story is, in fact, a good one, but also rather a long one, and confusing too. Or maybe it's just that José doesn't know how to tell it, doesn't entirely understand it and so gets lost in the details, mixing up the order of the letters and confusing what comes before and after. As he talks, he is aglow with the light of the flames, which cast flickering shadows over his face and his words.

At first it was all very easy. So he says. And there is reason to believe him: when he talks about that period, those first weeks after Carlos's desertion, his speech seems freer, less mechanical. The letters they wrote then were humorous, or else so terribly serious that they made him and Ventura laugh. And so they laughed a lot and sometimes wrote a little, in the opium den, at the billiards table, in the Club Unión, in the stands at the bullring, in the brothels of Monserrate. They were overflowing with ideas, some of them contradictory and fearless, others absolutely ludicrous, but sooner or later they ended up putting them all down on paper. And it seemed that Juan Ramón enjoyed that wild Georgina, José insists, because his replies became longer, and in a way also contradictory, and fearless, and ludicrous.

But the poem — where was their poem? In those first months, they still quivered with excitement as they opened each envelope. Their hopes gradually went cold as they waited for the ever-absent dedication: just another dull letter to add to the collection — thirty-two — a little postcard with the Retiro pond in the distance, sometimes a few lines inspired by another woman.

Poems dedicated to Blanca Hernández-Pinzón, to Jeanne Roussie, to Francine, but none to him — that is, to her. Of course Ventura and his friends didn't care about that. (They are not writers, after all; they do not read poetry.) They may even have grown bored with this joke that was never really a joke. They would rather smoke and drink and carouse than engage in a tedious game when it no longer mattered to them whether they won or lost, whether Georgina was demure or dissolute. Whether Juan Ramón wrote the poem or didn't. But of course it matters, says José, what else could possibly matter if not this: writing a poem that, in one way or another, will make us immortal, serve as a reminder that we have lived, a posterity composed of lines and letters — but above all, in the end, a poem.

What was it about Georgina Hübner that the Maestro did not like? He was tempted to ask him. To write a letter calling the poet an ingrate, an imbecile. Instead, he did just the opposite. Georgina's missives became ever more passionate, more tender — all his ire was converted into adjectives, sentences that trailed off like sighs, intimate seductions. And also a great many adverbs and ellipses, as Carlos's lessons had not been entirely in vain.

Perhaps he overstepped certain bounds — José is willing to acknowledge that. He was in the grip of something like a fever, an irrepressible urge to make Juan Ramón fall in love at last. With him, with her. It was akin to the passion with which he had hounded first the Gálvezes' chambermaid, and then dozens of lady's companions, young women at their coming-out parties, vaudeville actresses, Sacred Heart schoolgirls, seamstresses. And he always accomplished what he set out to do — as Carlos knew all too well. Hadn't he felt that emotion once himself? Hadn't his desire for Juan Ramón to fall in love been strangely reminiscent of the desire to seduce a woman, to seduce all of them?

Carlos listens without offering any expression of agreement, without meeting José's eyes. He stares at the embers in the grate. It looks like he's listening to a story — indeed, listening with utmost attention — but the fire is the one telling it to him. And José — the fire — sometimes breaks off, takes lengthy pauses, possibly for dramatic effect. Or possibly not; maybe José really needs those breaks to figure out what he wants to say, because the novel has started to get complicated. At least that's what José reports. In reality, it's just the opposite: suddenly the story he's telling has become quite simple — certain characters disappear, the plot lines grow clearer, the love story is finally taking off — but in José's telling of it, he uses that grim word, *complication*. Suddenly eight letters arrive, each of them written a day after the previous letter and then all collected together in the hold of the same ship, and those letters seem to change everything.

In the first one, Juan Ramón talks for the first time about long-ago love affairs; he even refers to proper names, certain doleful farewells, kisses whose memory no longer causes him pain, feelings that one believes to be everlasting and, as it turns out, my lady, wither as quickly as they blossom. The second speaks of the (imprecise) boundary between love and friendship. The third, of the (finite) dimensions of the Atlantic Ocean; of how he sometimes imagines her traveling its ten thousand leagues in the same transatlantic steamer that bears her letters; imagines her, his dear friend, having her trunks carried up the gangway onto the ship; clutching her hat and holding up her skirts as she disembarks in some Spanish port. The fourth is about solitude: his need to be alone, his fear of being alone, his inability to be alone. The fifth rejects the arguments of the second: the line between love and friendship is not imprecise but rather utterly imaginary, a utopia, a boundary that is worked out between two people, that is invented and frequently adjusted, forgotten, expunged, fantasized, because in the cartography of sentiment — those are the very words he uses — there are no rivers or mountain ranges that one might use to orient oneself; an emotion can fit in the palm of one's hand today and be as vast as a continent tomorrow. The sixth returns to the ocean: a sailor in Palos de la Frontera once told him that a man's first voyage on the high seas expands his soul and transforms his perspective. The seventh doesn't talk about anything — it is brief and desultory, vainly attempting to hold forth on trivial matters. And finally there's the eighth, which in a sense ties all of the previous letters together. Six sheets of nervous handwriting and even blotches of ink that speak urgently of the possibility of a journey, of the need for a journey; in the past few weeks, he has been gripped by a wild obsession and begun planning a tour of lectures and poetry readings through the Americas and Peru, what do you think of that, Georgina — traversing the (finite) limits of the ocean to read poetry and discover the (imprecise) boundaries of love and friendship along the way, because for some time now he has been unable to think of anything but her. He is ashamed to admit it, though there is really no reason why he should be. Why should it make a man tremble simply to be sincere, to give voice to certain dreams, to explain how much he has come to feel for a woman whose face he has never even seen — why do you still refuse me that photograph, Georgina? And above all, why should he blush at telling her that on some nights he even maintains the ludicrous hope — ludicrous? — that perhaps with time, with patience, she might end up reciprocating; an emotion can fit in the palm of the hand today and be vast as a continent tomorrow; just imagine it, me in Lima, taking you by the hand and ardently telling you so many things, what do you say to that, dear Georgina, what is your answer?

It seems incredible, but that's what the Maestro's letter said; that's what José tells him now.

◇

He pauses again. Takes a swig from the bottle of pisco. Like the drafts of his letters, José's words seem to be filled with erasures, with silences. Holes in which whole chapters are dismantled page by page; fragments of things he will never tell Carlos, because perhaps they do not matter. And this pause is so long that by the time he speaks again, a couple of chapters have simply vanished. And now José has ended up all alone with his own novel. It's as if there's been a corporate dissolution, one of those separations of estates that they studied in their labor law class. After the divvying up, Ventura and his friends have gotten the opium den, the bullring, the club, the billiards tables, and the brothels of Acequia Alta and Monserrate. José has only the letters and a predicament: how to reply to Juan Ramón. He keeps writing, and the others keep carrying on more or less the same old way in the same old places, now without poems or commitments or novelistic dénouements to consider.

At first he weighed the two options he and Ventura had planned out: the pious ending and the spicy ending. Trot out Georgina the married woman or Georgina the nun, and the Maestro would abandon his plans to set sail. But it was too late to try to cram religious vocation into the novel, and much too late to cook up a marriage. Neither the convent nor the church was an option, then, and it was all Juan Ramón's fault, since he'd pushed the plot along too quickly. *The great works of Literature,* averred Professor Schneider in one of his mandates, *never succumb to the temptation of the unanticipated or sensationalist ending.* Didn't Carlos remember that counsel? Was it at all reasonable that, after a mere forty-one letters, after eighteen months without a poem, one of the protagonists would decide to make no less monumental a gesture than crossing the Atlantic? He hadn't even seen a photograph! *You ask, my dear Juan Ramón, if I am aggrieved that you requested a portrait? No! I hope you do not believe me to be so ungenerous in spirit. Only wait, it will come, but first it is only fair that you send me one of you.* Would a beautiful woman ever pass up an opportunity to reveal her face? Georgina might be fat, or homely, or deformed, or pockmarked—a poxy lover is such a difficult thing to accept! Or, more likely, she might simply be ordinary, indistinguishable from the Spanish women who pass beneath the poet's balcony each morning. That sort of blind heroism, traveling halfway around the globe to pull back the curtain on a dream, is the kind of thing you see in serial novels and bad melodramas, you know it's true, Carlos. And how could José have known, how could anybody have suspected that the Maestro would turn out to be such a dreadful protagonist?

And so he had only one option: The ending that wasn't really an ending, that was hardly more than a pause or a blank page. Georgina, fallen ill. Would Juan Ramón venture to board a ship if his beloved were far from Lima in a sanatorium and surrounded by her family? José imagined not, so he inflicted upon his Georgina a series of fevers that knocked her out for days—nay, entire weeks!—at a time. How about this: *I received your latest epistles while not yet fully recuperated from an illness that kept me confined to bed for weeks,* read the letter. And then a dash of drama, because her family, alarmed, had taken her to a sanatorium in Barranco, and then to another in La Punta, believing her to be on her deathbed—*I must ask you to postpone that journey you've mentioned, please understand, though I cannot tell you not to come, the doctor insists that I should not experience any surprises or strong emotions, and the feelings you describe are too immense to be contained in a body as frail as mine; a dry cough still occasionally racks my chest.*

And that plea should have been enough, but it was not enough, because Juan Ramón is afire and will not hear reason. Maybe the letter frightened him, or maybe he surmised it was a case of tuberculosis — though José would never be so boorish as to make his protagonist succumb to tuberculosis, of all the cheap clichés — or, worse, maybe he remembered the plot of Jorge Isaacs's *María* and thought that his beloved, too, might inexorably die, that there was no time to lose. In any event he answered just yesterday, I shudder to think of it, Carlos, just a single sheet of paper with a few frantic scrawls — *Why wait any longer?* says the letter. *I will take the very first ship, the fastest one, which will bear me swiftly to your side. You can tell me in person, the two of us sitting on the seashore or in your fragrant garden with birdsong and moonlight.* Birdsong and moonlight! See, Carlos? Birdsong and moonlight, no less, as if it were the tawdry dialogue from a serial novel, an installment with the prince and the whore of the who-the-hell-knows seas, the kind of garbage that only housemaids and seamstresses enjoy. And what am I going to do now, what are we going to do? I haven't been able to sleep all night! Who's to say that imbecile hasn't set sail, that he isn't already in El Callao, sniffing around Georgina's door, my door, right this moment? You have to help me, Carlos — you're the only one who can come up with a happy ending for this novel.

◇

The fire is dying down, and Carlos has to get up several times to feed it. It's been so long since he's written letters or poems that there is no scrap paper left, so he ends up digging through the rubbish piled up in the corners. He patiently pulls out dusty cloths, pieces of broken furniture, burlap sacks. Pries loose a few planks.

José starts to get up.

"Let me help . . ."

"No need."

Carlos pokes the rags and splintered wood in through the door of the potbelly stove. José watches him silently. He seems to recognize a seriousness, a new determination in Carlos's movements. Actually, the whole scene is eerily reminiscent of his fantasies of artists living in a Montmartre garret: clochards warming themselves by burning their poems and, when those run out, piece by piece pulling apart the walls, the ceiling, and even the floor until they are huddled in the heat of the stove under the implacable Parisian sky. But José doesn't have time to think about that tonight. Instead, he keeps repeating the same thing: Carlos, what are you doing, sit down already, aren't you going to say anything?

After a few minutes, Carlos sits down at last. It seems like he's going to say something, but then he doesn't. José waits patiently — at least he tries to wait, tries to be patient. He doesn't manage it. He has decided to count to fifty before he speaks, to give Carlos fifty opportunities to speak first, but by the time he makes it to twenty, the question is already coming out of his mouth.

"Are you going to help me?"

Carlos only glances at him. He shrugs.

"You should ask Professor Cristóbal for advice. I don't have anything to do with that anymore."

There is no bitterness in his voice, only the neutral tone of someone expressing an incontrovertible truth. José fervently objects. Of course not, what is he talking about, hasn't he heard a single word he's said? He tries to apologize, to tell him they wouldn't have made it this far without him, that there's no getting out of this predicament without him, that the novel is his too and always has been, how could he doubt it.

"Anyway, I already talked to the Professor. Just this morning. I went to see him in the plaza and told him everything. That Georgina wasn't anyone's cousin, that it had all started as a joke and then got out of hand, that there was no malice in it. Brought him up to speed, basically. You know what he told me? He said he knew it from the start. The rascal! I don't buy it, though—I know we fooled him, just like we fooled everybody else, even if he's pretending to be clairvoyant now. And then there's the question of those ethics he's always going on about. Why would he have broken those famous rules of his to cultivate a romance if he knew it was a farce? I asked him that, naturally."

Carlos doesn't move, but his eyes are suddenly alert.

"And what did he say?"

"The first thing that came into his head. That I must remember that the first rule, the most important one, the one that trumps all others, is never to swim against love's tide. But whose love? I asked him. He laughed, of course—what could he say? I don't buy it, I don't buy it . . ."

As for advice, the Professor hadn't said much. He'd only laughed again and noted that Georgina sounded ill, quite gravely ill, those coughs and chills in her chest are a bad sign this time of year, she might very well be dying on them. Wouldn't that be liberating? he'd added with a wink. And so José needs Carlos now — can you believe it, even that charlatan friend of yours has given up, has no idea how to get out of this fix, but I know you're different, I know you'll find a way. And as he says it he holds out the bundle of letters with a beseeching expression. Everything's here, he adds, the latest chapters of our novel.

Our novel — that's what he says.

Carlos hesitates a moment before finally accepting the packet of letters. He weighs it warily in his hand, finding it surprisingly light for its size. It is a mechanical gesture with no anxiety in it but no joy or curiosity or sadness either. He can't find the right words to answer José, which, to paraphrase the Professor, means he doesn't know what to think, doesn't know how he should feel. He has waited so often for this moment — José's apology, Georgina's return — and now that he's holding that bit of fulfilled desire in his hands, he doesn't know what to do with it. José humiliated; José pleading with him for help, to help him save their novel; José needing him for the first time in his life — but for some reason that humiliation, that plea, that need, elicit no emotion in him. His true desire, what he has been searching for so long, is something else — but what? As he grasps the packet of letters, he knows only that it seems to contain something profoundly intimate yet utterly alien. That it is the most important thing he's done in his life and yet, at the same time, it's nonsense, a prank, a wearisome joke that's fallen flat. For a moment he feels the urge to take those pages and throw them one by one through the stove's little door and into the crackling flames. *Goodbye to Georgina,* he thinks, and the thought is both freeing and terrifying.

But he doesn't do it. Instead he surveys the bobbing pen strokes, José's superb forgeries. He pauses for a moment on a passage from Georgina's last letter. *I received your latest epistles while not yet fully recuperated from an illness that kept me confined to bed for weeks. Alarmed, my family took me to Barranco, a picturesque seaside resort, and then to a sanatorium in La Punta, another summering spot, this one quite lonely and sad.*

"The Santa Águeda sanatorium," Carlos says suddenly, with unaccustomed energy.

Perhaps because it's been so long since Carlos has spoken, José is startled by his words. Carlos's voice sounds unusually low, as if it belonged to someone else. It takes José a moment to react.

"Santa what?"

"The sanatorium that Georgina is talking about, in La Punta," he says without looking at him, as if he were thinking aloud. "She must be referring to Santa Águeda."

José blinks, confused.

"Well . . . I don't actually know. I just said it to say something. I wasn't even sure there was one."

"It's a tuberculosis sanatorium."

"Tuberculosis," José repeats distractedly, perhaps thinking about something else.

Carlos does not read the letters in their entirety. He reads only a few scattered phrases, which, through some mysterious happenstance, seem curiously linked. The bundle of letters must contain more than two hundred pages. Let us suppose, to offer a likely figure, that it contains exactly 249. Carlos begins reading on that page — *I will take the very first ship,* the poet has said — and moves from there to page 248, page 247, page 246. This is a new novel, an unfamiliar one in which the answers precede their questions, in which missives are sent futilely into the past and in which a friendship's initial tenderness gradually calcifies into ever more ceremonious formulas — *Dear friend, Most distinguished Ramón Jiménez, Most esteemed sir* — until its characters decide to ignore each other entirely and never speak again. He begins at the pinnacle of a passion that dwindles the way romances never do: slowly. He knows full well what he will find in those last, first pages: a false Georgina, somewhat crude, charmingly vulgar, her mouth full of inappropriate words, rough-mannered and inelegant, who will little by little regain the characteristics of her original purity. And at first he delights in her vulgarities, in that stranger's missteps, as if he were admonishing a young child for whims that will be corrected only a few letters later. Who would say such a thing, why on earth would he write such a stupid letter, what was José thinking when he had her put down this sentence, and this one, and that one? In his imagination, he removes those words, those idioms, those jokes, as if he were scrubbing makeup from a marble statue.

And beneath all that must be Georgina. Except that suddenly it turns out that she's not really there: behind that makeup there's nothing. Though perhaps it is untrue to say it happens suddenly. It is a sudden discovery that nevertheless only much later becomes a certainty: a slow, cold surprise that lasts many minutes and dozens of pages, letters that pass through his hands one after another, faster and faster. First he goes back to page 206, more or less the moment at which the tragedy begins, and then to the strike, and then even farther back, almost to her birth, and yet there's nothing. Georgina no longer seems like Georgina; she is like any other woman, a stranger, a ridiculous puppet. A Frankenstein fashioned out of organs and limbs pillaged from different graves, phrases from *Madame Bovary,* from *Anna Karenina,* from *The Dangerous Liaisons,* even certain expressions they've read in Galdós's latest novel — but not a trace of the real Georgina. Did she ever exist at all? Around him, Carlos sees only lifeless wreckage. It reminds him of when the doctor and his father and even the servants began to scold him if he talked to Román, forcing him to say again and again that his little friend didn't exist, that the silver pitcher had been hurled to the floor by Carlos alone, not some other unruly boy; that there was nothing in that chair, on that sofa, in that garden, except air. And after a while he had heard them say it so often that he began to see it too — the air, you know — he saw the air, and in it the whips, and the stretchers, and the rifles, and the fly-swarmed corpses, and so very many real children with yellow eyes and swollen bellies, as if they were pregnant with hunger. At this point, that's all he sees: air — that is, words — and maybe that's why he suddenly remembers Sandoval's words, how one must bore down to the reality of circumstances, the materiality of things, because all ideology is only a false consciousness, not the product of the material conditions of existence. He thinks those words now and repeats them to himself, and suddenly Georgina becomes only what he is holding in his hands, a crinkled sheet of paper, a few carefully chosen words, a way of returning to certain themes and commonplaces, a coffee stain on a draft that they used as a coaster, the way the *i*'s and *t*'s rise up as if they were trying to escape the page — that is, to reach heaven.

Carlos wonders what has become of the novel that was once vividly rendered with each letter, as if it were being projected in the milky half-light of a moving-picture theater. A girl swinging her parasol from one shoulder to the other; a gloomy arbor in which someone is sighing or sobbing; the grille of a confessional, the grate on a window, and the wrought-iron fence around a garden with gravel paths and governesses; another cage, and in it a parakeet morosely being fed, pinch by pinch, its ration of birdseed; a missal clutched devoutly to a chest, the better to hide a bundle of letters inside it. He no longer sees any of those images that used to accompany the words. Not a trace of the real Georgina, if she ever even existed: only the faces of all the grotesque impostor georginas all around him. He sees the Panteoncito waif in the expensive dresses he gave her, costumes that were never quite able to wipe the whore off her. He sees the Polish prostitute, not a girl anymore, who no longer has her summer dress or her pink bows or her canopy bed, who doesn't even have teeth now; all she has is the corner of a trash heap where she sells herself for a copper or a few swigs of wine, a toothless mouth that murmurs *Cheistormoro* to her customers, tall and short, young and old, fat and skinny — *Cheistormoro,* which might mean "hurry up and come" or "you're hurting me" or maybe "I wish I were dead." And he also sees himself lying languidly in bed, patiently kissing, with complete, pathetic earnestness, the back of his own hand. His eyes closed. And then he no longer feels a desire to reproach José or sadness for Juan

Ramón or nostalgia for Georgina; instead, he feels only cavernous shame, and something like disgust. He recalls a dream he's had many times and always forgets upon waking, a fantasy in which he sees a beautiful woman reclining on her divan, majestic as a Fortuny odalisque or a Doré engraving. Her body voluptuous, white, like something straight out of a painting, seems to become more and more real, drawing nearer, unbearably near, as if instead of eyes he had microscope lenses that someone was adjusting, or as if she, the beautiful woman, were growing so immense that soon she would swallow everything. A suddenly enormous chest, the areola of the breast covered with a purple rash, a repulsive acne, hairs growing thick as forests and wrinkles as deep as valleys, and under the skin a vertigo of secretions, viscosities, entrails, bacteria, sounds of digestion and excretion, menstruations, hot flashes, cells that replicate and die and replicate again. He always wakes from those nightmares feverish, soaked in his own sweat, shivering with fear from the weight of that awful, immense beauty.

He feels almost the same desperation now as he pushes aside the bundle of letters. He feels deep repugnance, something he cannot express in words (but the Professor says that if there are no words, then the inexpressible thing is nothing), and he understands at last, or at least he thinks he does. It is a longing for everything to be over, to declare that Georgina is dying.

That's what he thinks: *Georgina has to die.*

Actually, he says it out loud.

"We have to kill her."

And José turns to look at him and laughs. A long, exaggerated guffaw that breaks off as Carlos's meaning dawns on him.

"Kill whom?"

Then José tries to object, to say anything at all, but Carlos rushes on. His voice does not sound like his voice; indeed, it no longer is his voice. It sounds a bit like José's, but it's not that either. It sounds like, and in fact is, the authoritarian voice of Román: a voice that demands deference and quiets José in an instant. It is rather amusing to hear Román say that an imaginary friend must be killed — but really it isn't amusing at all. It is true.

Is it true?

Carlos seems quite sure of himself. As if Román had lent him not just his voice but also his confidence, that determination with which he used to play pranks or declare the rules of a game. As he talks, only the slightest gesture reveals the emotion he's feeling: the way his fingers are fiddling with the edges of the bundle of letters. It is as if he could go forward and backward in time at will, returning to the novel to select just the scenes and examples to buttress his words. He says: Weren't you the one who insisted that all of this was just literature? The one who quoted Aristotle and talked about verisimilitude? The one who kept saying our novel's ending needed a bit of drama, because the best love stories always end in tragedy? That Petrarch had to have a woman die on him, and Dante a girl, and Catullus a young man, so that a great poem could be written. Isn't that what you said, José? Well, there's your tragedy — Anna Karenina throwing herself under a train, María clenched with epilepsy, Fortunata bleeding to death, Emma Bovary swallowing arsenic. Because Georgina has consumption, don't you see? She has two cavities in her lungs as large as fists. How else can you explain her pallor, her seclusion, and the way the housemaid would scold her when she spent evenings in the garden watching the moths burning up in the lamp — don't you remember, José? And the cough racking the chest and the urgent admission to the Santa Águeda sanatorium — a surprising choice of disease, really. "I never said it was

Santa Águeda!" José sputters. That hardly matters now, Carlos continues, the main thing is there's only one sanatorium in La Punta, and that sanatorium is for consumptives — Juan Ramón can confirm it if he wishes. You wanted me to help you, and this is all the help I can offer: I'm just a reader of your novel, and as such I know that this story has to end with Georgina dead and Juan Ramón in mourning.

Can it really be true?

José sighs. All right, he says. Carlos may very well be correct in what he's said, at least about part of it; José is even willing to accept that he might be correct about everything. Lately the novel has been hurtling toward a tragic end, and that could be his fault. But surely there is still something they can do; even if we aren't the authors, let's get on with it, damn it, who else can write an alternative ending? One where Georgina does not die but they still find a way to keep Juan Ramón from boarding that ship, to make him write a poem instead.

Hearing José's insistence, Carlos smiles with a new expression. He has practiced it in front of the mirror many times, and at last he has the chance to use it: a look of superiority, of disdain. Of course you can do that if you like, he answers. Save her on the very last page, like in those flea-market novels that always end with an unexpected pardon from the Crown. Or the discovery of a hidden treasure. Or a mounted charge against the enemy's rear guard, led by a general who's never even been mentioned before. That's called deus ex machina, is it not? Well, there you go, then: perform a deus ex machina if that's what you want, and the hell with your novel — and the poem too. Have you forgotten about the poem? What will the Maestro write if Georgina survives? A few trifling verses that no one will even notice, guaranteed — an inconsequential lament for yet another maiden who became a nun or was forced to marry. Worse still: a poem about two scoundrels pretending to be a woman. And why should José be satisfied with that when he could have a poem that aches with real grief, a true and inconsolable wail; an elegy for a beloved who has died, snuffed out on the very eve of this long-anticipated encounter, maybe for no other reason than that such a beautiful flower simply could not last. But if he's not convinced, he can go for it. If he'd rather have a tacky junk-shop novel, the kind that's sold at a nickel a pound, then he knows what he has to write. Or he could just sit back and let Juan Ramón come to him; he and Georgina can get married and have paper children, for all Carlos cares.

Here Carlos pauses; he lights a cigarette. His hands are shaking, but this time it's not out of unease or trepidation. He feels a wild exultation, a furious euphoria that has driven him to his feet and inspired him to spit out those last words. It is a new emotion, or at least it seems new at first, but slowly he realizes that it also leaves a familiar aftertaste. He experienced something similar once before — he's just remembered. It was eight years ago, in the Polish prostitute's bed. Because if he's honest with himself, he has to admit that back then he felt more than just guilt and sadness, even if it is those emotions that have prevailed in his memory for all these years. When he awoke and saw the blood-stained sheets, he also felt, he remembers now, a more primitive pleasure that he didn't understand at the time. A sort of arousal tinged with the same frenzy his father used to exhibit when he beat their indigenous workers, and perhaps too with the pleasure that he himself had secretly enjoyed as he moved repeatedly over the young girl's body. Her cries like a sweet anesthetic in his ear, like a thermometer measuring his valor, his strength. The knowledge that, in spite of everything, he too could inflict pain. That he could dominate and destroy another human being and then simply leave, nonchalant. And now the same exhilaration washes over him, a furious elation that would destroy everything, as if the blood on that sheet belonged not to the Polish prostitute but to tubercular Georgina — the red sputum that she will keep coughing up till she breathes her last, just because he wishes it to be so.

José vacillates. He doesn't speak immediately. In the glow from the stove, his face is full of oscillations, of flickering dark shadows and red light. But Carlos doesn't need to hear what he's about to say. He knows that his hesitation is only a mirage — that in fact the decision has already been made, just as Román always knew that his friend Carlos would end up accommodating all his desires. It cannot be otherwise. And so he takes another drag on his cigarette, and as he does, he seems to anticipate everything that will follow: His father bribing the consul, or even the Peruvian ambassador to Madrid (*Tell me, you leeches, how much this poet's heart is going to cost me*); if necessary, forging a death certificate for Georgina, just as he previously invented the records of all those illustrious ancestors. Georgina's death contained in the space of a telegram, because her final words will journey not in the hold of a ship but in a diplomatic cable. Thirteen words, to be exact, the maximum allowed in urgent messages, and he and José scrawling on sheets of paper, crumpling them up until they find the right ones. Thirteen words, perhaps something like these: *Please inform poet Juan Ramón Jiménez that Señorita Georgina Hübner of Lima is dead* — "That's fourteen," the telegraph operator will point out, and Carlos, after thinking a moment: "Then cross out the *poet* bit." And the telegram, without the word *poet*, traveling across the ocean as Georgina dies in a tuberculosis hospital — or, better still, Georgina dying and in her delirium dreaming of a telegram that travels across the ocean; the nuns coming and going with their white wimples and surgical trays and cold compresses; electric pulses rattling down thousands of miles of undersea cable, invisible as a dream; Georgina awake, in the throes of death, and behind her eyes a telegram soaring over ocean ridges and shipwrecks, seaweed forests and mud flats, shelves and trenches briefly illuminated by a feverish lucidity; her nightmare spinning the telegraph bobbin, the inked roller, the strip of paper that is filling up with words, with silences, with dots and dashes so much like her broken breathing. The nun's hand reaching out to close her eyelids, and the strip of paper in the hands of the telegraph operator, in the hands of the messenger boy, in the hands of the guard, of the servant, of Juan Ramón at last; once more his fingers unrolling the telegram, his hands steady at first, though soon they begin to tremble.

Somebody is pounding on the door. It is six in the morning, and the noise is so loud, it sounds like whoever it is is trying to tear the house down. The gendarmes again, thinks Madame Lenotre as she hurries downstairs, attempting to fasten her shawl. It's been four years since the incident, but impossible to forget — a squad of armed men rapping sharply on the door to arrest one of her customers, a tiny man, almost a dwarf. They took him into custody right then and there, his cock still erect and a look on his face like he'd never broken a dish in his life. Seeing him so defenseless, so small, so childlike in the hands of all those men, some of the girls wept. Finally someone explained that he'd escaped from the penitentiary, and that on previous nights he'd attacked four women at other brothels, slitting their throats and hacking them to pieces. The girl who'd been with him was dumbstruck when she found out, and the other girls peppered her with questions about him. They wanted to know what he was like, how to distinguish a normal customer from a deviant, a madman. Her eyes still wide and her tongue stiff and clumsy, she answered that he was just a man. No gentler or rougher, no chattier or quieter than any of the other customers she saw, some two dozen a week.

But tonight there are no fugitive prisoners in the house; there aren't even any customers. The last one left at least a couple of hours ago, and Lenotre told the girls they could go to bed, that nobody else was likely to come. So there are no men, and no girls awake to see them, and when she opens the street door it turns out there aren't any gendarmes either. Just young Master Carlos, thoroughly soused, clinging to the knocker to keep from falling down. It's hard to believe this polite, formal boy has caused such a ruckus. And yet there he is, his chin held high and his gaze defiant. There's a new determination in his voice and expression, a profound gravity that comes not just from drunkenness but from something else, someone else. Yes. That's exactly what Lenotre finds herself thinking for a moment: *Young Master Rodríguez has become another man.* And this stranger needs to see the girl — he's yelling it at the top of his lungs. He knows that it's six in the morning and the house is closed, but he must see her immediately; he is very sorry, it must be at once. His money is as good as anyone else's, and as he says this he pulls wads of bills out of his pocket like fruit rinds. Empty casings that first spill into Lenotre's bony hand and then fall across the rug.

The girl is sound asleep, and everything that happens after that seems to her like the continuation of a dream. Lenotre claps loudly at her bedside, shouting that the young gentleman is here. What young gentleman? Well, who else, the young gentleman is the young gentleman, Mr. Gob-Smacked, the one with the hymen, the son of the rubber magnate. He's out of his mind, he says he must see you at once and he's brought a pile of cash — put on one of those dresses he likes so much and do whatever he wants. She jumps to her feet in a flash; she almost leaps across Cayetana's body. She runs to look at herself in the cracked moon of the mirror. Why would the young gentleman be in such a hurry? His desperation, his urgency can mean only one thing. Only one? As she hastily applies makeup and gets dressed, she makes a deal with God: if he is waiting for her in the private rooms on the ground floor and not on the second, then it means he's come to say to her what she so longs to hear. It's a fair deal; not having a crucifix, she seals it with a kiss on her fist. As she descends the staircase, everything around her seems unreal: the carpeted stairs, the still-life paintings on the walls, the sickly light that is beginning to sift in through the windows, giving the house a dreamlike atmosphere. No, it's not a dream — it is a passage from one of those novels Mimí is always reading to her. And she is the protagonist, of course; she looks like a young lady and everything, with her white dress and her matching hat and gloves. His favorite outfit. She has opened the parasol, too, and is carrying it against her shoulder. She's not superstitious about that, at least; how could she be, when lately only good things have been happening to her, even when she opens umbrellas that aren't really umbrellas indoors.

No, she's not superstitious. But she smiles to discover that there's no one in the rooms on the second floor. And so she goes down to the bottom floor. She pushes open the only door that's ajar. And on the other side is the young gentleman, who abruptly drops his hat and lunges at her. It is such an unexpected movement that she instinctively closes her eyes, as if bracing for a blow. But it's not a blow. It's a frenzied kiss, one that tastes of alcohol and fever and blood. It takes her a moment to react. Could the gesture mean more than the words he isn't saying? Is God keeping up His end of the bargain? She doesn't know. She only feels her body go weak when he begins to press against her, furiously fumbling at the laces of her bodice. For the first time, the young gentleman's hands aren't shaking. Indeed, they are quite steady as he takes her in his arms and drops her onto the bed. A little rough, perhaps. The prince would never have done such a thing, but of course she is not an odalisque of the southern seas but just another tart on Calle del Panteoncito.

She thinks that — *just another tart* — and the word won't go away. *Tart*, while the young gentleman tears at the seams of her dress. *Tart* when he pulls up her skirt to cover her face. Her, the tart, her legs forced open under the weight of his body. She's supposed to wash her customers' cocks in the basin, it's the house rule, but before she can say anything, he is already inside her, violently driving into her. If she could move her hands . . . but she can't, because the young gentleman is holding them down. If she could speak . . . but she tries, and the young gentleman — gentleman? — screams at her to shut up, just shut up, you tart. Her, the tart. If she could see — but she can only feel the white gauze of the dress covering her face, the stifling humidity of her own breath. Through the fabric she hears Carlos's animal panting, his hot gasps and hoarse grunts. If only it hurt a little, but there's not even that. She barely feels him moving inside her, and that's the most absurd, horrible part of all. He's just another customer, murmuring the same old filthy words in her ear, crushing her with his body and digging his fingers into her flesh. Is it really him? He could be anybody. At the very least he's as repellent as all the others, his movements produce the same nausea, the same need to fly far away in her thoughts. To fly — but where? She has nowhere left: he is not waiting for her in a distant palace with a turban and beautiful poems but instead is right here, holding down her wrists so fiercely that it hurts.

She has stopped struggling to get free, stopped trying to uncover her face. There is nothing she can say, nothing she can do. She knows that the way to make this finish as soon as possible is to stay very quiet. And since there is no longer any prince to dream of, she finds herself thinking about everything else. About the window bars. About the bed she shares with Mimí and Cayetana, and Madame Lenotre's account book, and the pieced-together portrait stored under the straw mattress. And she understands for the first time that she will never leave that house, never finish paying off her debts, never see her mother again the way she was in that photograph. She feels an urge to shout. To put her lips close to that body jerking inside her and howl her own name, to shout it out at the top of her lungs so that the stranger hears it, so that he never forgets it. To tell him that she too exists, that she's there right now. But at the last moment her voice freezes up inside her. The man's breath gets faster, grows hoarse and staccato — in the end, he's the one shouting. And she, her mouth still open, murmurs the only words that men want to hear from her lips.

"Oh, like that, you strong man.

"Like that, you stud.

"Like that, faster, harder, deeper — like that. Yes, like that."

IV

A Poem

◇

The novel ends right where its authors leave it — that is to say, one night in the final weeks of 1905. At least that's what they will believe for the next fifteen years: that they have written a tragedy, and that their tragedy ends with Georgina dying. They are mistaken, but that's no surprise, as they were never great writers, and perhaps not even good readers. They have not realized that something is still missing, an epilogue that shows up late, when no one is waiting for it anymore. And after that, it's done.

It is 1920. Up until very recently, the world seemed to be living out a tragedy worthy of the pages of their novel. In addition to Georgina's death there was also the Archduke Ferdinand's, and then the fifteen million dead of the Great War; the massacres of the February and October revolutions; the Spanish flu and its seventy million victims; the execution of Czar Nicholas, the czarina, their five children, and their four servants. But something seems to have changed now. There is no more flu, no more war, no more revolution or counterrevolution. There are even those who claim that the young Princess Anastasia is still alive, hidden away somewhere in Russia. It is not a question of reviving Georgina too — at this point, Georgina is as dead as the Austro-Hungarian Empire. But at the very least it is a sign that no catastrophe is absolute, that even in the greatest tragedies there is room for mercy or hope.

If the ending of their novel is not a tragedy, then what is it?

The ending is a poem. But it is also a conversation, a reencounter in a café on Calle Belaochaga. A café that did not exist fifteen years earlier. Because Lima has changed a great deal, and José and Carlos have changed along with it. They are fatter, older, better dressed. Time has made them the same in a way, and now it is difficult to tell them apart. Indeed, it is impossible. They are sitting together in a private room in the café, shielded behind identical smiles, and it is impossible to tell which of them is asking the other about his business affairs, which one is answering that he's muddling along as usual, just muddling along.

Or maybe it is possible to tell them apart, and the problem is that the distinction no longer matters. That José and Carlos not only look alike but in fact have become the same person.

But they do not speak or smile with ease. They address each other with the somewhat brusque air of people who do not see each other often. As if this conversation were not the product of an encounter dictated by friendship or chance but a meeting carefully arranged after a lengthy silence. That might be precisely what is happening: that they haven't spoken in fifteen years or seen each other in nearly nine. And now they have to sum up those years in a few minutes, in a few lines. The answers are as predictable as the questions. They are both married. They both have children. The way they refer to them, the way they describe them in a few sentences, one might think they were talking about the same people. That they have married the same wife and raised the same children. This is not the case, of course; each of them has his own family, his own longings, his own secrets and sorrows, but neither is going to say that. After all, people are members of the bourgeoisie not so much because of what they say aloud but because of what they keep quiet. The vast swath of themselves that they have learned to mask behind a discreet, decorous silence.

One might say, in fact, that up until now they haven't talked about anything. That everything worth saying, everything they want to hear from each other, has been hidden beneath a veil. And so it is for the next few minutes, as they idly inquire about the people they knew fifteen years ago. Like two old friends trying to catch up on each other's lives. Or like a couple of mediocre writers who can't figure out any better way to mention their novel's secondary characters one last time. What ever happened to Sandoval? asks one of them, and the other replies that for a few years he was starting up and shutting down newspapers, calling for and calling off strikes, and is now running a doomed campaign for the legislature. But that in the end that nonsense about the eight-hour workday actually came through and has just been passed by the parliament—who would have thought it. And their professors? Most of them retired or dead. And Professor Cristóbal? Who knows. They know only that he no longer comes to the plaza to write—there are fewer and fewer people who need letters written for them, and even fewer who fall in love. Because that's what getting older means: meeting fewer and fewer people who are in love.

And what about the other destitute poets? They've had some news of all them, all of it good. What's more, they no longer have to pretend to be poor—they only have to pretend to be happy. Their fathers? Here the balance is unequal: one is dead, the other still alive. They don't bother asking after each other's mothers, who never figured prominently in the novel to begin with. And finally they talk a long while about their business affairs, the companies they head, as if, in a way, the two of them were also characters. But now they're no longer secondary. Now the plush offices, the stocks and bank drafts, the deals struck at galas and cabarets, the trips to the estate, seem to fill everything, to take center stage.

Then, all at once, the conversation collapses. Their relationship is paralyzed, nearly dead, sustainable only through endless questions and answers, sips from their coffee cups and drags on their cigarettes, cardboard smiles that make their faces ache. The coffee runs out. They must decide whether to order something else or take advantage of the empty cups to make their excuses and go their separate ways. One of them even starts to make that gesture, to say goodbye, but the other remains seated. He must do one more thing: pull out a book of poetry. Their novel cannot end until he does that: opens the book of poems and places it on the table.

"A gift," he says, with the hint of a smile.

And that is enough. The title of the book, in a mute shout, says the rest.

Labyrinth.

Juan Ramón Jiménez.

He picks up the book cautiously, without asking any questions. And as he flips through it, the other offers irrelevant explanations. That it was published in Spain in 1913. That the Great War had prevented any copies from reaching Peru until now. That it was difficult, incredibly difficult, to find.

All of a sudden, the rapid turning of pages ceases.

It is called "Letter to Georgina Hübner in the Sky over Lima." It is a long poem that takes up three pages, but he manages to read only the title. The rest he takes in all at once, in an instant, as effortlessly as one might contemplate a landscape. First the title and then the ending too, because the last line has a question mark that automatically draws his attention, a rhetorical question — rhetorical? — that he reads once, twice, three times.

Then he looks down at the blank space that comes after the last line. It is an empty void and yet he stares at it as if it contained something more important than the poem itself, a silence that is somehow the answer to the question he cannot get out of his head. Then he slowly pushes the book away.

"Aren't you going to read it?" the other asks. He gives a forced smile, out of a mutual understanding that no longer exists.

No, he's not going to read it. He understands a number of things all at the same time, and that is one of them. He will not read it, not ever. He also knows or thinks he knows that they must be very beautiful verses, perhaps the best that Juan Ramón has ever written. Worse still, he knows that the poem that does not belong to them, the poem he's not going to read, is better than they themselves will ever be. That it is worth more than their wives and children, more than their factories, than the contract to bring Chilean nitrate to market, than their summer residences, their mistresses, their pasts and futures. He understands all that in an instant, just by looking at the last stanza.

He doesn't know what to say. And yet something must be said — anything at all — even if it's inappropriate, even if it will never be as beautiful as what Juan Ramón has written in his poem. For example, he could tell his friend — friend? — that over time he has almost entirely forgotten the women they seduced back then, the games they used to play to amuse themselves, the poems they wrote or read together, the voice of his dead father, but that nevertheless he remembers Georgina's face in the minutest detail. But he cannot tell him that, because it would be, in some way, like starting the novel over again, and all he wants is to finish it once and for all. Close the book. Finally reach the last page, and then keep on living.

And for that they need only to write the ending, an answer to the question that the Maestro poses in his poem. And he decides to do that right there, in that blank space, just below the final line: Carlos Rodríguez. A slow, laborious signature that tears at the paper, as if instead of scrawling his name he were carving an epitaph. And in spite of everything, José doesn't understand at first, and Carlos has to explain it to him again, once, twice, attempting to pass him the pen, to hand back the book: It's our life, he says, this is the best thing we've ever done, the best thing we'll ever do, so now we're going to sign it. It seems like a joke, and when he hears it, José laughs. But it's not a joke, it's the ending to their novel — quite a serious matter — and when he finally understands, his expression grows sober, concentrated. He, too, takes a long time to sign his name. He, too, is careful to make it a good signature, the one he uses for checks and formal documents.

Then they pay the bill and walk together three or four blocks to the corner where their paths diverge. Maybe they chat about something else before saying goodbye. They may try to lighten the dramatic tone of their parting, the solemnity of their names interwoven on the page of the book of poems. They will spend the rest of their lives doing that: pretending that the ending has not yet arrived, that a great many things are still to come, that what succeeds that poem and that novel still matters. But they will do all that on their own, once more on their own. Because when the last chapter is over, they will never see each other again. That, then, is their ending: a poem, two signatures, a farewell.

◇

They part on the very corner in San Lázaro where their garret once stood. Like all coincidences, this one is meaningless, but on his way home Carlos amuses himself by coming up with different explanations.

It is a new brick building with freshly painted bars on the windows and electrical wires running up the walls. He stops and looks at a particular spot on its façade. A place where, in fact, there is nothing to see, somewhere between the third and fourth floors. His memory has to painstakingly rebuild the rest: a crumbling attic, a roof with splintering rafters, a window. Two young men looking down from on high. And it seems to him that if his nearsighted eyes were twenty years old again, he would be able to see their hats and bow ties, all from another era, and, of course, their ridiculous mustaches; and that if it weren't for the automobiles and the honking horns, he could even make out what the two men are saying to each other.

"And what about that fellow?"

"Which one?"

"The fat one . . . the one looking up at us. The one stopped in the middle of the street, carrying a book under his arm."

"Oh! Well . . . he looks like a portly millionaire out of a Dickens novel, don't you think?"

"To me he looks more like a bored middle-class man from one of Echegaray's plays."

"Or a greedy landlord out of Dostoyevsky, with the addresses of all the tenants he's going to evict written in that little book."

A silence.

"Not at all! Take a good look. Now that I observe him more closely, I think he's really just a secondary character . . ."

And down there on the sidewalk, the millionaire, the landlord, the secondary character, looks back at them and smiles.

Letter to Georgina Hübner
in the Sky over Lima

Juan Ramón Jiménez

The Peruvian consul tells me: "Georgina Hübner is dead ..."

... Dead! Why? How? On what day?
What golden rays, departing from my life one eventide,
would have burnished the splendor of your hands,
so sweetly crossed upon your quiet breast
like two lavender lilies of love and sentiment?

... Now your back has felt the white casket,
your thighs are now forever shut,
and in the tender green of your new-dug grave
the sinking sun will set the hummingbirds aflame ...
La Punta is much colder and lonelier now
than when you saw it, fleeing from the tomb,
those far-off afternoons when your phantom told me:
"So often have I thought of you, my dearest friend!"

And I of you, Georgina? I cannot say what you were like —
fair? demure? melancholy? I know only that my sorrow
is a woman, just like you, who is seated,
weeping, sobbing, beside my soul!

I know that my sorrow writes in that graceful hand
that soared across the sea from distant lands
to call me "friend" . . . or something more . . . perhaps . . .
     a part
of all that throbbed in your twenty-year-old heart!

You wrote: "Yesterday my cousin brought your book to me."
Remember? Myself, gone pale: "A cousin? Who is he?"

I longed to enter your life, to offer you my hand,
noble as a flame, Georgina . . . In every ship
that sailed, my wild heart went out in search of you . . .
I thought I'd finally found you, pensive, in La Punta,
with a book in your hand, just as you'd told me,
dreaming among the flowers, casting a spell on my life!

Now the vessel I will take one evening, searching for you,
will never leave this port, nor cleave the seas,
it will travel into infinity, its prow pointing ever upward,
seeking, as an angel would, its celestial isle . . .
Oh, Georgina, Georgina! By heaven! My books
will wait for you above, and surely you'll have read
a few verses aloud to God . . . You will tread the western skies
in which my fervent fancies are snuffed out . . .
and learn that all of this is meaningless —
that, save love, the rest is only words . . .

Love! Oh, love! Did you feel in the nights
the distant thrall of my ardent cries,
as I, in the stars, in the shadows, in the breezes,
wailing toward the south, called out to you: Georgina?

Did, perhaps, a gentle zephyr bearing
the ineffable perfume of my formless longing
pass by your ear? Did you hear something of me,
my dreams of your country estate, of kisses in the garden?

Oh, how the best of our lives is shattered!
We live . . . for what? To watch the days
with their funereal hue, no sky in the still waters . . .
to clutch our foreheads in our hands!
to weep, to long for what is ever distant,
and never to step across the threshold of dreams.
Oh, Georgina, Georgina! to think that you perished
one evening, one night . . . and I all unknowing!

The Peruvian consul tells me: "Georgina Hübner is dead . . ."
You are dead. You are, soulless, in Lima,
opening white roses beneath the earth.

And if our arms are destined never to intertwine,
then what heedless child, born of hatred and pain,
made the world, unwitting, while blowing soap bubbles?

José Gálvez   Carlos Rodríguez